SLEIGHT OF HAND

THE KINGS: WILD CARDS BOOK 3

CHARLIE COCHET

D1526912

Sleight of Hand

Copyright © 2021 Charlie Cochet

http://charliecochet.com

This is a work of fiction. Names, characters, places, and incidents either are the products of author imagination or used fictitiously. Any resemblance to actual persons, living or dead, business establishments, events, or locales is entirely coincidental.

Cover content is for illustrative purposes only. Any person depicted on the cover is a model.

Cover Art Copyright © 2021 Reese Dante

http://reesedante.com

Edited by Deniz Durand

Proofing by Brian Holliday

Content Warning: *Please note this novel contains scenes and/or topics dealing with sensitive issues that may trigger some readers, including sexual abuse, kidnapping, PTSD, and the trauma of military service and loss.*

ACKNOWLEDGMENTS

To all the amazing people in my life who helped make this book happen. Thank you for your input, support, friendship, and love.

For Minerva, the sassy German Shepherd who inspired Chip. You may not be a military dog, but you're a fierce warrior at heart.

To all our military heroes and their K9 partners. Thank you for your service.

FOUR KINGS SECURITY UNIVERSE

WELCOME to the Four Kings Security Universe! The current reading order for the universe is as follows:

FOUR KINGS SECURITY UNIVERSE

STANDALONES
Beware of Geeks Bearing Gifts - Standalone
(Spencer and Quinn. Quinn is Ace and Lucky's cousin)
Can be read any time before *In the Cards*.

FOUR KINGS SECURITY
Love in Spades - Book 1 (Ace and Colton)
Ante Up - Book 1.5 (Seth and Kit)
Free short story
Be Still My Heart - Book 2 (Red and Laz)
Join the Club - Book 3 (Lucky and Mason)
Diamond in the Rough - Book 4 (King and Leo)
In the Cards - Book 4.5 (Spencer and Quinn's wedding)
Free short story

FOUR KINGS SECURITY BOXED SET

Boxed Set includes all 4 main Four Kings Security novels: Love in Spades, Be Still My Heart, Join the Club, and Diamond in the Rough.

THE KINGS: WILD CARDS

Stacking the Deck - Book 1 (Jack and Fitz)
Raising the Ante - Book 2 (Frank and Joshua)
Sleight of Hand - Book 3 (Joker and Gio)

RUNAWAY GROOMS SERIES

Aisle Be There - Book 1 (King's cousin Gage)

SYNOPSIS

Former Special Forces Green Beret, Sacha "Joker" Wilder, is well-versed on the subject of demolitions. As a silent partner of Four Kings Security, Joker spends his days working alongside his brothers-in-arms and his best boy, Chip—a bomb-sniffing Belgian Malinois with sass. Years of military and private security experience have prepared Joker for almost anything, except the explosive attraction between him and Giovanni Galanos.

When Gio returns from his travels abroad, everyone is charmed by the handsome billionaire philanthropist, but in Joker's experience, anyone who's too good to be true usually is. Gio is hiding something, but the more time Joker spends around Gio, the more his walls start crumbling, leaving him exposed and at risk of losing his heart, something he swore he would never do. Love is for suckers, and that's not him.

For years Gio has dedicated his life to his charity work, helping people around the globe, but when things go horribly wrong during one particular trip, Gio decides it's time to come home for good. The desire for family, and a certain ex-Green Beret with a chip on his shoulder, has Gio eager to restart his life Stateside. For all of Sacha's blustering and griping, no one makes Gio feel safer. If only Sacha could see how right they are for each other.

Danger lurks in the shadows as someone sets their sights on Gio, and secrets are forced into the light. If Gio and Joker are to have any kind of future together, they'll have to face difficult truths, because where love is concerned, it'll take more than sleight of hand to make things work.

ONE

SHIT.

Joker froze.

Never had he faced this level of peril, not even as a Special Forces Green Beret. In the span of his military career, he'd gone up against a host of evil, from terrorists to savage warlords and everyone in-between, but never had he encountered anything like this. Thankfully, they hadn't spotted him. He could still make his escape.

Having memorized the exits at the start of his shift, he quickly considered his options. Backstage was out of the question. He could duck and cover behind the sound equipment or—

"Hey!"

Fuck.

Five men headed in his direction, each one more terrifying than the last. Individually, he could take them, but together? He didn't stand a chance. At least he wasn't alone. That's right! He *wasn't* alone. He had a furry weapon of mass distraction.

"You're trained for this, pal," Joker told Chip, scratching

behind his giant pointy ears. Chip side-eyed him, making Joker laugh. "Yeah, all right. Better you than me. Brace yourself. Here they come."

The Boyfriend Collective.

What did a billionaire, a hairstylist, a cowboy, a computer genius, and a fashion photographer have in common? They were all attached—or in Colton's case, married to—one of Joker's brothers-in-arms. That wasn't the scary part. Oh no. Because each of his brothers-in-arms was disgustingly in love and in a committed monogamous relationship and Joker wasn't—and *never* would be—a lovesick sucker, the Boyfriend Collective had decided he was some kind of homeless puppy in need of coddling, feeding, and petting.

Okay, so it wasn't *all* bad. Plus, Joker had gained the bonus of using said newly acquired powers to drive his brothers crazy. If Colton wanted to feed him, and Fitz wanted to hug him and play with his hair, and Laz wanted to introduce him to gorgeous models, who was Joker to turn down such heartfelt gestures? So what if Leo provided Joker with an endless supply of snacks in the hopes of finding him his signature snack? Was Joker supposed to crush his precious little heart? And Mason, well, Mason was just fun to fuck with.

The scary part came when the Collective unanimously set their minds to something or when someone stupidly pissed them off. The leader of this terrifying group was the billionaire, Colton Connolly. The man who started it all. The moment Colton came into their lives and Joker's buddy Ace fell in love, the rest of them toppled like dominoes. Sappy, hearts-in-their-eyes, tents-in-their-pants dominoes. Shameful. Absolutely no self-control.

Even their giant grumpy-ass fearless leader, King, who

Joker had been sure was too smart to get sucker punched by love, fell for a cute little computer geek. What was the world coming to? Back when they'd served, Joker had watched a fucking *building* fall on King, and the man had walked away from it with only a few bruises and scratches. The guy falls in love with Leo and *bam!* Next thing they know, King is baking his boyfriend fish-shaped sugar cookies. With sprinkles. *Sprinkles.*

"Go get 'em," Joker murmured to Chip.

Chip barked and bounded off like a huge black rabbit, tail wagging so hard his butt looked like it might fly off any minute. It never failed. The Boyfriend Collective turned into a puddle of baby-talking dorks, cooing and lavishing love on Chip, who soaked that shit up like it was his favorite freeze-dried salmon treats. Joker couldn't blame them. It was those Belgian Malinois ears. They were impossible to resist. Fitz lifted his gaze, and Joker sighed. Of course. Every time. Damn it.

"All right," Joker said, motioning with both hands for Fitz to bring it.

With a laugh, Fitz glided over, because the man was tall and sinewy like some Hollywood starlet, so he didn't walk but fucking *floated*. He threw his arms around Joker and hugged him tightly, their height difference meaning Joker's head got plastered to Fitz's chest. Why couldn't his brothers date men who weren't fucking redwoods? Even Leo was taller than him. Fucking tall-ass motherfuckers.

Joker's earpiece came to life, and he smiled evilly. He wrapped his arms around Fitz and hummed as Jack's voice came through.

"Hey, cameras are online. Where are you?"

Joker hummed again. "Center stage, feeling up your boyfriend."

Silence. Then, "What?"

Fitz laughed softly. "You're so evil."

"Center stage," Joker repeated.

Wait for it...

"If your hand gets any closer to his ass, I'm going to upload your profile to every dating app in the country," Jack hissed. "Detach yourself."

"But he's so warm," Joker murmured, closing his eyes and smiling happily.

The low growl made Joker laugh, and he released Fitz. "Your boyfriend is going all caveman on you."

Fitz lifted his gaze to the nearest camera and blew a kiss at it. A ridiculous sigh met Joker's ear. Yep, total sucker. He shook his head in shame. Then again, his best friend and partner in crime had always been a sentimental sap.

"Yeah, you enjoy that smugness while you can," Jack said. "One of these days, when you least expect it, love is going to hit you so hard, you're going to get whiplash."

Joker thrust a finger at the camera. "You take that back, asshole!"

"Nope, and I'm going to be there when it does, laughing my ass off and enjoying every fucking minute."

"That's it. Your best-friend status has been revoked. From this point forward, Ace is my best friend."

"Yes!" Ace whooped over the line. "I'm going to have matching T-shirts made!"

Joker pinched the bridge of his nose. "Never mind. Jack, your best friend status has been reinstated."

"Oh no!"

They could all but hear Ace pouting.

"I'm still having matching T-shirts made. Mine will say, 'Say hello to my little friend,' and yours will say—"

Joker groaned. "Don't you say it."

"Little Friend."

The guys all cackled in his ear, and Joker flipped them off. "Fuckers." He was *not* going to get suckered into love like the rest of them. Nope.

Someone walked through the heavy black curtain onto the stage and headed toward Chip. It was *him*.

Joker's heart sped up, and he hissed at Fitz, "What's *he* doing here?" And with the Boyfriend Collective? Okay, so the guy was best friends with Colton, and Laz was his brother, but he wasn't a Boyfriend. After all, they were out of Green Berets. Well, except for Joker—and no. Never gonna happen. Fuck *no*. Joker wouldn't fall for Giovanni Galanos if he were the last human on the planet.

Fitz followed Joker's glare. "Oh, Gio's the one who got us tickets to the concert and backstage passes. Did you know he and Nia are good friends?"

"Of course they are," Joker grumbled. Saint Fucking Gio. Media heartthrob, philanthropist, billionaire, friend to one of the hottest pop stars in the world. And just how "good" was his friendship with the gorgeous singer? Not that Joker cared. None of his business. He was here to do a job.

The arena, one of the largest in Florida to date, had hired the Kings to work security for one of the biggest concerts to hit the state in decades. Tickets sold out in minutes. Over twenty-five thousand people would be in attendance tonight, meaning the Kings weren't the only ones working security. The venue hired the Kings to secure the interior of the arena and Nia's people during setup. A second security company would handle the actual concert, while Nia's security was taken care of by her usual team.

With that many security teams in place, they had a high risk for fuckery, which was why he was glad King was in charge. If anyone tried to give him or any of their team shit, it only took one look from his friend to send them crying home to momma. The guy might bake his boyfriend cookies, but he'd also been their unit's second-in-command. No one was stupid enough to fuck with Ward Kingston, and if they did, they'd be regretting their life choices real quick.

"I've never been in an arena before a concert," Fitz said, taking in all the scaffolding, scattered equipment, and various pieces of machinery.

Joker shrugged. He'd been working the entertainment side of security for years now. He'd seen it all. "It's not much to look at right now, but in about another six hours, it's going to be pretty impressive. Speaking of six hours, what are you guys doing here so early?" He'd been here several hours already, and the last thing he needed was Gio hanging around while he worked. If he'd known Gio was going to be around, he wouldn't have volunteered to work a fucking twelve-hour shift. For events this size, overtime meant he got to take the next couple of days off.

"After the backstage tour, we're all going out to an early dinner to some fancy VIP restaurant before Nia's got to come back for the concert."

Joker frowned. Dinner for who knew how many at a restaurant with one of the hottest singers on the planet? Talk about a logistical nightmare. "Whose bright idea was that?"

"Nia's manager. Nia wanted a private dinner with us, but he didn't want her to miss such a big promo op."

Gio laughed, and Joker's eyes darted to him on instinct. "Promo op?" He forced his gaze back to Fitz, who blinked at him.

"You don't know?"

"Know what?"

"Gio was the one who discovered Nia. Every few years he travels to Greece to visit the village his mother was from." Fitz waved a hand. "Anyway, he was in a little village in Greece a few years ago. I can't remember its name, only how heartbreaking it was to hear Gio describe the poverty there. It's an amazing story. You'll have to ask him to tell you one day."

Not likely. Joker didn't say as much, but Fitz rolled his eyes like he knew what Joker was thinking. They'd gotten to know each other pretty well since Fitz started dating Jack. If it concerned Gio, Joker didn't want to know. Everyone might have fallen for the guy's charms, but not Joker. If it was too good to be true, it *always* was. No one was perfect. No man could be beautiful on the outside and inside, be a billionaire and a saint. Gio was hiding something.

As if sensing Joker, Gio turned in his direction, his smile widening and reaching his dark eyes, forming little lines at the corners because the guy was always fucking *smiling*. Who the fuck smiled all the time? A curl of Gio's pitch-black hair fell roguishly over one side of his brow, the rest of his hair untamed. It happened whenever his hair got a bit too long. Not that Joker paid attention to that sort of thing.

Like every other time Joker had seen him, Gio looked impeccable, from his designer shoes to his charcoal-gray dress slacks and slim-fitting black button-down shirt. His naturally tanned skin—thanks to his Greek roots—wasn't flawless like so many of the hot young models Joker had fucked over the last few months. Not that Joker had given any thought at all to Gio's subtle freckles and tiny nicks, or that his top lip was fuller than the bottom. He must have made a sound because Fitz poked him in his side.

"What?" Joker growled.

"Behave," Fitz told him.

Joker arched an eyebrow at him, making him laugh. "I don't know what you're talking about. I'm a fucking paragon of politeness."

Mason and Leo arrived in time to hear his remark, and Mason threw his head back, letting out a booming laugh.

"What's so funny, cowboy?"

"Nothin'," Mason replied in his thick Texan drawl. "Just where Gio is concerned, you have a habit of squattin' on your spurs."

Mason and his damn cowboyisms.

"I don't know what that means, but I'm gonna respond with this." Joker flipped Mason off, making him laugh again. "What the hell are you doing here, anyway? I thought you listened to shit country music."

"Fuck off. I listen to good country music." Mason scratched his stubbled jaw. "And I'm here because certain individuals insisted I come along." He tilted his head toward Colton, who stood a couple of yards away talking to Laz and Gio.

"Still haven't figured out how to say no to him, have you?" Joker snorted at Mason's wide eyes.

"That man is terrifying."

Leo tilted his head in thought. "Really?"

Oh, sweet Leo. So oblivious. But that was part of what made him Leo. He was like a tiny fluffy bunny—a fluffy bunny who happened to be the most dangerous man in the room because of his brain. The guy had been kept a secret from the government by his Army general dad out of fear of what they—and any other government—would do to get their hands on Leo, and they would have succeeded if it hadn't been for King.

Gio might be Chip's favorite human, but Chip guarded Leo like no one else, especially from strangers. Like he knew

Leo was a precious snowflake who needed to be protected at all costs. Speaking of...

Joker turned to Leo. "I didn't think this was your kind of scene." Outside of their family, people in general were not Leo's scene, much less a loud arena packed with thousands of people. It was the opposite of Leo in every way.

Leo snapped his attention away from the guys moving computer equipment. He pointed up and behind them to the owner's skybox.

"I'll be watching from up there. As for being here, are you kidding?" His eyes went all huge and sparkly. Uh-oh. Leo was about to have one of his nerdgasms. "Do you know the kind of coding and tech that goes into a Nia show? She's got her own dream team who make her ideas a reality through coding and engineering. All of it perfectly in sync with her dance choreography and music. Her use of holograms is state of the art! And the best part is, Gio's going to introduce me to her team. A couple of them used to work for NASA! I have so many questions."

Joker nodded. "I bet."

"Oh, I brought you a new snack." Leo reached into his jacket pocket and produced a small packet of something. He held it out to Joker, his smile bright. "Plantain crisps. I know you've had plantain chips, but these are thinner and crunchier. They're so yummy. Not as epic as Goldfish Crackers, but then nothing is."

Joker took the bag from Leo with a wink. "Thanks." He stuck the bag into one of the pockets of his black tactical pants as a bark caught their attention. Chip, the traitor, was losing his furry mind, as per usual. Because, of course, his dog's favorite human had to be the one guy Joker preferred to avoid.

"I'm so happy to see you too," Gio cooed as he made his

way over, laughing and conversing with Chip, who shared his woes with Gio through a combination of barks, whines, and howls. His whole body wagged as he licked whatever part of Gio he could get to with his doggie tongue. If they'd been at Colton's house or anywhere else Chip had toys, he would have brought Gio a toy or one of his bones, because he loved the fucker that damned much. Asshole.

Gio stopped in front of Joker, his smile soft. "Hello, Sacha."

"Giovanni," Joker said through a grunt.

Gio gave Chip one last ear scratch before Chip returned to sit at Joker's heel. Gio opened his mouth to say something as Ace and Lucky appeared to say hello to the guys, or more likely because they couldn't be at ease if they weren't breathing the same damn air as their men.

"You look handsome," Gio told Joker.

Joker peered at him. "You've seen me in this before." Same black tee with the Four Kings Security logo on the front left breast pocket and the company name on the back in bold white letters, black tactical pants, and boots. "I'm wearing the same uniform everyone else is."

Gio leaned in, his lips quirked at the corners in that roguish way of his. "But no one looks as good in it as you do." His voice was low and silky, not that Joker was paying attention to the throatiness of Gio's voice.

Joker glanced toward the end of the stage, where Saint stood, the sleeves of his T-shirt straining against his bulging biceps. He was over six feet tall, all broad shoulders, thick thighs, and sculpted male perfection. The guy looked every bit the Navy SEAL he'd once been. Gio turned his head to see what had caught Joker's attention, then turned back to Joker, his smile knowing.

"I stand by my statement."

Joker snorted. "Right." Not that he had any hang-ups about his body. He was toned, fit, and had twice the stamina most of the guys at Four Kings had, even the guys younger than him. He could run circles around all of them. He was agile, adept at sports, and a natural gymnast. Maybe if the universe hadn't been such a dick, he'd have been given a little more height, but whatever.

"Will you and Chip be at Colton's tomorrow for the barbecue?"

Joker replied without thinking. "Well, yeah. Obviously." *Shit, wait...*

"Great! I'll see you then."

Damn it. Joker should have known. Fuck it. At first, he'd avoided any event where Gio might be but quickly realized there was no point. Gio was back for good and a part of their lives whether he liked it or not, even if Joker couldn't figure out why the sudden return. The guy had traveled the world for years doing who knew what in the name of charity, and out of the blue, one day he calls Laz up and says he's coming home for good? Why?

"Sacha?" Jack's voice came through his earpiece.

Joker sighed. He hated to be called by his real name, but Jack had known him for decades, long before one of their fallen brothers-in-arms had given them their nicknames. "What?"

"One of the stagehands bumped camera three with a prop he was carrying onto the stage. Must have knocked it pretty hard. It's out of alignment. Can you go check it out?"

"Sure thing."

Aw, what a shame. "I need to go. Duty calls."

"Stay safe," Gio said, his expression sincere.

Joker nodded. He ignored the way his heart did a stupid little flip. None of his friends understood why he was such an asshole to Gio, which was funny, considering Joker was pretty much an asshole most of the time, but something about Gio got to him, and *that* pissed Joker off like nothing else. From the moment they'd first spoken, Joker had a visceral reaction to the guy, and he hated it. No one was going to have that kind of control over him. *No one.*

"Come on," he told Chip. They headed backstage, where he removed the small tablet from his pocket and signed into the secure event portal Jack had created for this job. He located camera three and frowned. It was just outside Nia's dressing room. Giving the command, Joker sent Chip to sniff around.

They'd already checked this area several times, but over the next few hours, they'd be making several more rounds. His earpiece came to life, and King's low grumble sounded in his ear.

"Listen up, guys. Nia and her crew are on their way. Check in with your teams."

"Copy that," Joker replied, along with Ace, Lucky, and Jack. He followed Chip as his partner left no corner unsniffed. Joker stopped in front of camera three outside Nia's dressing room and peered up at it. The camera hung at an odd angle. "Jesus, what did he hit it with, a brick?" He'd just returned the tablet to his pocket when Chip gave his low warning growl. Turning, he found Chip with his nose pressed to the bottom of Nia's closed dressing room door. Joker tapped his PTT button. "Jack, is Nia onsite?"

"Not yet, but members of her entourage have started arriving."

"Copy that. Chip's not liking something in her dressing room. I'm going in to investigate."

"Let us know if you need backup."

"Will do." Joker hissed out another command in

German, and Chip swiftly returned to Joker's heel. They slowly approached the dressing room from one side. He silently turned the knob, but found it locked. This couldn't be good. He knocked on the door. "Security. Is everything okay in there?" No answer.

"Security." He pounded on the door. "I need you to respond. Now." Still no answer.

Chip growled again, his hackles up, and Joker took a step away from the door.

"Okay, if you don't answer or open this door, I'm coming in. You have five seconds. Five, four, three—"

The door cracked open, and a pair of blue eyes glared at him. "What do you want?"

Joker arched an eyebrow. "Who are you?"

"Who are *you*?" the guy snarled. A low growl rumbled from beside Joker, and the guy snapped his gaze to Chip. His eyes went huge, and he swallowed hard. "I mean, uh, hi, sorry. Can I help you?"

Joker grabbed the edge of the door with a smirk. "Yeah, you can tell me who you are and what you're doing in there."

"I'm Jiles. I work for the props department."

"Doesn't answer why you're in this dressing room, Jiles."

The guy opened the door and stepped to one side so Joker and Chip could enter the room. Chip immediately began sniffing everything, and Joker remained alert as he scanned the huge room. The doors to the two bathrooms were open, the curtains to the changing rooms also open. It was a brightly lit space decorated in black and white with pops of bright pink. Multiple mirrors and vanities were positioned across the seating area.

Something red blinked from a vase of flowers on the

bigger vanity, and Joker strolled over. Considering Chip hadn't given him the signal, he was confident it wasn't an incendiary device. He reached into the flowers and pulled out what looked like a small camera. Turning, he held the camera up to Jiles, who'd gone so pale Joker wondered if the guy was about to pass out.

Jiles didn't pass out. He took off running like someone had shot him out of a cannon.

"Fuck!" Joker shoved the camera into his pocket as he shouted a command to Chip, who bolted after Jiles. Upon seeing the black demon dog on his heels, Jiles shrieked loud enough to shatter glass and plowed through the curtains onto the stage.

Jiles's first mistake had been to run. His second and *biggest* mistake had been to run toward Leo, who was so absorbed in whatever was on his phone screen he didn't hear Joker shouting at him. Gio, however, did hear Joker and sprang into action, putting himself between Jiles and Leo right as Chip tackled Jiles.

Jiles plowed into Gio, knocking him off his feet, the two hitting the stage hard, with Chip's jaws around a mouthful of Jiles's cargo shorts. Where exactly Jiles thought he was crawling to with a Belgian Malinois attached to him was anyone's guess. Jiles yelped as Chip dragged him away from Gio as if he were nothing more than a sack of potatoes.

Several of their guys reached Jiles, so Joker gave Chip the command to disengage and then turned to help Gio, only to find Saint with his arm around Gio's waist as he helped him to his feet.

"Shit, man. You okay?" Saint asked, a hand to Gio's chest.

What the fuck? Gio hadn't been hit that hard. There

was no need for him to be held. Either way, Gio was up now, so Saint could let go.

Okay, this needed to stop. Joker shook himself out of it. First of all, who the fuck cared if Saint was touching Gio? Saint was Joker's friend. He was also *straight*.

"Yes, I'm fine," Gio replied, running a hand through his hair. "Thank you, Saint."

Saint smiled brightly, his cheeks looking a little... flushed. "You're welcome."

That was *not* how a straight man smiled at another man. *Wait, what?* The adrenaline must have gone to Joker's head, because that thought had to be the most ridiculous thing to ever cross his mind. With a snort, he turned back to Jiles. Behind them, a large figure emerged from the shadows, and Joker grinned. King had walked on stage, and he looked *pissed*.

Joker patted Jiles's shoulder. "Nice knowing ya." He waited while King went straight to Leo, gently moving him to one side so he could talk to him privately. He took hold of Leo's chin and murmured something to him. Leo nodded, his cheeks pink as he said something in return that led to King hugging him tightly. It was a quick hug, but enough for those who knew King to know he'd been shaken at the possibility of Leo being hurt. King stopped next to Gio and put a hand on his shoulder.

"Thank you for protecting him."

Gio shook his head. "No need to thank me. Any one of us would have done the same. I was just closer."

"Regardless, I appreciate it."

Joker groaned. Great, because Gio wasn't on a high enough pedestal already. King patted Gio's shoulder, then stalked over to Joker, who handed him the camera he'd found.

"This was in some flowers on Nia's vanity. My guess is Jiles here was the one who took out camera three, then locked himself in her dressing room to plant it. I'd have someone sweep the room in case there are more in there."

King took the camera, looked it over, then lifted his icy-blue gaze to Jiles. "Bring him to the security office," he growled as he stormed off.

They hauled Jiles away, and Joker was pretty sure that before the police arrived, Jiles would be all too agreeable. Whether he was a perv or had been intent on making a quick buck by filming Nia, he was in for a world of hurt. With that handled, Joker headed over to Leo, who now stood with Gio.

"It's okay, Leo," Gio said, placing his hand on Leo's shoulder. "I'm fine. I promise."

Leo nodded, but he still looked upset. Only one thing—or rather one fur ball—could change that. Joker scratched Chip's head and murmured, "Go give Leo a kiss."

Chip bolted over to Leo and repeatedly jumped like a kangaroo so he could assault Leo with doggie kisses. There was no way to keep a serious face as Leo laughed and giggle-snorted while he attempted to stop Chip, who was determined to give Leo all the kisses in his canine arsenal.

Joker stopped next to Gio, who laughed at Chip's hijinks. "Thanks for doing that," Joker grumbled. "Though maybe next time, just move him out of the way instead of turning yourself into a human shield."

"Were you worried about me?" Gio asked, his smile reaching his eyes. Joker was about to squash that sentiment, but Gio went pale and threw a hand out, gripping Joker's shoulder.

"What's wrong?" Joker asked. Not even thinking about

it, he wrapped an arm around Gio's waist, his free hand going to Gio's chest. "Talk to me, Giovanni."

"I think I'm a little dehydrated."

Gio needed to sit before he fell.

"Over there." Joker motioned to a closed steel trunk a few feet away.

"Gio, are you okay?" Leo asked worriedly. Chip whining at Gio's side was not a good sign.

"I'm fine. Simply a little dehydrated."

Joker helped him over to the trunk and pressed his PTT button. "Saint, bring me a bottle of water."

In no time flat, Saint returned with the water and handed it to Joker, who twisted the cap off and held it out to Gio.

"Drink."

"Thank you." Gio took the bottle from him, his fingers covering Joker's, surprising a shiver out of him. Pretending he hadn't felt the jolt and ignoring Gio's knowing look, Joker took a step back. He turned to Saint.

"Thanks."

"Everything okay?" Saint asked, concerned.

"Yeah, he needs water. You can get back to it."

Saint appeared momentarily shocked by the dismissal. Why? Joker had no idea. It wasn't the guy's first time working with him. He had a job to do, and it wasn't to hover around Gio. "Oh, right. Sure thing." With a nod, he walked off.

"Are you sure this isn't my fault?" Leo asked quietly, his boyish face filled with worry.

"Not your fault," Gio assured him. "I promise. I had a charity brunch this morning that was outdoors, and I should have hydrated more." He lifted the bottle of water. "I'm feeling better already."

"Okay."

Colton called Leo over, and Leo excused himself.

Not wasting any time, Joker frowned at Gio. "Not drinking water while outdoors is stupid."

"Agreed."

"You're in Florida now. Hydration is important. Even when it's cloudy, the sun will still bake you."

Gio nodded. "I know that now."

"Well, make sure you don't forget it," Joker growled. "Drink the whole bottle." It wasn't like this was Gio's first trip to Florida. The man had been born and raised here.

"Yes, sir." Gio saluted, and Joker rolled his eyes. Smartass. At least the color had returned to his face. Gio lifted his eyes to Joker's. "Thank you."

"For what? Sending someone to get you a bottle of water?" Joker waved a hand in dismissal. He wasn't that much of an asshole. Not even to Gio. Springing into action when something was wrong was his default, and had been since his years in the military. Just because he and his brothers weren't serving anymore didn't mean they forgot years of training or life experiences.

"You must know a lot about dehydration, working these kinds of events," Gio said.

"Yep. It's serious shit. August will be the worst. Our guys spend a good deal of the time bringing people water at outdoor events because people forget how fucking brutal the heat and humidity can be."

Gio finished the bottle of water and stood. Much to his annoyance, Joker caught himself reaching for the guy. He quickly dropped his hand.

"All good?"

"Yes, thank you." Gio smiled sweetly, and Joker forced himself to avert his gaze. He was going to say he had to get back to work when someone called out from across the stage.

"Gio!"

A gorgeous woman with flawless tanned skin and waves of shimmering black hair, dressed in a black silk robe precariously tied around her slim waist, hurried toward them.

Nia was even more stunning in person than she was on screen, with ample curves and long legs that put her at least four inches taller than Joker, and that was without the three-inch heels she had on. Her lips were full and pouty, her eyes so dark they were almost black, and her presence was so *raw* it seemed to sucker punch everyone she swept past. She looked more like a goddess than a pop star, and she headed straight for Gio, arms wide.

"When they told me what happened, I couldn't believe it!" She threw her arms around Gio, hugging him. "I was so worried! Are you okay?" She pulled back enough to cup his face.

"It was nothing. Really. It's so good to see you."

"I've missed this face." She kissed one cheek, then the other, her smile dazzling.

Well, that was his cue. Joker turned to leave, but Gio called out to him.

"Wait! Sacha."

Joker stopped and rolled his eyes. Now what? All Joker wanted was to get through his shift and have a couple of beers after work, and maybe a steak. Was that too much to ask? He turned, his expression telling Gio exactly how unimpressed he was.

"Yeah?"

"Sacha, I'd like to introduce you to Nia. Nia, this is Sacha Wilder. He's the one who found the man in your dressing room and caught him." Chip barked from behind Joker, and Gio laughed. "I'm so sorry. Chip was technically the one who caught him."

"Oh, he's beautiful," Nia cooed. "Such a brave boy."

"Yes, he is," Gio said, his gaze on Joker rather than Chip, who Nia fawned over, though to her credit, she hadn't tried to touch Chip.

Chip wagged his tail slowly, suspiciously, as he stared at Nia, making Joker hold back a snicker. *That's my boy.* Chip looked from Nia to Joker and waited for the verdict.

"Say hello," Joker finally said. It wasn't Nia's fault she was stunning. Besides, if she was interested in Gio, it was none of his business. She'd also known Gio longer than Joker had, which didn't matter since Joker wasn't interested in Gio.

As soon as Nia finished greeting Chip, she turned to lavish her attention back on Gio. Time to get gone. Joker excused himself. He had a job to do, and it didn't include babysitting the billionaire and his "good" friend.

Chip came to heel and remained at his side as they headed backstage to make another round. They'd just turned away from the dressing rooms when Nia and Gio emerged through the curtains, their heads close together as they spoke quietly, her arm wrapped possessively around his as they headed for her dressing room. Whatever they were talking about seemed to have Gio mesmerized.

Chip whined, and Joker dropped his gaze to his furry friend. "It's fine. Like I care?"

"And once more with feeling," Ace said, his grin stretching from ear to ear.

"Where the fuck did you come from?" Joker hadn't even heard Ace, and that was a freaking terrifying notion because when *didn't* you hear Ace?

"You must have been too busy being fine over the hot pop star wrapped around the guy you definitely don't care about."

Joker narrowed his eyes at Ace, and his friend threw up his hands in surrender.

"Only an observation."

"If I want your observation, I'll give it to you. Now fuck off."

With a chuckle, Ace walked away. If his friend thought he'd meddle in Joker's love life, he had another think coming. Not that Joker *had* a love life. Which was exactly the way he liked it. He had a sex life, and a very active and glorious one at that. Love had nothing to do with it.

Okay, so maybe he was in the middle of a dry spell, but it would pass. Work had been busy, and he'd been doing a lot of overtime, so he hadn't been to Sapphire Sands in a while. None of the hookups on his app had been particularly enticing. Didn't mean a thing.

"It's fine," he assured Chip. "A momentary setback. We're good. It's all good." He got another side-eye from Chip. "Listen, mister. I don't need any of your sass, okay. Get to work. Earn your extortionate bone-and-toy budget." Chip barked and trotted off ahead of Joker to do his thing.

The rest of his shift went on without incident, and he certainly didn't spend any time at all thinking about Gio or what he and Nia might be getting up to in her dressing room. Thankfully, his shift was officially over. The arena was a thrum of bustling activity as teams of people ran around making sure everything was ready while crowds of people lined up outside.

Ace approached him by the security office. "Hey, Colton and Gio got the Boyfriend Collective a bunch of rooms at that swanky guitar-shaped hotel about twenty minutes from here. My shift ended, so I'm gonna hang out in our room and order room service while Colton's at the concert. Wanna come? You can feed your beast and chill."

"Sure, why not." The rest of the guys had been invited to watch the concert from the manager's box with Leo, and Joker wasn't about to turn down some tasty—and more importantly *free*—room service from Colton's fancy hotel suite.

They checked in with King before hopping in Ace's red Corvette Stingray Coupe. Being married to a billionaire certainly had its perks. Colton loved to spoil Ace, and Ace loved to be spoiled. Joker wasn't sure exactly how they managed it, but the two were disgustingly happy and in love, so whatever they did worked.

A couple of hours later, they'd ordered enough food to feed a small army and eaten every single delicious morsel. No one could eat his weight in french fries like Ace. With all three of them fed, they popped open a couple of beers and settled in to watch some TV. Chip was out of his work vest and lay on the couch on his back, paws in the air and head on Joker's lap, because why would he lie on the floor like a sucker when there was a comfy couch and someone's lap?

"Your dog is ridiculous," Ace said, his smile wide. Chip let out a huff, making Ace laugh. "He seems to have really taken a liking to Gio."

"Wow, was that you trying to be subtle? Because I hate to break it to you, pal, you're about as subtle as your Cuban mama."

Ace barked out a laugh. "She asks about you every time she calls."

"I'm sure she does," Joker said with a hum. Heaven

forbid one of her boys not be in a relationship. "Tell her I'm perfectly happy having lots of amazing sex."

"If you think I'm going to even hint to the word *sex* while talking to my mother, you're nuttier than I thought."

"Maybe if you two didn't gossip about everyone's love life, it wouldn't come up."

Ace blinked at him. "But then how would I know that my cousin Lolita's best friend's father's second cousin's nephew showed up to his sister's quinceñiera party with his *straight* best friend, and the two got caught making out in the janitor's closet?"

"I..." Joker shook his head. "I don't even know what to say to that."

"See? That's vital intel."

"Of course it is." Joker snickered and shook his head. They went back to watching TV and ribbing each other over nonsense. Joker had just dozed off when Ace's phone rang.

"Hey, baby. Miss me— *What*? Are you okay? Are you safe? Hang tight. I'm on my way."

Joker jolted awake. "What happened?"

Ace hung up and shot to his feet. "I gotta go. Colton went to meet Gio at Nia's tour bus when someone shot at Nia and Gio."

"*What*?"

Chip rolled off Joker as Joker jumped to his feet, his heart pounding in his ears.

"Security thinks they meant to hit Nia and Gio got in the way. Either that or the guy, lucky for us, had shit aim. They tackled him and restrained him. The police are on their way."

Joker grabbed Ace's arm. "Is Gio okay?"

"I think so."

"You *think* so?" Joker asked, incredulous. He was going to kick Ace's ass.

"Colton said he looked okay."

"Jesus Christ! He *looked* okay? I'm going with you."

"Why?"

"Because you'll be busy with Colton and Red's in the middle of a job over an hour away. Plus, he'll have his hands full with Laz. The moment Laz finds out about Gio, he'll freak out."

Ace pursed his lips. "Your argument is sound."

"Shut up and let's go." Of course his argument was sound. He quickly made sure Chip had water in his bowl and some dry kibble, just in case. With a scratch on the head, he told Chip to stay, then quickly left the room.

As soon as Laz discovered someone had shot his brother, he'd lose his shit. "Have you told Red?"

"Unless Colton called him, he doesn't know. Laz was with Fitz, waiting for Leo and the others."

Which meant Laz didn't know. They had some time.

"Colton won't call Red or Laz," Joker assured him.

"How do you know?" Ace asked as they hurried to the elevator. Joker did his best not to think of worst-case scenarios. If Colton said Gio looked okay, then it was probably nothing. That's twice in one day Gio had put himself in harm's way. For fuck's sake. The guy was a trouble magnet.

"Gio won't let him. He's a stubborn shit."

"Yeah, I mean, trying to protect his little brother." Ace shook his head, his lips quirked in amusement. "What an asshole."

"Shut up."

With the concert let out, traffic was a nightmare. They'd had to park blocks away and run to the arena. Joker made no apologies to the assholes who didn't heed his warning and get out of his fucking way. They were still dressed in their uniforms, so flashing their credentials meant they were allowed past the barriers and security behind the arena, where Nia's ginormous tour bus was parked.

"Where the fuck is he?" Joker demanded of no one in particular. The crowd parted and people got the hell out of his way as he thundered toward the ambulance and the tall figure with broad shoulders he'd recognize anywhere, much to his annoyance. From the looks of it, Gio was alive and well. How dare the bastard cause him concern!

A growl rose up in Joker's throat. "What the fuck did you—" He stilled at the sight of the bloodied shirtsleeve. He swallowed hard as Gio turned to face him, the left side of his torso bare, his shirt hanging off one shoulder to reveal the white bandage around his arm. It was a stark contrast against his tanned skin.

"Sacha," Gio said, warmth filling his tone, a warmth that reflected in his dark eyes.

Joker snapped himself out of whatever stupid trance he'd been in and narrowed his eyes at Gio. "Don't call me that."

"What are you doing here?" Gio asked softly.

"I'm here because you got yourself shot, asshole." Why the hell did the guy look so amused? He'd just been shot. Fucking Gio.

"Why do you say that so accusatory?"

"What happened?" Joker demanded.

Gio cocked his head to one side, his lips quirked up in the corner. "Someone shot at me."

Sweet Jesus, give me strength. "And someone's about to shoot at you again," Joker hissed. "What the fuck happened?"

A weary sigh escaped Gio, and Joker's anger subsided despite his better judgment. It was only then that Joker noticed the dark circles and harsh lines. Gio was exhausted. *No. Nope. You are not going to feel bad for him. He's an asshole, remember?*

"The truth is, I don't know what happened. One minute Nia and I were leaving the bus, the next minute someone screamed and I saw the gun. I pulled Nia behind me and felt my arm burn. By then the man had been tackled to the ground. I've never seen him before in my life, and believe me, I have an excellent memory when it comes to people." The heat in his eyes told Joker exactly which memories he was revisiting. Not that Joker thought about that night backstage. Nope. Not ever.

Don't meet his gaze. Don't look him in the eye. It's a trap, and you know it.

Joker's jaw muscles tightened. Fuck that. He was no coward. Defiantly, he lifted his chin and met Gio's gaze. A slow, wicked smile spread across those full lips, and Gio took a step closer. He stood looming over Joker and leaned in, his lips next to Joker's ear. His breath was hot, his words a low, sultry purr.

"I was hoping you'd come for me."

Fuck.

TWO

Gio didn't dare smile at the thought. Not when faced with the explosive whirlwind and contradictory force of nature that was Sacha Wilder. The man captivated him. From Sacha's first growl, he'd been struck. Why? At first, he hadn't been certain, but the more Gio interacted with Sacha, the more he wanted to know him, talk to him, be around him. Gio had never met anyone so... passionate, so expressive, so damned honest.

When Laz had told Gio about the Kings' charity bachelor auction, Gio had asked his brother if Sacha would be one of the bachelors. At Laz's confirmation that he would be, Gio spent an obscene amount of money to not only make sure he was there that night, but that he'd have the winning bid. No way was he losing out on an opportunity with Sacha Wilder. It was the first time they'd met face-to-face, and oh! What a face. Gio had been swept away.

The man's online photos didn't do him justice. Mainly because there wasn't one photo where Sacha wasn't growling, scowling, or glaring. The intensity in his eyes, his intimidating stance, and the set of his jaw screamed, "Danger! Approach with caution!" Yet Gio couldn't seem to keep away.

That night at the auction, in a moment of shock when Sacha had stared up at Gio, every stunning feature had been on display. Bright, sharp blue-gray eyes, the most expressive eyebrows Gio had ever seen, a heart-shaped face, cupid-bow lips, stubble, and tousled honey-colored hair. His personality made him larger than life, but physically, he was petite and slender, with a body that appeared better suited to a dancer than a soldier. He was absolutely beautiful.

Sacha's lips had parted ever so slightly, revealing a minor imperfection Gio found charming. His two top front teeth were ever so slightly longer than the rest. With Sacha's defenses momentarily down, Gio had said hello, placed his fingers under Sacha's chin, and kissed his flushed cheek. His sharp intake of breath, his blown pupils, and more importantly, the slip of vulnerability had sealed the deal for Gio. In that heartbeat, he'd made his decision.

Sacha Wilder needed to be his.

"Are you fucking listening to me?"

"Always," Gio replied with a smile.

Sacha grunted. "Why are you so annoying?"

"Why are you so delightful?"

"You know what the worst part is? Most guys would say that and I'd know they were fucking with me, but you actually mean it."

"I wouldn't say it if I didn't."

"Hence why you're annoying." Sacha snorted. "I'm a lot of things, pal, but believe me, delightful is not one of them."

Gio chuckled. "If you say so. The answer to your

question is none. I have no security detail." He shrugged. "Why would I need security?"

Sacha's eyebrows flew up, and he thrust both hands in the direction of Gio's bandaged arm. So dramatic, his sweet man.

"I'm sure this was a one-time incident. There's no need for a security detail. I've faced far more dangerous men than that."

"I don't want to know, and I don't care. You're getting a security detail. I'm assuming you have a whole itinerary of saintly do-goodery events scheduled?"

Gio smiled, captivated by Sacha's wrinkled nose. He was too endearing. "I have several charity events scheduled over the next few months, yes."

"Send me your schedule. I'm going to put a security team together, and you're getting assigned executive protection."

"That's not necessary." While traveling abroad, he'd had security with him at all times, naively believing they'd keep him safe. He'd been foolish, and it had cost him. He quickly pushed that thought away. It didn't matter now. He was back in the United States with his friends and family. Round-the-clock security wasn't needed.

"Gio!" Laz's frantic cry broke through the crowd, and Sacha's evil grin was not lost on Gio.

"Not necessary, huh? We'll see about that."

Gio sighed, knowing the argument was over before it began. With a warm smile for his little brother, he opened his arms, and Laz threw himself against Gio, who made the mistake of wincing when Laz accidentally brushed against his injured arm. Laz jerked away, his eyes huge and his gaze locked on Gio's arm.

"Oh my God."

"I'm okay," Gio promised, bringing Laz back into his embrace and squeezing him with his uninjured arm. He hated worrying Laz. His little brother had been through enough. The familiar guilt of not having been there when his brother had needed him most tried to overwhelm him, but he remembered his therapist's words. *You can't feel guilty for not being somewhere you didn't know you needed to be. You couldn't have known.* Sometimes it helped, but even if he hadn't known what Laz was going through at the time, he still felt that if he'd been around more, maybe Laz wouldn't have landed in the hands of that predator.

Sacha's voice intruded on his thoughts. "I'm putting a security team together for your brother."

"Oh, that's perfect! Thank you so much, Joker."

"Laz, that's not—" His little brother's glare could have turned him to stone. Gio cleared his throat. "Right. I suppose a little security wouldn't hurt."

Sacha snorted and smacked Gio in the abdomen. "Not like you can't afford it."

"I'll accept any security proposal from you, on one condition."

Narrowed eyes met Gio's. So much suspicion. Gio had noticed a trust issue with Sacha from early on, more so than with his brothers-in-arms. What had happened to cause such deep-rooted distrust?

"I'm not going to be a part of it," Sacha replied, arms crossed over his chest. "So don't even think about it."

"Not you. Chip."

Sacha looked endearingly puzzled. "What?"

"I will accept any security you decide, providing Chip is part of my security detail."

"Is that so?" Sacha said, one thick eyebrow arched.

"Yep." They both knew Chip only worked with Sacha.

"I see." Joker widened his stance; his chest puffed up as he seemed to consider it. Laz turned to Sacha, big eyes pleading.

"Please, Joker. I've been trying to get him to hire security for eight months now. He's already had the press show up at his office. How much longer before all the media outlets find out he's back for good and where the new house is? It wouldn't be the first time they'd show up wherever he was staying."

"Jack installed a very robust security system in the new house," Gio reminded his brother. If anyone so much as approached his property without the proper credentials, a security team would be alerted.

"And I suppose the house is going to secure you when you're not in it?" Laz asked, looking unimpressed. He turned his attention back to Sacha. "Please."

"Fine," Sacha said through a grunt. "I'll let you know when the proposal is done."

"Wonderful," Gio replied cheerfully. "And thank you for coming to check on me."

"Yeah, um, okay." Sacha turned to Laz. "He staying with you guys tonight?"

Gio frowned. "That's not—" The warning look he received from Sacha had Gio holding back a smile.

"Yeah, it is."

"Of course," Laz said, scowling at his brother.

"Good. I'll discuss it with King, and we'll have someone assigned as your executive protection first thing in the morning."

Executive protection? "I really don't think—"

"Well, I think it is. Now, how about you go home with Laz and stay out of trouble." With that, Sacha stormed off.

Laz continued to fuss over him, and Gio sighed. "Laz, I'm fine. It's just a scratch."

His brother's glare told him he disagreed. Feeling a little dizzy, Gio didn't have the energy to argue, so he simply nodded, even if the only thing he wanted to do right now was take a nice hot shower and get into his own bed, though it was probably best he not be alone. Twice in one day. He needed this kind of excitement not to become a habit.

Colton appeared and gently placed a hand on Gio's shoulder. "Why don't you come home with us," Colton said, then moved his gaze to Laz. "We'll look after him."

"That's a wonderful idea," Gio replied, perking up. "Then I'll already be there for the barbecue."

Colton blinked at him. "You don't want to reschedule it?"

"Are you kidding? No. I've been looking forward to it. Starting next week, I have a full schedule of events." Now that his move back was official and his affairs were all in order at home and the office, it was time to get back to it.

"Are you sure?" Laz asked, uncertain.

"Positive." Gio hugged his brother once more. "Give Red a hug from me and tell him not to worry."

"You call me if you need anything, you understand?" Laz demanded, and Gio promised he would. When had his little brother become so forceful? It was good to see. At one point, Laz seemed to have lost all his self-confidence. Or more likely, it had been slowly stripped away by his bastard ex-boyfriend.

Once Gio hugged Laz and promised him for the hundredth time that he'd rest and call if he needed anything, Laz went off with the guys, and Gio climbed into the back seat of Ace's car. The two lovebirds murmured from the front seats, holding hands. Gio was so happy for

Colton. Never in a million years would he have predicted his best friend would end up married to a man like Ace, but after spending only a few minutes in their presence, Gio understood.

Colton laughed softly at something his husband said, and Gio smiled. Once upon a time, Colton had been so serious, devoting himself to nothing but work, afraid to risk his heart after the utter betrayal from his previous relationship. He'd been cold and detached. He laughed and smiled easily these days, his eyes filled with life and love, even when Ace drove him mad. All Ace had to do was pull Colton into his arms and murmur a few soft words and Colton dissolved; his anger evaporated much like the rain on a hot and humid Florida day.

An image of bright blue-gray eyes came to mind, and Gio found himself smiling again. Sacha put on a formidable front of dislike for Gio, but the truth was Sacha did care. Why he seemed so against showing it had Gio stumped. He recalled the night of the auction, replaying the memory for what had to be the thousandth time.

After the kiss to Sacha's cheek, Sacha had stormed off backstage, and Gio had quickly followed him to a darkened corner away from the busyness of the stage area. Sacha whirled on Gio, hissing at him like a bristled wild cat with sharp fangs and sharper claws.

"What the hell are you doing here?"

The way his eyes shone, even in the dim lighting... Good God, he was beautiful. "You're stunning."

Sacha stared at him before seeming to shake himself out of it. "What the fuck, Gio? You're supposed to be halfway around the world."

"And miss taking you out on a date?" Gio shook his

head. "Never. Besides..." He shoved his hands into his pockets and shrugged. "I'm home. For good."

That seemed to shock Sacha more than Gio's sudden presence. "You... You're staying?"

Gio stepped closer to Sacha, and with a warm smile, tentatively reached out to move a lock of Sacha's hair away from his brow. "Yes, I am. Consider this my homecoming." A host of emotions crossed Sacha's face, none of them decipherable.

"Holy fuck! You just paid a hundred thousand dollars for a *date*."

"With you."

Sacha didn't appear impressed. Not that it had been Gio's intention. Quite the opposite. Sacha's reaction had him even more captivated, but then Gio shouldn't be surprised. A man like Sacha had little interest in pompous gestures. He'd been aware of Gio's wealth from the beginning and couldn't have cared less. He seemed more suspicious of it than anything.

"The truth is, I spent a hundred thousand dollars on a very worthy cause."

Sacha regarded him with narrowed eyes. So suspicious. "Why?"

"You and your family saved my little brother's life. More than once, in fact. The more I've gotten to know Red, and through him your family, the more I want to help where I can. Tonight provided me with the perfect opportunity. A date with you is simply a lovely bonus."

Sacha glared at him and thrust a finger at him. "Whatever your game is, I'm not playing; you got that?"

Gio moved closer, and Sacha quickly retreated a step, unaware he had nowhere to go until his back hit the wall behind him. His eyes widened.

"I never play games," Gio whispered, cupping Sacha's face. He ran a thumb over Sacha's bottom lip, his pulse racing when those gorgeous eyes fluttered shut and Sacha leaned into Gio's touch. His lips parted ever so softly, and Gio lowered his head to brush his lips along the side of Sacha's mouth. Heat flared through him at the sound of Sacha's sharp intake of breath. A barely-there moan escaped from between those sweet lips. "Let me give you what you need."

Sacha shivered beneath his touch. Then his eyes popped open, and he glared at Gio. "I don't need anything from anyone, especially *you*. Get the hell out of my way."

Gio held up his hands in front of him and stepped aside. After that, Gio had canceled the date. Of course, he'd still donated the money, but he wasn't going to force Sacha into doing something he didn't want to do. To his absolute bewilderment, Sacha texted him several days later, informing him the date was back on. Gio had no idea what had prompted the change of heart, but he'd been thrilled. The heat and tension between them had almost killed him, but spending that time alone with Sacha had been worth every second.

"Home sweet home."

Ace's voice interrupted Gio's thoughts, and he climbed out of the parked car. He followed the two into the house from the garage, thanking Ace for everything. Colton led Gio to one of the many guest rooms and went to find him some clothes he could change into, along with something to wrap his arm in so he could shower.

"Thanks, Colt."

"You let me know if you need anything, okay? And don't worry if your bandage needs changing. Ace can do that for you." He smiled brightly. "Having a former Green

Beret for a husband is pretty handy." His eyes widened. "Just don't ask him to fix anything."

Gio frowned. "I would have thought he'd be good at fixing things."

"Oh, he is. The problem is that when he goes to fix something, like oh, let's say the bottom board on the steps of the walkway leading from the deck to the beach, upon further inspection, he discovers how uneven the rest of it is and ends up tearing the whole thing up." Colton looked slightly traumatized. "Our house might get swept away by a hurricane, but the military-grade walkway will survive. Also, he fixed the Roomba, so unless you want to get sucked into another dimension, stay away from it."

Laughter bubbled out of Gio so hard, he had tears in his eyes, and Colton was right there with him. They were so loud, Ace appeared, a bemused smile on his handsome face.

"You two are adorable. By the way," Ace told Colton, "the showerhead broke in our bathroom, but don't worry, I fixed it."

Colton and Gio exchanged glances before they started laughing again. Gio could barely breathe.

"What?" Ace said. "What's so funny?"

Colton wiped a tear from his eye and wrapped his arms around Ace's waist. "Nothing, baby. Let's go to bed. Goodnight, Gio."

"Goodnight, you two." Gio shook his head and closed the door behind his friends. It was so good to be home.

As much as Gio would have loved to take a long hot shower, it wasn't a good idea after the night he'd had, so he made it quick, mindful of the bandage on his arm, and then changed into the pajamas Colton had brought him. He was a little lightheaded but okay. Knowing he wouldn't be getting much sleep despite his exhaustion, he stepped outside onto the balcony that ran along the back of the house facing the beach.

The March weather was perfect. Still early enough in the year for a cool evening breeze, but late enough for the winter chill to have gone. He'd forgotten how peaceful it was to be on the beach.

When he'd returned home, he'd stayed with Colton and Ace while his broker found him the perfect house. Laz had been hurt at first that Gio hadn't stayed with him, but Gio gently reminded his brother that moving back to the States meant his life was going to be chaotic before it settled, and the last thing he wanted was to interrupt Red's routine.

As someone who lived with PTSD, Red needed to keep to his routines as much as possible. He also required quiet time, and the constant phone calls coming through Gio's phone to the video conferences and meetings were anything but quiet. Red was a good man, and he'd done so much for Laz, Gio refused to do anything that would cause him any setbacks.

After just a few days of watching the sunset from his bedroom balcony, Gio informed his broker to find him something on the beach. He'd also insisted on being near his brother. His broker had come through for him, finding him a gorgeous five-bedroom house on the beach smack in the middle between Colton and Ace's Ponte Vedra mansion and Laz and Red's condo in St. Augustine Beach.

Gio closed his eyes as he listened to the lulling sound of the waves crashing against the shore. The night sky was cloudless, with twinkling stars scattered here and there. When sleep crept up on him, he dragged himself inside. He locked the balcony doors behind him, then dropped onto the comfortable recliner, his feet propped up. He drifted off soon after and managed to get about four hours of sleep.

By the time he'd dressed and wandered downstairs, Ace was in the kitchen serving Colton breakfast.

"Good morning," Gio chirped. "Thank you again for letting me stay last night."

Colton waved a hand in dismissal. "As if there was any question. Did you sleep well?"

"I did," Gio lied. His best friend didn't need to know he rarely slept, or when he did, the nightmares were so terrible they left him shaken and even more tired in the morning.

"How's your arm?" Ace asked.

"Sore, but on the mend." Gio slid into the chair at the counter next to Colton and thanked Ace for the plate of scrambled eggs, bacon, and toast placed in front of him. He still marveled at his new family. At one point, it had just been him, Laz, and Colton. Now his days were filled with the boisterous sound of laughter and hijinks, thanks to the rowdy and lovable mischief-makers who'd embraced Gio upon his return without hesitation. It's what Gio hadn't even realized he'd been missing for so long.

After breakfast, Ace kissed Colton. "Okay, I'm heading out to get the new showerhead and the, uh, the stuff to replace the tile. Let me know if you need anything while I'm out."

Gio opened his mouth to ask, but Colton gave a slight shake of his head, his smile barely suppressed.

"I will," Colton replied. He waited until Ace had left before turning to Gio. "Fancy a morning run?"

"Sure. What happened to the showerhead? I thought he fixed it last night?"

"He did," Colton said, standing. "He also fixed the water pressure. The showerhead is now embedded in the tile. Thankfully, he hasn't lost his killer reflexes, or the showerhead would have knocked him out when it shot off the wall."

If Gio hadn't known Ace, he would have thought Colton was exaggerating. The two of them laughed on their way upstairs to change for their run. One thing was for sure —his best friend would never be bored.

Once changed, they headed down to the beach and the wet sand by the shore. The day was beautiful, and although still hot even at this time of the morning, a nice cool breeze was coming off the ocean. They jogged up the beach, greeting fellow joggers and several dogs. Gio stopped to pet each dog, because how could he not? He loved dogs, had always wanted one, but his busy schedule didn't leave room for a furry friend. It wouldn't be fair to either of them, especially with all the traveling.

"And here I thought you'd slowed down," Colton teased.

How he'd missed Colton. "Are you saying I'm getting old?" He wiped the sweat from his brow and slowed to a walk.

"Never. Especially since we're the same age."

"Ah, of course." Gio smiled warmly at him. "Though I have to admit, some days I can certainly feel myself aging."

Colton's smile turned sympathetic. "When was the last time you took some time off? And I mean real time off. You haven't stopped since you got back, and I can only imagine what kind of schedule you kept while you were abroad."

"What are you talking about? I've traveled the world for years, met all kinds of amazing people. I'm incredibly lucky."

"And you've made such a difference in people's lives. You're an inspiration, Gio. I mean, look at Nia. You helped her make her dream come true."

Gio waved a hand. "I'm just a guy with a shit ton of money."

Colton didn't appear impressed, but then no one knew Gio like Colton. "Right. Tell me, which other billionaires were out there with you, living in unholy conditions, almost *dying* while transforming people's lives?"

"Thank you, by the way, for not telling my brother about my brush with death." Gio hated lying to his brother, but Laz had spent so much time worrying about Gio while he was away, the last thing he needed was to know Gio had been in some makeshift hospital somewhere fighting for his life. What good would it have done?

Gio never discussed the dangers he faced while abroad with Laz. His brother wouldn't have understood why Gio had to be the one to go out there, spend time with the people he was trying to help, live in the conditions they did, get to know the challenges they faced. Some problems couldn't be solved by throwing money at them. What he did was more than charity. He helped people set up and maintain a new, better life, one they'd been too afraid to dream of. After that, he made sure they had the support they needed every step of the way to continue operating in their new life, checking in with them and offering support.

"I only did it because you promised me you'd tell him eventually." Colton stared off at the ocean. "I felt like such a bastard, telling him you had no phone signal when we had no idea where the hell you were. If I had known you were in some godforsaken hospital hanging on by a thread, I would have gone out there and dragged you home myself."

Gio smiled and patted Colton's arm. His best friend didn't even know the half of it. "I know you would have." Colton would have at least tried. Lord knew, there would have been nowhere for any kind of plane or helicopter to land. Hell, the tent they'd set up as a hospital for the tiny village would have been nearly impossible for anyone to find. Would Sacha have found him? Gio was pretty sure Sacha could do whatever he put his mind to.

"You're thinking of him again."

Gio lifted an eyebrow. "Oh?"

"Yep. You get this look of deep concentration on your face whenever you think about him."

"You know me too well." Gio wiped his brow again. The humidity was intense, and it was still early in the morning.

"Yep. Which is why, as your best friend who knows you so very well, I'm going to say this with nothing but love. Please be careful. Joker isn't like anyone you've ever dealt with."

"Oh, I know." The mention of him had Gio's entire body buzzing.

"I'm not saying he's not a good guy, because he is. If you're in trouble, in danger, hell, if someone so much as looks at you funny, he'll probably launch a counterstrike."

The thought warmed Gio all over. "You think so?"

"You're family, so yes. You've seen the way Ace and the guys are. Family is everything, whether through blood or bond. Joker might act like a jerk at times, but he'll never let you down."

"An admirable quality in a partner, don't you think?"

"Yes." Colton's brows furrowed, his expression one of confusion. "He's... so unlike anyone you've ever dated, Gio."

"And you and Ace are alike?"

"We both know that's not what I'm saying. Joker is... intense. He's got a lot of baggage, and he doesn't open up the way the rest of the guys do."

"Who doesn't have a lot of baggage?" Gio had plenty,

that was for damned sure. Between his father, his brother, what happened before he ended up almost dying, and the ramifications of it? He had his own airport terminal's worth of baggage.

"He's also the most volatile. The guy has one hell of a temper."

"He's... expressive."

Colton laughed. "Is that what we're calling it?"

"Do you think he's dangerous?"

"Do I think he's dangerous to you physically? No. Of that, I'm certain. Do I think he's a danger to your heart? Absolutely. Gio, he doesn't date. And believe me, we've tried."

Gio narrowed his eyes behind his sunglasses. "Are you still setting him up with people?"

"Um, no. Joker's been too busy with work lately. Or so he says."

"That so?" Interesting. Gio's heart did a little flip. "I've been around him long enough to know that everything you're saying is true, and I appreciate your concern, but there's something about him that calls to me. I think he needs me."

Colton's eyebrows shot up. "Is that so?"

Gio nodded. "He simply doesn't know it yet."

"And you need him?"

"I think I might," Gio replied softly, his gaze off toward the house as they approached.

"What aren't you telling me?"

"I'll let you know once I've figured it out myself. In the meantime, please, trust me."

"Always have. Please be careful. I don't want to see you get your heart broken."

"Don't worry. I'm rather experienced when it comes to broken hearts."

"Gio..."

"It's okay. Thank you." Dating when he'd had nothing had been a challenge. Between working several jobs, taking care of his little brother, and going to school, Gio had barely had time to sleep, much less date.

Dating once his investments paid off and made him rich had been a more significant challenge. Suddenly people who'd never given him a second look were calling him, messaging him, flirting with him. On the few occasions he'd taken a chance, he'd ended up with a broken heart. One guy had even tried suing him, stating Gio breaking up with him had caused him such deep anguish he couldn't work—but not enough anguish to keep him from going clubbing and fucking some stranger in the back room. Suffice to say, the guy hadn't gotten a penny.

They returned to the house in companionable silence and spent the morning and afternoon hanging out. Gio managed to doze for a couple of hours while Colton watched a movie and Ace fixed the showerhead, water pressure, and tile. Soon the house was filled with rowdy conversation and laughter as the guys started to show up. Colton and Ace's house was a home away from home for everyone, and it showed.

Outside on the pool deck, Mason stood at the barbecue with Red, chatting and drinking his beer, while Laz sat with Ace, Lucky, and Colton, laughing so hard he was in tears. Gio made his way down the private walkway that led to the beach and stopped at the end, where King sat on the steps, smiling contently as he watched Leo running and laughing with Fitz and his black poodle, Duchess. A Frisbee whizzed by, chased by Chip, who leaped and caught it before darting back to Sacha and Jack.

Gio was mesmerized by Chip's skills. The speed at which he took off after the Frisbee, the way he tracked it as it soared through the air, knowing precisely when to leap and chomp down to catch it, landing gracefully on his paws. He then trotted proudly over to Sacha and dropped it at his feet, tail wagging. The second Sacha picked up the red disc, Chip took off in anticipation.

"How's the arm?" King asked in his deep rumbling voice, his gaze still on his boyfriend. He moved over, and Gio took the hint, sitting beside him.

"Sore, but healing." The sharp pain had lessened to an annoying throb, but in a couple of days he wouldn't even need a bandage.

"Glad to be back?"

"I should have returned sooner," Gio admitted. "I owe you and your brothers a debt."

King shook his head. "You owe us nothing. Laz is family, as are you. We take care of family."

"Thank you." Gio's words were quiet. No matter what King said, Gio would forever be grateful to King for what he'd done. The man had flown across an ocean and hunted down the bastard who'd hurt Laz. He'd brought the monster back to the United States and handed him over to the FBI, where the guy faced a lifetime in prison for the dozens of young men like Laz that he'd preyed on.

Despite King's words, should he or his brothers need *anything*, Gio would make it happen. He might not have the skills the Kings had to pull off a manhunt across the globe, but being rich had its perks, and if he couldn't use his wealth to help those he cared about, what good was it?

"I approved Joker's security proposal. Frankly, you

should have had a security detail the moment you landed back on US soil."

Gio could feel King's gaze on him, which was impressive, considering the man wore sunglasses.

"Google is a thing," King grumbled. "All it takes is for the wrong people to look you up and realize you don't have security. What were you thinking?"

"That I'd settle in and have somewhat of a normal life before I was back to having suits standing outside the bathroom door while I took a piss."

"I hate to break it to you, buddy, but you gave up normal a long time ago. Hard to remain anonymous after all the press you've had."

Gio sighed. King wasn't wrong. He'd appeared on the cover of *Forbes* magazine more than once and even been featured in *People* magazine, as well as several other high-profile editorials. He'd lost count of how many interviews he'd done over the years, how many charity events he'd attended or photos he'd posed for.

"Now that I'm home, I'm thinking of pulling back a bit. Enjoy time with my family." Chip barked, getting his attention. He smiled at Sacha playing tag with his best boy.

"You strike me as the kind of guy who doesn't shy away from a challenge," King said, surprising Gio.

"You'd be right."

King seemed to think about something, then nodded. "Good. He's worth it."

"I know," Gio replied quietly, his stomach doing somersaults. There was something special between him and Sacha. He just needed to figure out why Sacha was so afraid to let Gio in, give them a chance.

They sat in companionable silence, watching the guys play with their furry friends until Mason called out that dinner was ready. Standing, King laughed softly when Leo ran to him and jumped on him. He wrapped himself around King's back, arms around his neck as King carried him down the walkway, asking him if he'd had fun.

The two were incredibly sweet. Individually, no one would believe they worked as a couple. Still, the adoration on Leo's face when he gazed at King and the very gentle and obvious way King cherished Leo removed even the tiniest shred of doubt that they were meant for each other.

"Hey, Gio," Jack greeted cheerfully as he walked by, his hand in Fitz's. They laughed as Duchess pranced past them, her fluffy tail wagging happily.

A familiar bark had Gio turning around, and he dropped to one knee, arms wide for Chip, who bounded over excitedly, tail going at full speed, tongue lolling out as he howled and barked, telling Gio of his adventures.

"Is that so? Oh my goodness! Well, you've certainly had a busy day."

Sacha snorted, and Gio stood.

"Hungry?" Gio asked.

"Starving. If he had it his way, we'd be playing day and night," Sacha replied, playfully smacking Chip's doggy butt. Chip spun in a circle with a series of happy barks before darting off, making them laugh.

"He must have been quite a handful when he was a puppy."

"Training is brutal when the dog you're training is as smart as you are, not to mention just as stubborn, but with any shepherd breed, it's essential. They're going to push you, try to take charge. Chip had to learn I was the boss, not him. He accepted it, but he reserves the right to bitch about it, and he does. Often."

Gio laughed. "He's very vocal, isn't he?"

"Oh yeah. He's also a master of the side-eye. No one gives attitude like my boy."

They reached the pool area and joined the guys as they served themselves from the buffet. He'd never seen so much food, but then at the rate Ace and his brothers-in-arms put away food, Gio understood the need for quantity, and thanks to Ace, Lucky, and especially Red's culinary skills, they were also gifted by quality. The guys liked their good food.

"Here."

Gio lifted his gaze, surprised to find Sacha standing beside his lounge chair, holding out a cold bottle of water.

"What did I say about staying hydrated?"

With a smile, Gio took the bottle from him. "Thank you."

"Not what I said."

Gio held up an empty bottle and waved it at him. "I've been a good boy."

Sacha's pupils blew, and his nostrils flared, but he didn't reply. Trying a different tactic, Gio held back a smile when Sacha sat in the lounge chair next to Gio's. Chip hurried over and sniffed the air near Sacha's plate.

"Hey. Manners."

Chip whined and sat, his tail wagging and his gaze locked on the steak on Sacha's plate.

"How do you resist that face?" Gio asked.

"Very skillfully."

"How do the rest of the guys resist that face?"

"They all know not to feed him, but Ace is the biggest sucker." Sacha shook his head. "He thinks he's all sneaky when he slips Chip a piece of steak or b-a-c-o-n."

"I'm guessing there's an excellent reason you spell that word."

"My boy will shank you for some b-a-c-o-n, so yes."

As if knowing Sacha was talking about him, Chip whined and lifted onto his haunches, his front paws up.

"Don't beg," Sacha said, shaking his head in mock shame, his eyes filled with amusement. "That's beneath you. You're embarrassing yourself."

Chip barked, making Gio laugh. He was adorable. Sacha reached into his pocket and pulled out a plastic baggie and removed a treat that he tossed to Chip, who caught it in midair.

"Now settle."

Chip did as he was told, lying down on the cool floor between their lounge chairs. The two of them ate, making small talk about how good the food was, the weather, how spoiled Duchess was, as evidenced by the way Fitz cooed at her and had her in his lap on the lounge chair like she didn't weigh over fifty pounds.

After a few heartbeats of silence, it was obvious Sacha wanted to say something. He'd open his mouth, then close it. Gio was going to ask, but Sacha finally spoke.

"So, did you and Nia have a good time last night?"

Gio managed to keep his expression neutral despite the urge to beam at Sacha. "We did. It was nice to catch up."

"I bet," Sacha grumbled.

"She's a beautiful woman."

Sacha grunted.

"And so talented."

Another grunt, then silence. Sacha shifted in his seat. "So, uh, what's the deal with you and her? She seems *comfortable* around you."

"That's because she is. We're good friends. Stay in touch."

Sacha nodded, his gaze off in the distance.

"But then I stay in touch with all the people I've helped."

"You do?" Sacha whipped his head around to stare at Gio. "Why?"

"Despite what many people believe, I don't simply show up somewhere and make it rain money. My charity invests in people who are unable to find help from the usual places. We spend time with them, work out business proposals, plans, schedules, and walk with them through every step of their new journey. We teach them to start and run their own business. Some of them are artists, some inventors, entrepreneurs, athletes, you name it."

"How'd you meet Nia?"

"Every few years, I travel to Crete, where my mother was born. When I was little, she'd tell me about her home, how beautiful it was, her big family, and how much love surrounded her. It's my way of remembering her. Anyway, I was at a cafe when I overheard a loud conversation regarding Greek singers, who were the best, that sort of thing, and one of the men said the best Greek singer he'd ever heard wasn't famous. She was a young woman who lived in an impoverished, tiny village he'd visited the previous month. He talked about how tragic it was that the world would never hear her voice."

"So you rode in like a white knight and rescued her?"

Gio laughed softly. "No. I gave her the tools so she could rescue herself. Nia was in a difficult position. Her family was very poor, her father ill and unable to get out of bed, much less work. She worked tirelessly to earn enough money for his medication and to put food on the table, and some days she went without so her father wouldn't starve. When we met, she was understandably very wary of me."

"Of *you*?" Sacha cocked his head to one side as if he

were studying Gio from behind his sunglasses. "Yeah, I can see how you might come across as shifty." His tone was light and teasing.

"Yes, well, I was used to it. Believe it or not, people distrust strange men showing up out of nowhere, offering money and help without wanting something in return. It took me a month to convince her I was telling her the truth, and that was only after I was finally able to bring in a full medical team to tend to her father. When she finally spoke to me, I'd just received the news that his transfer had been accepted. He was being moved to the best hospital in Athens. We spent days talking about her dreams, what she would do if money weren't an issue. If her father was receiving the best care."

"Wait, had you heard her sing yet?"

"Not yet."

"What if she'd been a horrible singer?"

Gio shrugged. "We would have remained committed to helping her father. Depending on her skills, we might have hired her a voice coach. Lucky for me, she was even better than we imagined. I set up meetings with an agent and several people from the music industry who were thrilled and eager to work with Nia."

"And now she's a very wealthy, award-winning pop star. No wonder she looks at you like you hang the stars."

"Like I said, I simply provided the opportunity and the means. I don't have the power to make anyone a success. Like so many of the others my charity has helped, Nia's forged her own path and worked hard for what she's achieved."

Sacha nodded but didn't respond. He stared off into the distance, and Gio would have given anything to know what he was thinking. Instead, he enjoyed Sacha's company, loving the way they could sit together observing their friends and family without needing to fill the silence. It was such a change from a few months ago when Sacha didn't even want to be in the same room as Gio. He couldn't remember the last time he'd been so... relaxed.

Jack and Fitz decided to stay in one of the guest rooms since both had been drinking, and wherever Jack stayed, Sacha was never far, so he and Chip took another guest room, the one next to Gio's.

After two hours of lying in bed, staring at the ceiling, it became painfully clear he wasn't about to fall asleep. With a sigh, Gio got up and left his room. He went into the living room and lay on the long couch near the glass wall. It was unlikely he'd fall asleep, but at least he could still hear the waves crashing against the shore.

Shadows moved around the room, and Gio startled awake, nothing but pitch-black surrounding him. He could have sworn he'd heard something. Probably just the wind or an animal outside. He'd been about to lie down again when a hand clamped over his mouth and several hands grabbed him. His heart thundered in his ears, and his breath caught.

"Gio!"

A familiar voice pierced the haze.

"Gio, wake up. It's me. It's Sacha."

Gio's eyes flew open, and he sprang forward, grabbing the man's shoulders. Blinking through the wetness and fog, he stared into wide blue-gray eyes.

"Sacha?" The word left his lips on a whisper.

"Yeah, it's okay. You're okay." Sacha cupped his face, his brows drawn together in concern. "What the hell aren't you telling us?"

Gio swallowed hard. He shook his head. "It was just a bad dream."

The expression that crossed Sacha's face told Gio precisely what he thought about that bullshit. With a sniff, Gio pulled back and ran a hand through his hair.

"I'm all right."

"That's not what I asked you."

As much as he wished he could confide in Sacha, he was far too exhausted even to contemplate the conversation that would entail. "Please."

Sacha nodded, but he wasn't happy about it. "How often do you have these dreams?"

"More often than I'd like," Gio admitted.

"I know you don't want to talk about it, and you don't have to talk about it with me, but you need to talk to *someone*."

"I know." Gio had hoped the nightmares would end with time, but after almost a year of them, nothing had changed.

"When was the last time you had a full night's sleep?"

Gio couldn't remember, so he didn't reply.

"Well, that's just great," Sacha grumbled. "There a reason you're sleeping on the couch instead of the queen-size memory foam bed?"

"It's... easier to fall asleep. What about you?"

Sacha motioned over his shoulder to Chip, who sat watching them. "Potty break." He went thoughtful. "Okay." Sacha straightened, then walked off.

Gio sat confused. Had he said something wrong? Sacha was unpredictable at the best of times, but he never simply walked off without a few more words, at least. Before Gio hurt himself wondering what he'd done, Sacha returned with a couple of pillows and blankets. He tossed a set to Gio, then dropped his pillow onto the couch across from him.

"What are you doing?"

"What's it look like?" Sacha lay down and covered himself with the blanket. "Go to sleep, Gio. Chip, time for night-night."

Chip padded over to Gio's side, licked his hand, then curled up on the floor next to Gio's couch.

"There you go. If a frog so much as farts, Chip will hear it, so go to sleep." Sacha rolled over and pulled his blanket over his shoulder, his back to Gio.

Gio's smile couldn't get any wider or his heart any fuller as he lay down. "Thank you."

"You're welcome."

Knowing he was safe, Gio drifted off to sleep. For the first time in many months, he dreamed of being wrapped in the warm embrace of an untamable whirlwind with blue-gray eyes.

THREE

"I DON'T GET IT."

"Get what?" Jack said through his earpiece.

"This whole modern art bullshit," Joker said discreetly, motioning around him at the vast gallery lined with wall-to-wall artwork. "Standing in front of a bunch of scribbles and paint splotches with a constipated expression, pretending you see something, then being all"—he put a hand to his chest and gasped—"it's incredible. Just look at these lines, the colors. See how it represents our crumbling environment and the decimation of man brought on by our mutual propensity for self-destruction."

"My God," someone gasped to Joker's right. He turned and arched an eyebrow at the tall, lanky man who sported thick square-rimmed glasses encrusted in rhinestones, a chunky knit turtleneck sleeveless sweater—the collar of which was so ginormous and fluffy it looked like it was swallowing him whole—and a pair of matching harem pants. Oh, and translucent sandals. Let's not forget those.

"You are *so* insightful," the man drawled, hand to his chest. "Do you know the artist?" He studied Joker, his eyebrows lifting when it became apparent Joker was not a guest but security. A look of distaste quickly followed. "My mistake." He caught sight of Chip and mewled, "Aw, what a pretty puppy!"

Sweet Betty White.

The guy completely ignored the tactical vest Chip wore and the *five* noticeable patches with white block letters that stated: "DO NOT PET. I'M WORKING." He took a step forward, hand out, and Joker quickly stopped him. "Sir, please do not pet the dog. He's working."

The man blinked at him. "But he's just sitting there. Can I touch his ears? They're so big!" He leaned toward Chip, and Joker sighed.

"I hope you're a lefty."

The man paused and blinked at him. "What?"

"I said, I hope you're a lefty because you're about to lose that hand."

Chip let out a low growl, and the guy squeaked before snatching his hand back. He power-walked the hell away from them, throwing glares over his shoulder as he did.

Cackling filled Joker's earpiece.

"Shut up," Joker said through a grunt.

"Oh my God, I can't breathe."

"That back there is why murders happen. The point is, I'm right."

"You are," Jack replied. "Because you are *so* insightful."

"And you are *so* dead when I get my hands on you, Constantino. And what the fuck? Just because I don't look like a cross between Elton John and an alpaca, I don't know art?"

"But you *don't* know art," Jack reminded him.

"Not the point, Jack-ass."

Jack snickered.

"I don't know how Ace does it."

"Maybe you should ask him."

Maybe he would.

Joker hummed as he slowly made his way around the giant room, which was several rooms with moveable walls. The Saint Gio Charity Tour had officially started. For the next month, Gio had numerous charity events, auctions, brunches, lunches, and dinner meetings in several cities across Florida. None of which was unusual for someone like Gio. Frankly, his calendar wasn't all that different from Colton's, but Joker didn't work Colton's security. That wasn't his job. Executive protection wasn't his job, which was why King had assigned Saint to be Gio's executive protection. Still, entertainment and events *were* Joker's job, which was why he'd agreed to be part of the security team assigned to Gio. For now, anyway.

Gio and King had spoken at length. Although Gio hadn't decided whether he would hire a permanent security team—he seemed reluctant for some reason he wasn't divulging—but he agreed to have security for the next month and then reassess with King after that.

Two hours into the charity art exhibit and Joker still didn't get it. The place was crawling with people who had more money than sense and little finger foods that couldn't fill up a hamster, some of which looked more decorative than edible. They were all dressed in outrageously expensive clothing, talking about yachts, vacation homes, private jets, celebrities, the latest this or that, portfolios and profiles, and any number of rich-people topics. Admittedly, a few conversations Joker overheard were about helping people, but those usually involved Gio.

How the hell did Ace do this? Mingle with these people, have conversations with them? What the fuck did

Ace talk about? He couldn't imagine Ace's brand of humor going down well with this crowd. Then again, Ace could be a charming son of a bitch when he wanted to be, and if it was for Colton, Joker didn't doubt his friend could pull it off. But didn't it get exhausting?

Joker caught a glimpse of Gio in the middle of a small crowd, his smile wide as he regaled guests with some tale. They were enraptured, hanging on his every word. Shaking his head, Joker continued on his route. Annoying, that's what it was.

No matter where in the room Gio stood, Joker was aware of his presence. While walking the perimeter, he instinctively sought the man out and found him. But then that was part of his job, wasn't it, knowing where Gio was? Not that Saint didn't know where his client was, but still. They were part of a team. It was *all* their responsibility to be vigilant.

Taking up position by the wall, Joker stood at attention as he surveyed the crowd. It became apparent who the star of the show was, and it wasn't the art.

Gio stood surrounded by people, all vying for his attention, their smiles wide, eyes focused on his face, and hands on some part of him. The men put a hand to his shoulder or upper arm, while women touched his hand, chest, or arm. Why did he let these people touch him? Then again, Gio appeared genuinely pleased to see them. He took their hands, his handshake firm for the men or a kiss to the back of the hand for the women, his smile always bright.

They laughed at whatever he just said. Nothing about Gio came across as fake. Joker frowned. For years he'd heard stories about this man from Laz, Red, or Colton, about how great Gio was, how he'd spent most of his adult life helping people, giving away vast amounts of money to help others. He'd come off as a saint, and Joker had declared bullshit. No one was that good. Not that he thought Gio was good. Or beautiful. Okay, he needed to stop thinking about the guy.

Was it possible he'd been wrong? Joker quickly shook himself out of it. A few smiles weren't going to sway him. For all he knew, Gio was an exceptional actor. The man exuded confidence, after all. His smile never faltered, and he seemed to know everyone who approached him.

Goddammit, he was thinking about him again. *For fuck's sake, get your shit together!*

That night at Colton's invaded his thoughts, and he found himself frowning. Gio hadn't been acting then. Whatever he'd had a nightmare about was real. Something had happened to Gio while out there traveling the globe. Was that why he'd suddenly returned home? Laz clearly didn't know whatever it was, and Joker had to wonder exactly how much Colton knew.

"My God, the man is gorgeous."

Joker moved his gaze to a brunet and her male companion who'd stopped near him. They hadn't noticed him or most likely hadn't seen Chip at Joker's left heel. People tended to notice the dog before they noticed the guy wearing the tactical uniform. The dog was the only reason most people didn't lose their shit. It was the ears. Hard to freak out when faced with a dog that looked like a giant black bunny.

"I know," the man replied with a groan. He definitely liked what he saw. The way he raked his gaze all over Gio had Joker clenching his jaw. No question what he would do to Gio, given the opportunity. "Filthy rich, handsome, *and* a good guy? Ugh, I'd never let him leave my bed."

"You should go talk to him," his friend said, nudging him.

Joker stiffened. The man undressing Gio with his eyes was stunning—tall, broad-shouldered, golden-blond, big green eyes, a chiseled jaw, and a suit that probably cost more than everything Joker owned.

"Oh, honey, I tried," the guy lamented. "He was so damned charming when he turned me down, I wasn't even upset about it. The man has talent."

"I bet," his friend purred.

"What about you? You're a knockout. Why haven't you snagged him?"

The guy wasn't wrong. His friend was just as gorgeous. Her ample curves filled the slinky black cocktail dress beautifully. She brushed her big soft curls away from her slender neck and pouted plump red lips. "You think I haven't tried? No luck either."

"You think he has someone?"

Joker listened intently, though he knew there was no one in Gio's life.

Except you.

Joker rolled his eyes at himself, though he couldn't help his smirk. He lifted his gaze to the crowd at the very moment Gio looked his way. Their eyes met, and Gio's smile turned soft.

"He never talks about his personal life," the brunet replied and shrugged. "Who knows?"

Was it possible? All these rich, beautiful people and Gio wanted *him*? Why?

A striking man in a flashy tuxedo stepped up behind Gio. He placed a hand to Gio's shoulder, but instead of turning and smiling as Joker expected, Gio stiffened, his smile dropping from his face. He turned toward the man, his smile back in place, but this time it didn't reach his eyes. Joker spotted Saint near Gio, but Saint didn't know Gio the way Joker did. He didn't see the rigid way Gio held himself, the subtle tension in his jaw, and the way he quickly took a step back, forcing the man's hand off his shoulder.

Joker had been observing Gio since his return almost nine months ago in an attempt to figure the guy out. By now he was all too familiar with Gio's quirks—when he was genuinely happy to see someone, when he was simply being polite, or when he was uncomfortable and wanted the asshole in front of him to get gone.

Gio shoved his fists into his pants pockets, something Joker had noticed Gio did when he was anxious around someone. Joker didn't hesitate. He made his way through the crowd, and everyone moved out of his and Chip's way. Some looked startled, as if seeing him for the first time, while others seemed amused, their smiles and gazes on Chip. Seeing Joker heading for Gio had Saint on the move, and he stood behind Gio to his right while Joker stopped behind Gio just to his left. He caught part of the quiet argument.

"The answer is still no," Gio replied through his teeth. "And quite frankly, I can't believe you have the gall to show up here and ask. You should have known better, William."

"How many times do I have to apologize? Why do you always have to be so stubborn? Please. Have dinner with me. We can discuss this, and you'll see—"

"No."

"Goddamn you, Giovanni. Just fucking listen. I want—" William reached out to grab Gio, and Joker caught his wrist. The man stared down at him.

"He said no." Joker let his voice go low, the warning clear.

"Who the fuck are you?" William jerked his hand out of Joker's grip.

"Don't be rude, William." Gio narrowed his eyes at William before turning to put a hand on Joker's shoulder. "Thank you, Sacha. I'm fine."

"You sure?" Joker didn't take his eyes off the asshole, who glared at him.

William moved his gaze to Gio, then sucked in a breath, his face draining of color. He looked like someone had punched him in the gut, and then he let out a harsh laugh that sounded somewhat unhinged.

"Oh, this is good." William shook his head, his lip curling up in disgust. "Are you fucking kidding me?"

Joker was lost. What the hell was this guy's problem?

"This is who you replaced me with? A prepubescent mall cop?"

Joker's eyebrows flew up near his hairline. *The fuck did he just call me?* He opened his mouth, but Gio placed himself between Joker and the douchenozzle.

"Sacha is a military veteran. You *will* show him respect."

"That guy? Let me guess; his job was to polish the real soldiers' boots."

Anger flared through Joker, but it was swiftly replaced by stunned disbelief when William went stumbling back into a crowd of people and landed on the floor on his ass, his nose bloodied.

Holy fuck! Joker gaped at Gio, who shook his hand out, his murderous glare on William. Ace had joined Saint, waiting for the word.

"Gentlemen, please escort Mr. Deveaux out."

They grabbed William and hauled him to his feet. With a snarl, he jerked his arms out of their grasp.

"You can't be serious," William spat. His eyes darted to Joker, and if looks could kill, Joker would have been annihilated on the spot.

"I would choose my next words very carefully if I were you, William." The low, menacing tone was one Joker had never heard from Gio before. It was kinda hot.

"This isn't over," William growled, stomping toward the gallery exit. Ace and Saint grabbed him again, and Joker ordered Chip to stay with Gio. He quickly caught up and took hold of William's elbow in a bruising grip, ignoring the man's snarl as Joker escorted him outside. William snatched his elbow away and whirled to face Joker, who got up in his face to murmur quietly.

"If you go anywhere near him, I will *end* you."

William scoffed. "You think I'm scared of *you*?"

Joker's grin had William taking a quick step back. "You should be."

"I don't know what your angle is, but if you think giving him your ass is going to get you a rich daddy, you're in for a disappointment. Giovanni Galanos is a frigid, selfish son of a bitch."

"If *your* ass isn't gone in the next five minutes, you're going to learn the real meaning of frigid," Joker warned. He left security to keep an eye on William and went back inside, hurrying to Gio, who assured guests everything was all right. They believed him and quickly went back to schmoozing. Everything might be all right, but Gio wasn't. Joker put a hand to the small of his back and led him to one side.

"Are you okay?"

Gio inhaled deeply through his nose, then exhaled through his mouth. He smiled warmly and nodded. "Yes, thank you. I need a moment. Would you mind accompanying me?"

Joker was going to suggest Saint since he was Gio's personal protection, but Gio looked a little pale all of a sudden. "Yeah, sure." He turned to Saint, murmuring, "Stay close."

Saint nodded, and they trailed behind Gio as he made his way through the crowd, assuring everyone everything was okay, smiling, excusing himself, and promising he'd be back soon. Gio picked up his pace, and Joker knew something was wrong, especially when Chip whined.

Gio headed for a door at the back of the art gallery, and when they stepped through, Joker frowned. Whatever he'd expected, it hadn't been the small empty room with the lone couch. A large plastic bottle of water sat on the floor beside it.

"Thank you," Gio said, sounding breathless. He turned and sat on the couch. Joker had been about to ask what the hell was going on when his pulse picked up. Chip stared up at Gio and whined.

"Shit." Joker pressed his PTT button. "Red, I need you. *Now*. And bring your bag. We're in the room at the end of the gallery."

"On my way," Red replied.

Saint looked from Chip to Joker and back. "What's going on?"

Joker quickly sat next to Gio. "Talk to me."

The soft smile Gio gave Joker squeezed at his heart. His face had drained of color, and his brow was beaded with sweat. He shivered, but his smile remained. "It's okay. I'll be okay. But I'm going to pass out first. You'll be here when I wake up, won't you?"

Joker nodded. "Of course."

"Thank you." Gio closed his eyes, and Joker's reflexes kicked in, catching him before he could fall forward. Getting up, Joker carefully laid Gio down. Red slipped into the room and hurried over.

"What happened?"

"We were out on the floor, and he suddenly went pale. He got all sweaty and shivered and told us he was going to pass out. Chip tried to tell us something was wrong. I think he knew."

Red quickly went to work checking Gio's vitals. "His heart rate and blood pressure have dropped, which would explain the fainting. Check his wrist."

Frowning, Joker did as Red asked. "What am I looking for?"

"A medical alert bracelet. If Gio was prepared, it's because this has happened enough times for him to know the signs."

Joker checked both wrists. "No bracelet."

"Okay. If he doesn't come out of it in the next few—"

Gio stirred. "Sacha?" He reached out, and Joker took his hand.

"I'm here."

Red helped Gio slowly sit up, and with a quiet "Thank you," Gio took the water bottle Red handed to him.

"What's going on, Gio?" Red asked, concerned.

"I'm so sorry I worried all of you. I was so busy making sure everything was perfect for tonight that I forgot to eat. I should have done better at hydrating as well. It's not the first time, I'm afraid."

"Drink," Joker growled at him, exchanging discreet glances with Red as Gio quickly gulped down the water, all in one go. This was more than dehydration. Did Gio believe they were that naive? That kind of bullshit might have flown with someone else, but not with them, and certainly not with Red, who'd been a Special Forces medical sergeant.

When Gio was done, he handed Saint the empty bottle. "Thank you." He made to stand, and Joker grabbed his arm.

"Whoa. Where do you think you're going?"

"I have to get back out there." With a warm smile, he patted Joker's hand. "I'm okay. I promise."

"You need to eat," Red said. "Skipping meals is never a good idea."

With Joker's help, Gio stood. "I'll grab a few hors d'oeuvres. The exhibit will be over in an hour, and then I'll have dinner."

Red eyed him with suspicion, and Gio laughed.

"I promise."

"Good," Joker said. "Because my shift will be over by then, so I can make sure of it."

Gio's eyebrows shot up, and Joker gave him a pointed look that dared him to refuse. The guy was exhausted. He was like the saddest panda that ever sadded, so how could Joker not make sure he ate and didn't fucking pass out again? Gio was a smart man. This was hardly the guy's first event. Something was going on. Clearly, Red had no clue, which meant neither did Laz.

"Great," Red said cheerfully. "Call me if you need anything."

"Red," Gio called out, his smile apologetic. "Would you mind not telling Laz about this? He'll worry for nothing."

Red appeared conflicted, and rightfully so. In the end, he let out a heavy sigh. "Don't skip any more meals."

Gio held up a hand. "I promise."

"Okay then."

Joker turned to Saint. "Would you mind stepping

outside for a moment? I need to have a word in private with Gio."

Saint nodded and did as Joker instructed. As soon as the door was closed behind him, Joker rounded on Gio. "What the fuck is going on? And don't give me that bullshit about not hydrating."

"Wasn't it you who told me dehydration was very dangerous?"

"Your heart rate and blood pressure dropped, and it wasn't from dehydration. What's going on with your health, Gio? Why aren't you wearing a medical alert bracelet, and why won't you tell your brother?"

"There's nothing wrong with me," Gio snapped, surprising Joker.

"Gio—"

"I apologize. I didn't mean to snap at you. I'm just a little tired, but I promise you, I'm fine. Now, if you'll excuse me, I have guests to attend to."

And Jack called *him* stubborn. Did Gio think Joker was oblivious? Was he simply hoping no one would figure out something was very wrong? Between the dizzy spells, the "dehydration" issues, and Gio's nightmare the night of the barbecue, it was clear something had happened while Gio was out there traveling the globe. How long did he think he could keep this up? More importantly, how long did he think he could keep his secret from his brother?

Following Gio outside, Joker murmured to Saint, who stood by the door. "Keep a close eye on him."

Saint nodded, and they escorted Gio back out to the party. Saint stayed close, as did Joker and Chip. When it looked like Gio was losing himself in conversation, Joker pulled him to one side and shoved a small plate of hors d'oeuvres at him.

For a moment, Joker thought Gio would argue with him, but instead, he smiled warmly and thanked him. Joker grunted and got back to his rounds. He kept an eye on Gio the entire evening, reminding him every so often to hydrate. To his credit, Gio never got annoyed at Joker's interruptions. He seemed thankful. It should have pissed Joker off, but for some reason that he couldn't fathom, it didn't.

Once the exhibit was over, true to his word, Joker was there right beside Gio, waiting. Not that Gio seemed surprised by this, as if he'd trusted Joker to keep his word. He'd appeared so sure of it, Joker overheard him decline several dinner invitations. Why the hell he'd rather have dinner with Joker than his fancy friends was beyond Joker. The rest of the security team packed up and headed back to the hotel, except for Saint and Joker.

"What would you like to eat?" Gio asked Joker.

Joker blinked up at him. "Me?"

"Saint informed me he's already eaten."

Saint nodded his confirmation. "An hour ago, when Ace took over for me."

"And I'm certainly not going to have dinner while you sit there watching me. I know you haven't eaten. You must be starving. Where's Chip?"

How did Gio know he hadn't eaten? Had Gio been keeping an eye on him? "Chip is with Jack. I didn't know what you'd be doing for dinner, and not all restaurants welcome dogs—service or otherwise."

Gio frowned at that. "Well, a restaurant that doesn't welcome Chip is a restaurant I don't want to eat at."

The guy was a nut. "What?"

"You heard me."

"You'd give up eating at one of your fancy restaurants

because Chip wouldn't be allowed in?" No one had ever said anything like that to him. True, he'd never spent enough time with any of his one-night stands for them to make that kind of offer. Still, on the very few occasions where he'd met up with potential dates after work and had Chip with him, the cute-dog factor wore off as soon as they realized their choices were limited thanks to Joker's furry companion. They were always so surprised when he picked his dog over them. As if there was any question.

"Of course. Besides, I only go to fancy restaurants for business. I like good food, and you can find that without spending a fortune. So, what are you in the mood for? There are several options close by, or I can ask Saint to take us somewhere."

Since Gio didn't drive and Saint provided round-the-clock executive protection, he'd been assigned one of Four Kings Security's specialized SUVs to drive Gio around in. Typically, Gio had a chauffeur, but the guy had been given some time off until Gio decided what to do about his security on a more permanent basis.

Gio removed his phone from his pocket and stifled a yawn. "Excuse me." He looked exhausted. Sometime in the last couple of hours, the circles under his eyes had darkened.

"Or," Joker prompted, "we can order room service."

Gio clearly hadn't expected the suggestion. "Room service?"

"It's been a long-ass, eventful day. How about you treat me to some expensive hotel food and a beer since..." He checked his watch. "I'm officially off the clock."

The smile that split Gio's face could have lit up the entire Florida power grid, as if Joker had given him some fantastic gift and not the suggestion of room service. Not a big deal.

"That sounds perfect." Gio turned to Saint. "Do you mind driving us back to the hotel?"

Saint shook his head in amusement. "You don't need to ask me. It's my job, remember?"

"I know, I know," Gio said, waving a hand. "But you're my bodyguard, not my chauffeur. I'm still getting used to it."

"Okay. Come on. Let's get the car from valet."

In less than twenty minutes, the three of them were back at the hotel. The place was expensive, with all marble floors and pillars, sparkling chandeliers, and gold accents. They took the elevator up to the top floor, where Gio had booked the penthouse suite.

Two of their security agents stood at attention outside the double doors, and they nodded a greeting as they approached. Since Gio's suite was the only room on the top floor, along with a hospitality suite and conference room—both of which they'd made sure weren't booked during Gio's stay—Gio agreed to let Saint stay in the second bedroom attached to his huge suite. The agents outside the door would rotate throughout the night, so there were always two agents posted outside Gio's room, while Saint remained close to Gio.

When they stepped into the suite, Joker whistled. His entire apartment would fit inside the living room area. The spacious suite included a kitchen and what looked like two bedrooms, everything decorated tastefully in neutral colors. "Nice."

"Thank you." Gio removed his suit jacket and draped it over the back of one of the pristine cream-colored couches. "The menu's just there on the coffee table. Order whatever you like."

Joker snatched up the menu and plopped himself down onto the couch with a flourish, making Gio laugh. "Don't mind if I do."

Saint headed for his room. "Let me know if you need anything," he told Gio, who nodded his thanks.

As Joker scanned the menu, he sneaked glances in Gio's direction, noticing how he closed his eyes and rubbed at the back of his neck. If these events took this much out of him, why did he do them? Then again, Gio didn't strike him as the kind of guy to let a little thing like his health get in the way of his do-goodery.

Gio removed his shoes and took a seat on the couch opposite Joker. "Anything look particularly good?"

"There's a couple of steaks with potential."

"Wonderful. I'll have whatever you're having. Medium, please."

Joker snickered. "You're gonna want to rethink that. I might not look it, but I eat *a lot*."

"I'm not surprised."

"Hm. And why's that?" Joker braced himself for some flirting.

"You need a lot of energy to keep up with Chip."

Well, that was unexpected. "Um, yeah. Malinois are high-energy dogs. They like to be challenged." He stood and walked over to the phone to put in their order. "What do you want to drink? They've got all kinds of fancy wine and cocktails."

"I don't drink alcohol."

Joker had suspected as much. Since Gio's return, anytime they were in the same place, he'd never seen Gio drink alcohol, raising another red flag. There many reasons why Gio might not consume alcohol, but with everything he'd seen so far, his gut told him it was connected to whatever the hell was going on with Gio's health.

Once he'd put the order in, Joker returned to the couch. Only then did it occur to him that he and Gio were alone. Together. He hadn't considered that when inviting himself to dinner. They were rarely alone, and when they were, it was usually a few minutes. He rested his right ankle on his left knee and tapped his fingers on his boot.

"You didn't have to punch that guy, you know. I'm used to guys like that underestimating me."

Gio's expression darkened. "No one disrespects you in my presence." Joker opened his mouth, and Gio shook his head. "No one."

Joker nodded but didn't respond to that, which was probably for the best. Although he wouldn't have allowed William to continue his verbal attack, he'd restrained himself for Gio's sake. Of course, had Joker not been in the middle of a job, things would have turned out a little differently. He recalled William's words about Gio being frigid and selfish.

"Who was that asshole anyway?"

"William and I were together for three years."

The words hit Joker harder than he'd expected, and he shifted in his seat. What the fuck? Why did he care if Gio had dated that asshole? Gio had probably dated plenty of people. Hell, Joker had fucked his way through most of St. Augustine, so who was he to judge?

"It ended almost two years ago. We met in Paris during a charity summit. He was everything I thought I wanted in a life partner. It turns out I was very wrong."

"What do you mean?"

"It took me three years to discover he was nothing but a sycophant. The only reason he was with me was for my money and connections. He's a real estate financial broker, and when we met, he'd just opened his own business and started operating internationally. In the beginning, he refused to let me help him, stating he wanted to get ahead on his own and didn't want to take advantage, but as time went on, he started throwing hints." Gio loosened his tie, then slid it out from around his shirt collar. Joker shifted in his seat again, his pants suddenly feeling a little constricting.

"I wanted to help him, so I connected him to several wealthy acquaintances who were looking for someone with William's skills. For over a year, everything was lovely. We traveled together, even had fun. Then one day he asked me to meet new clients of his. A couple of brothers he strongly believed my charity should help."

"Uh-oh."

Gio hummed. He absently unbuttoned the top two buttons of his white dress shirt, and Joker's mouth went dry. The guy needed to stop undressing, *or* Joker could not pay attention. That would be better. He really shouldn't find the divot of Gio's collar enticing, or the expanse of tanned skin he'd exposed below it.

"The brothers had a business proposal to breathe life back into their little coastal village in France. On paper, everything looked great. They were buying up abandoned properties and had plans to revive tourism." Gio unfastened his left cufflink, then started to roll up his sleeve. *Oh, for fuck's sake.* This was *not* happening. He wasn't attracted to Gio.

"However, William should have known better. My charity never blindly agrees to anything," Gio continued, unaware of Joker shifting in his seat again. "That's not how it works, especially when something feels off. I've always been good at trusting my instincts. So I traveled to the village, and sure enough, there were several abandoned homes and businesses, but as I spent more time there and earned the trust of the villagers, I discovered something alarming."

Gio rolled up his other sleeve, and Joker also discovered something alarming.

He was attracted to Gio.

Fuck.

Not only that, he'd been attracted to Gio for months.

Double fuck. Fuckity fuck fuck. This was not happening.

"The brothers weren't buying abandoned properties. They were forcing villagers out of their homes, terrorizing them, and forcing them to sign over their homes."

That had Joker sitting up. "Wait, what? Did they not go to the authorities?"

"The brothers had the local authorities in their pockets. If that wasn't bad enough, William was brokering the deals between the brothers and the foreign investors they'd acquired to buy these properties at obscene amounts with the promise of turning the village into the latest must-visit tourist destination."

"So they were stealing these properties and selling them at a fortune. But then why did they need you and your charity?"

"Because the purchase of the properties was based on the shiny 'new' vacation villas, shops, and restaurants. Meaning someone needed to pay for the restorations and renovations."

Joker shook his head in disbelief. "And William believed that would be your charity?"

Gio pursed his lips and nodded. "When he found out

I'd flown out there, he showed up at my hotel, furious. Accused me of betraying him, lying to him about our relationship, and not trusting him."

"What a fucking asshole."

"Yes, well, I ended it. He pleaded with me. I refused. And then..." Gio sighed. "He broke my arm."

Joker jumped to his feet, his fists at his sides. "He *what?*" The no-good son of a bitch! Granted, Joker had pretty much hated the guy the moment he'd laid a hand on Gio, but now he wished William was in front of him. He'd show the guy what a *real* soldier could do.

"It was so unexpected I was dumbstruck. I hadn't anticipated him to come at me, much less when my back was turned. Fighting isn't exactly my area of expertise, so I managed to fracture my wrist when I punched him, which led to him breaking my arm. I was able to fend him off long enough to call the authorities. Not that it helped. By the time I was out of the hospital, the charges I'd pressed had disappeared, and so had William."

Joker dropped back onto the couch. "And he had the fucking balls to show up tonight?" This guy was officially on Joker's shit list.

"He was trying to convince me to have dinner with him and discuss the proposal. My guess is things with his business partners aren't going well." Gio's eyes sparkled with mischief. "What a surprise, he hasn't been able to find any more investors."

"Talk about a piece of work." Joker shook his head at the nerve on the guy. Then again, he knew little about the investment world. Just enough to know where money was concerned, it could get ugly.

"Knowing William, he's spent money that's not his and doesn't know what he's going to do to get it back. I don't doubt he'll find a way, though. He's resourceful like that."

If William knew what was good for him, he'd get resourceful somewhere else. The guy had already assaulted Gio once. No way was Joker letting William anywhere near Gio again.

"What are you thinking?" Gio asked.

"I think we need to teach you some self-defense."

"Are you going to teach me how to throw someone over my shoulder?"

"You want *me* to teach you?"

Gio looked confused. "Why not? You may not be my bodyguard, but you were a Green Beret, same as the others. You're a big part of Four Kings Security, same as the others. I trust you."

Joker refused to acknowledge how those words made him feel. "Yeah, okay," he replied, his voice rough. He was often overlooked when in the company of his brothers-in-arms. When faced with the Kings, all of whom were muscled and over six feet tall, no one ever questioned them being Green Berets, and for the most part Jack, but most looked skeptical when Joker was included. Gio had never treated him as anything but equal to his brothers. A lump formed in his throat, and he quickly pushed it down.

"I'm sorry," Joker muttered.

"For what?"

Joker shrugged. "That you had to go through all that shit with William. You didn't deserve that."

"Thank you."

A knock sounded on the front door, and Joker stood to answer it. "Yeah?"

"Mr. Wilder," one of their security agents called in. "Room service is here."

Joker motioned for Gio to stay seated. He went over to the doors and greeted the waiter as he wheeled in a cart carrying several dishes covered with big silver domes. Everything was set up on the dining table, and Gio thanked the man as he signed the receipt.

Once the waiter was gone and the doors were closed, Joker dropped down into his chair. "Thanks for dinner."

"It's my pleasure."

Gio's smile did something weird to Joker's stomach, but he chose to ignore it. He was still trying to wrap his brain around his earlier revelation of finding Gio attractive. Not just attractive, but hot. Really fucking hot. Not that he planned to do anything about that. It was only an observation. He'd found plenty of people attractive or hot as fuck over the years. It didn't mean he pursued them.

Even if Joker was wrong about Gio, which wasn't outside the realm of possibility—he could be wrong on occasion—nothing would come of it. Outside of his brothers-in-arms and now the Boyfriend Collective, Joker didn't do attachments. Romantic relationships were nothing but a pain in the ass, and in the end, they always turned ugly. They always wanted to change him, turn him into someone he wasn't. When their expectations didn't match up with reality, they bailed.

Joker lifted his gaze to Gio, who sat with him in comfortable silence as he ate, his mind seeming to be preoccupied. Would Gio try to change him, like so many of the others? Of course he would. How else would Joker fit into Gio's world? Maybe not at first when things were new and the heat was all they could think about, but eventually he would, and unlike the others, who Joker had dropped and left without so much as a phone call, leaving Gio would be... complicated, and that was without considering their family circle.

Nope. The best thing for both of them would be to ignore the attraction and carry on as they were. They were finally getting along, so why rock the boat? Should be simple enough.

Gio sat back and ran a hand through his tidy hair, loosening the curls so they fell roguishly over his brow. His evening stubble had grown in, and he smiled at Joker, the corners of his eyes creasing, making him look so fucking happy. Like just being here with Joker made him happy. No. Nope. This couldn't—can't...

"I'm glad you're here," Gio said quietly, his near-black eyes intense. "No one has ever made me feel as safe as you."

Well, shit.

Joker was fucked.

FOUR

DISTRACTED.

A word Gio had never associated with himself. For the first time in a very long time, he wanted to be somewhere else—or more accurately, be *with* someone else—and he didn't quite know how to feel about it.

Every day Gio woke up eager to get the day started and dive into his work, organizing like-minded people, attending events, having long chats about upcoming projects and the various ways he could make a difference in the world. He loved to lose himself in discussions with his peers, people who contributed to bettering the lives of others. It gave him a rush like nothing else. He was passionate about what he did and couldn't picture himself doing anything else. He'd always been a people person and loved making new acquaintances. Attending social events energized him.

An old colleague of his, Ada Young, was hosting tonight's charity auction, the proceeds of which were going toward the resources needed for a small village in Africa to start sustainable businesses. The hotel ballroom holding the event was decorated elegantly in a black-and-white theme with pops of color, courtesy of the exquisite centerpieces of bright orange orchids, sugarbushes, monstera leaf, and fan palms. Several three-tiered gold-and-diamond chandeliers glittered from the ceiling as a live band dressed in white tuxedos played a lovely tune from a bygone era.

Hundreds of guests mingled in their finest suits or cocktail dresses, champagne flutes or glasses filled with expensive whiskey in hand. Instead of being swept away by the conversation, instead of getting inspired or excited to start his next new project, Gio was scanning the room for a certain grumpy former Green Beret and his furry companion. He seemed to be doing that more often than not these days.

Since Sacha wasn't his bodyguard, he wasn't around Gio the same way Saint was, but knowing Sacha was somewhere close put Gio at ease. If he needed Sacha, he'd be there without hesitation. Why Gio was so sure of that, he had no idea, but he was, and the times he'd spotted Sacha, Gio had been thrilled to see him searching Gio out.

Their relationship had changed, but Sacha seemed determined to continue fighting his attraction, and Gio was under no illusion that Sacha wasn't attracted to him. As much as Sacha tried to hide it, Gio felt it down to his core. It was in the lingering looks, the slight quirk of his lips, the way those bright eyes stormed over when their eyes met. Gio lived to hear Sacha's little intakes of breath or the way he shivered at Gio's touch.

Throughout the evening, Gio felt Sacha's eyes on him like a fiery caress, and the intensity of that attention, the heat radiating from him, had Gio thrumming with need at all times. Talk about uncomfortable and awkward. Sporting wood during a charity event was far from ideal. And yet something about Sacha calmed Gio, made him feel safe. Like Sacha could handle anything life threw at him, whereas these days, Gio wondered if he could say the same about himself.

Patience had never been a struggle for Gio, personally or professionally. His job required a steady dose of waiting on this government agency or that agency, on paperwork getting filed, signed, or delivered. At any given time, he waited on any number of items to be completed before he could move on to the next step, but when it came to Sacha, Gio experienced desperation he'd never encountered before, and he was more than willing to throw caution to the wind.

Movement caught his eye, and he shifted his gaze to the sinewy figure dressed in black moving across the floor by the far wall. As if sensing Gio's eyes on him, Sacha turned his head in his direction, a wicked little smirk tugging at the corner of his lips, as if he somehow knew Gio had been thinking about him. That look promised all kinds of trouble, and Gio welcomed it.

"Giovanni?"

Gio blinked, his face heating. "I'm so sorry, Ada. What were you saying?"

Ada craned her neck to spot the source of his distraction. She turned back to him, her hazel eyes sparkling with mischief. "Oh, honey, he's scrumptious."

"Don't let him hear you say that," Gio said with a chuckle.

Ada hummed and took a sip of her champagne. She was a gorgeous woman, the white Stella McCartney cocktail dress stunning against her flawless dark skin. Gio had known Ada for years. There was no one as genuinely kind and fearless. When she walked into a boardroom, she had everyone's attention, and not because of her beauty. "He looks like the best kind of trouble."

That was an understatement if he'd ever heard one. "Yes, well, I'm hoping to find out."

"Judging by the way he's watching you, I'm guessing you won't be waiting long."

"Really?" Gio resisted turning around.

"Mm-hmm." Ada fanned herself with her hand. "If he looked at me that way, we'd be getting to know each other in a much more intimate setting." She waggled her eyebrows, making Gio laugh. "I'm so glad you're back. You were away far too long."

"I know," Gio replied with a sigh. "I got so caught up in my job, I forgot what I was missing back home." It was his brief interactions with Sacha that had him wishing for more, for something he hadn't expected to find for himself—someone to come home to who'd love him and know what he needed.

Her red lips pulled into a frown, and she shook her head at him. "You've always worked so hard, Gio. When's the last time you did anything for yourself? For God's sake, man, enjoy some of that ridiculous wealth! Sweep your man off his feet and take him to some remote beach where clothing is optional."

Gio wondered how Sacha would react to Gio sweeping him off somewhere on some luxurious vacation. Would he refuse to let Gio spend money on him? Or would he embrace being pampered, the way Ace did with Colton? Something told Gio the answer—much like Sacha—would be a little more complicated than either option. But the idea of having Sacha to himself on a remote beach where they could sip cocktails and enjoy each other... It sounded heavenly.

"I might have to try that," Gio said, turning to find Sacha motioning him over. "Will you excuse me?"

"Go get 'em, tiger."

Gio left Ada and headed toward Sacha, who stood to one side of the kitchen doors, Chip at his heel. Saint remained close as usual, but far enough away not to call attention to himself. "Hi. Everything okay?"

"You tell me." Sacha arched a thick eyebrow at him. "You plan on eating something today?"

Gio blinked at him. "I'm sorry?"

"You will be if you don't eat." He motioned to the glass in Gio's hand. "You've also been nursing that same glass of water for the last two hours."

"I have?"

"Yes." Sacha took the glass from him and stopped a passing waiter. "I need you to bring Mr. Galanos a fresh glass of ice water." He handed the glass to the waiter, who nodded.

"Yes, of course. I'll be right back."

"Thanks."

Sacha turned back to Gio and waited. Had Sacha been keeping an eye on him this whole time? He must have known Gio hadn't eaten anything since his arrival. With all the guests he'd talked to, it sort of slipped his mind.

"Well?"

"I suppose now is as good a time as any to have a little something to eat."

"There's a couple of salmon things you might like."

Gio loved salmon. He smiled knowingly at Sacha, whose cheeks turned a lovely shade of pink. So he *had* been paying attention to Gio all these months.

The waiter arrived promptly with Gio's water, and Gio thanked him. "And thank *you*, Sacha."

Sacha had no idea how much it meant to Gio that he cared. Did he realize how sweet and attentive he was? Unlikely.

"Go on," Sacha said, motioning toward the buffet table with appetizers. With a smile, Gio headed off, took a small plate, and added several scrumptious-looking items, including the salmon appetizers Sacha had recommended. A couple of charity organizers he was familiar with approached him, and he listened to them chat about their upcoming events as he ate. He agreed to consider their invitations and asked them to send the relevant information over to his assistant.

The auction would be starting in half an hour. Catching sight of Sacha standing to one side of the room between one of the pillars and a set of curtains gave Gio all kinds of ideas. He excused himself from the small group he'd been standing with and left his empty plate on one of the many trays for used dinnerware. Discreetly popping a mint into his mouth, he headed in Sacha's direction. Saint moved closer, and Gio chose to ignore the little knowing smile that slipped onto Saint's face when he realized where Gio was going.

"Hi." Gio stopped in front of Sacha, blocking the room's view of him. Thankfully, Saint stood at attention on the other side of the pillar where he could see anyone approaching Gio, but not see what Gio and Sacha were getting up to, not that Gio expected anything to happen.

"Um, hi." Sacha's lips quirked in the corners. "Everything okay?"

"Yes. No. I'm having a bit of a crisis."

"Crisis, huh?" Sacha peered at him. "What kind of crisis?"

"I'm surrounded by all these people, and they're

charming people, yet I can't seem to stop myself from getting distracted."

"That so?"

Gio nodded. He leaned an arm against the wall to the left of Sacha's head. "Any suggestions on what I can do about it?"

"I don't know. That sounds like a *you* problem, not a *me* problem."

"Oh, but it's very much a *you* problem, and I think you know why."

Sacha's pupils were blown wide, and he stepped farther into the shadows. The curtained-off area led to a small empty room with extra serving carts, trays, and stacked chairs. Gio followed him past the curtain, his heart thundering in his ears when Sacha let him step close, his leg between Sacha's.

"You're very distracting," Gio murmured as he placed a hand on Sacha's hip.

"How's that?" Sacha asked, his face lifted toward Gio's. He dropped his gaze to Gio's lips before moving it back up to his eyes.

"Every time I see you, all I can think about is how I would much rather be with you. Alone." Gio brushed his lips over Sacha's temple, closing his eyes at the sound of Sacha's low groan.

"What the hell are you doing? I'm on the job. I can't be walking around with a hard-on."

The words caught Gio by surprise. Having Sacha admit he was in danger of sporting an erection because of Gio was almost as hot as the thought of Sacha's erection itself.

"At least then I wouldn't be the only one."

"Fuck." Sacha adjusted himself. "Gio…"

"Yes?" Gio slid his hand to Sacha's back and gently

brought their bodies together, their hardening lengths pressing against each other, making them both gasp for breath. With his heart pounding in his ears and his breath quickening, Gio moved his lips lower, kissing the corner of Sacha's lips as he rocked ever so subtly against Sacha. "You have no idea how desperate you make me feel."

"Yeah, I think I do," Sacha replied, breathless. He punched his hips forward and moved his face, his lips touching Gio's without kissing. Shattering plates made them both jump, and the atmosphere around them changed instantly. Sacha stepped around Gio with a growl. "I have work to do."

Damn it. With a sigh, Gio nodded and waited for Sacha to put some distance between them before he casually stepped out from behind the pillar. Sacha Wilder was going to be the death of him. Then again, it was one hell of a way to go.

Gio stood next to Saint, who smiled softly at him as he leaned in.

"If it's any consolation, I think he likes you."

"You think so?"

"Believe me. I've been around him when people have wanted to hook up with him and he's not interested. Let me just say they don't ask twice. He also doesn't keep an eye on anyone to make sure they eat."

Gio's heart did a little flip, and he couldn't help smiling. "Thank you." He kept Saint's words close to him as he returned to the event, forcing himself to focus on the auction and helping where he could.

The auction only lasted an hour, as the items were limited but high-value, from an eighteenth century Stradivarius to a 1947 Cheval Blanc. One particular item caught Gio's attention, and even if a certain someone didn't accept it, Gio would make sure the unique item was put to the best use. Thankfully, a certain someone seemed to be on a break during the auction, or Gio was certain he'd have felt Sacha's glare from here.

Once the auction was over, everyone went back to mingling. Gio had other ideas. He found Ada and thanked her for the invite. He also promised her they'd have lunch next week. As soon as he'd said his goodbyes to a few guests, he checked his watch and went in search of Sacha. Saint helpfully pointed out that Sacha had stepped outside the ballroom, so Gio hurried out with Saint close behind. Sacha had his bag slung over his shoulder as he stood in the hall, his phone in his hand.

"Hey," Gio said, casually strolling up to Sacha.

"Everything okay?"

"Yes, I'm finishing early. I have some work to catch up on." Which wasn't entirely untrue. "Fancy joining me for some room service? I hear the hotel makes a mean jerk chicken. My treat."

Sacha seemed to think about it. He shrugged. "Eh, why not? I've got Chip with me since Jack and Fitz are busy tonight."

At hearing his name, Chip lifted his gaze to Sacha and wagged his tail.

"Chip is always welcome."

"Okay." Sacha joined him and Saint as they left the hotel. As beautiful as it was, several events and conferences were happening alongside the auction, so Four Kings Security decided it best to stay at a different hotel for security reasons. That suited Gio just fine. He wasn't a fan of staying in overcrowded hotels in the middle of the city.

Outside, Saint handed the valet the SUV ticket. When the car was brought around, Saint opened the back passenger door. Sacha motioned for Gio to get in first, smiling when Chip jumped in after him. He sat in the center, tongue lolling as he waited for his person to climb in, then lay down across Sacha's lap, his tail wagging happily, making Gio laugh as he was forced to dodge getting whipped repeatedly by it.

"Watch out; it's lethal," Sacha said with a laugh as he patted Chip's bottom. Chip howled and barked in response, then proceed to attack Sacha with doggie kisses. "Yeah, thanks. I appreciate you bathing me with your tongue. That wasn't the kind of bath I had in mind for tonight, but sure."

In less than ten minutes, they were at Gio's hotel and riding the elevator up to his suite. They greeted the two security agents posted outside Gio's door, and he couldn't help smiling at the way their serious expressions broke when Chip wagged his tail at them. Sacha let Chip say hello, and Gio shook his head with a chuckle. The two huge men went from terrifying muscle to goo as they loved on Chip.

They went inside, and Chip hurried off to sniff every square inch of the place.

"Have you already eaten?" Gio asked Saint.

"Yep. I'm good." Saint cast a knowing glance at Sacha before moving his gaze back to Gio. "I'll, uh, be in my room. Let me know if you need anything."

"I will. Thank you."

Saint saluted and disappeared inside his room while Sacha took a seat on the couch and called Chip over. He removed Chip's vest and laid it on the floor by his feet, where Sacha placed what appeared to be a black tactical backpack. Chip happily went back to familiarizing himself with the room.

With a heavy sigh, Gio dropped onto the couch. He

motioned to the center coffee table and the menu. Sacha didn't need prompting. He picked up the menu and scanned it, going over the best-looking options.

"Hey, they have a Chimichurri salmon with roast vegetables and whipped garlic potatoes."

"Perfect," Gio replied. "I'll have that."

Sacha nodded and stood. He called down and put in their order, the salmon for Gio and a jerk chicken for himself, along with some kind of macadamia nut dessert that sounded heavenly.

Chip finished his exploration and trotted cheerfully over to Gio, tail wagging and mouth open. He stepped in between Gio's legs and laid his head on Gio's lap, big brown eyes looking up at him.

"Oh, you're good," Gio said, leaning forward to scratch Chip behind his ears and on his cheeks, which Gio had quickly learned was one of Chip's favorite spots. Chip leaned into the scritches, then seeming to need more, he surprised a laugh out of Gio by climbing onto his lap.

"Chip!" Sacha hurried over, eyes wide. "Shit, I'm sorry. He never does that."

Gio laughed, his arms around Chip as Chip licked his face. "It's okay."

"He's not exactly a delicate flower," Sacha said, seeming unable to keep himself from smiling. "Okay, that's enough. Chip, off."

Chip jumped down immediately and shoved his nose against Sacha's leg, then barked and hopped away.

"You accosted Gio, and you want to be rewarded for it with a toy?" Sacha crossed his arms over his chest.

"But he's so cute. How can you resist that face?"

"Because if I don't, he'd be even more spoiled than he already is." Sacha picked up Chip's backpack. "Mind if I toss him a toy? Fair warning, he might get the zoomies. If he does, I would just stay out of his way."

"Got it." The suite was plenty big enough for Chip to run around, the furniture minimal.

Sacha removed a tennis ball from the backpack and tossed it at Chip, who caught it in midair. He trotted over to Sacha and dropped it at his feet expectantly. The two played catch until, as Sacha had predicted, Chip got the zoomies. He darted through the room, racing around furniture at full speed. It was impossible not to laugh, though Gio now understood why it was important to stay out of his way. Poor Saint made the mistake of walking out of his room to investigate.

"What's going—" With a yelp, Saint dove out of the way a heartbeat before Chip zoomed by. Had he not, Chip would have sent the big man hurtling through the air like a bowling pin. "Holy shit." Saint pressed himself against the wall, a hand to his chest. "He's lost his doggie mind."

Sacha chuckled. "It happens at least once a day. Don't worry, he'll tire himself out in a sec."

As predicted, Chip decided he'd gotten enough wiggles out and flopped onto his side on the cool tile floor of the kitchen, his eyes closed as he panted happily.

"Now that I know you won't get sucked up by the furry tornado, I'll go back to my room. Let me know if you need anything."

"Thank you, Saint."

Standing, Gio stretched. Chip sat up suddenly, ears up and on high alert. A knock sounded on the door, one of the security agents calling out.

"Mr. Galanos, your room service is here."

Sacha opened the door for the waiter, who wheeled in the cart.

"Where would you like it?" the young man asked.

"By the dining table," Gio replied, removing some cash from his pocket and tipping the waiter as soon as he was done. When the guy left the room, they sat down to eat. "This smells amazing. Great choice."

"I thought you'd like it."

What Gio liked more than the food was getting to spend time with Sacha. Even the idle chitchat they made while they ate was nice. Considering how spirited Sacha was, he had a calming presence, at least for Gio.

Once they'd finished dinner, Sacha stood. "I'll get this cleared away. You go do whatever you gotta do." He shook his head, an amused smile on his face when Gio started helping him clear their plates and cutlery away on the cart. As Sacha rolled it to the door, Gio removed his phone from his pocket. Feeling a little frisky, he scrolled through his apps until he found his favorite music app. The Bluetooth speaker system came to life, a classic song from the seventies filling the room with its upbeat notes.

Gio stretched, aware of Sacha following the movement out of the corner of his eye. Pretending he hadn't noticed, Gio loosened his tie and removed it, then tossed it onto the couch. He swayed with the music as he undid the top two buttons of his dress shirt, then started rolling his sleeves up his forearms. Sacha's nostrils flared, his pupils dilating, and his fingers tapped his thigh as he walked over to the couch. With a smile, Gio started dancing, and Sacha snorted out a laugh. He shook his head at Gio.

"Now I know you're not right."

"Mm, yeah." Gio put his arms up and thrust his hips.

"Oh no, no, no. Don't make those noises. I never knew my grandfather, but I bet he danced just like that."

Gio laughed. "And you can do better?"

"Pft. Fuck yeah. Give me some music that doesn't suck and I'll show you what real dancing is." Sacha stood and motioned for Gio to toss him his phone. Gio did, amused as Sacha scrolled through the different stations. He tapped the screen, and the music changed to something modern and upbeat.

"You think you're that good, huh?"

Sacha rolled his eyes and motioned to himself. "Baby, this body was made for dancing. Now I'm no Bruno Mars, but..." He started dancing in time to the popular tune, and Gio was mesmerized. He'd briefly seen Sacha out on the dance floor in Sapphire Sands the few times they'd both been to the club with the rest of the group. But not enough to appreciate the hypnotizing way he moved his body. Was there nothing the man couldn't do?

Chip barked at seeing his person dancing around, and Sacha held his hands out to his furry friend, his smile wide when Chip got on his hind legs and placed his front paws in Sacha's palms. Gio laughed as Sacha danced with Chip, who stood as tall as Sacha, taller if you counted Chip's huge ears. Chip barked happily, his tongue lolling out of his mouth and his tail wagging as he bounced around with his favorite person in the world. Gio could watch them all day. He loved the way the two doted on each other. There was no one Sacha was more himself with than Chip.

Jack might be Sacha's brother, but Chip was very much his best friend. The sheer joy that filled his face when he was with Chip made Gio's heart swell. He'd never seen anything so sweet, so genuine. For all his gruffness, Sacha loved Chip with all his heart and an openness Gio doubted few got to see. He scratched Chip and kissed his face while Chip returned Sacha's love. Chip was more than a companion. He was a fiercely loyal protector, a dear friend, and a warm presence. Gio needed someone like Chip in his life, and if he had someone like Sacha, all the better. Okay, maybe not someone *like* Sacha, but the man himself.

Sacha lifted his gaze to Gio's, and his cheeks turned a lovely shade of pink. Not wanting him to feel self-conscious, Gio cleared his throat.

"How do you do that?"

"What?"

Gio motioned to his body. "Move your hips like that?"

"I'm very bendy."

"Oh, I have no doubt." Gio had spent many a night thinking about just how bendy Sacha might be. The intensity and heat in those blue-gray eyes threatened to set Gio on fire. "But seriously, I've been doing yoga for years, and I'm not as fluid as you are."

Sacha shrugged. "I did a lot of gymnastics when I was a kid."

"Really?"

"Yep. I loved sports. Anything that pushed me to my limits, I was all in, and I was good at it."

"Is that why you joined the military? To push yourself to your limits?"

Sacha's smile dimmed. "It's one of the reasons." He came to stand next to Gio. "Here. Do what I do." He lifted his arms and rotated his hips.

"You make it look so easy," Gio said with a laugh as he attempted to mimic Sacha's moves.

Chip barked and pranced around them as they danced, the music switching over to another upbeat song. Gio couldn't remember the last time he'd danced around like this for fun. Usually, his downtime consisted of non-downtime activities like work. He'd research, send emails, answer emails, watch documentaries. Good God, when was the last time he'd had any fun? He used to find time during his travels to enjoy the places he visited, immerse himself in the local culture, but over the last few years, he'd lost that joy, working himself into exhaustion with little sleep.

A sweet love ballad came on over the speaker, and Gio turned toward Sacha, ending up close to him. Sacha gazed up at him, lips parted, his chest lightly heaving from his exertion. He was so damned beautiful. Gio brushed the backs of his fingers down Sacha's stubbled jaw, making him draw in a sharp breath.

"I, um, I should probably go."

"You don't have to," Gio said softly. He cleared his throat and took a step back. "I, um, I've got some emails to send out if you want to take a load off. Hang out and watch some TV. I mean, your dog is snoring." Gio motioned to Chip, who lay on the floor on his back, paws up. "I'd hate to wake him after all that."

"Yeah, he works hard at being a nut," Sacha replied with a smile. "Okay. Just a while. You know, for my dog."

"Of course. I'm going to grab my laptop from my room. Be right back." Gio went into his bedroom. He'd send off some quick emails and then join Sacha in watching some TV. He enjoyed spending time like this with Sacha and Chip. Quite frankly, he would take all the time he could get with Sacha, didn't matter what they were doing.

Sitting on the couch, he opened his laptop, smiling to himself as Sacha flipped through the channels, stopping when he came across one of the Avengers movies.

"Do you like superhero movies?"

Sacha shrugged. "Yeah, of course. Good ones, though, not shit ones. Jack's the comic book nerd, though. Always was. In high school, his backpack weighed a ton because it was always crammed with comic books."

"And what did you have in your backpack?"

"A horror show," Sacha replied with a snort. "My backpack was the black hole of backpacks. I shoved everything in there. You could see my teachers physically bracing themselves when I handed in my homework, because they never knew what state it would be in. Meanwhile, Jack's homework was pristine, kept in separate color-coded folders. He was such a nerd." He scrunched up his nose in the most adorable way. "He still uses color-coded folders. Nerd."

Sacha went back to watching his movie, and Gio returned to his emails, his eyelids starting to feel heavy. He was not going to fall asleep with Sacha here. A few more emails and he'd join Sacha in watching his movie.

Gio stirred. Damn it. He must have dozed off. He opened his eyes to find Sacha frozen above him, a blanket clutched in his hands. He'd stilled midmotion, his hands over Gio's chest and his expression the perfect impression of a deer in headlights. Not wanting to spook him further, especially after the sweet gesture he'd been about to make, Gio remained unmoving despite his racing pulse. He'd have given anything to know the thoughts running through that sharp mind. Gio's heart thundered in his ears, and he held his breath as Sacha leaned in, laying the blanket on Gio without a word before he started to pull back and hesitated.

It seemed like an eternity, and just when Gio thought Sacha would close the distance, Sacha straightened and turned to leave. Desperate for him to stay, Gio sprang forward and took hold of Sacha's fingers, the blanket falling at Sacha's feet.

"Sacha..." The name left Gio's lips as a whisper.

The world seemed to slow, neither of them moving until Gio couldn't remain still any longer. Slowly, he rose to his feet, his gaze locked on Sacha's and their bodies so close he could feel the heat between them. Sacha pulled his fingers out of Gio's hand and turned, his jaw clenched tight and his brows drawn together. Despite his narrowed gaze, Sacha didn't step away.

Taking a chance, Gio cupped Sacha's cheek, his touch light as he rubbed his thumb over Sacha's bottom lip. *You're so damn beautiful.*

As if hearing his thoughts, Sacha's expression softened, and he swallowed hard. He brushed Gio's hand away from his face, and Gio's heart sank. With a small smile, Gio made to turn, and before he knew what the hell was going on, Sacha took hold of his face and kissed him. In a whirlwind of movement, the back of Gio's legs hit the sofa, and he fell back onto it with Sacha quickly straddling his lap, their lips once again joined in a scorching battle for dominance.

Gio had never tasted anything more sinful. Hunger and desire threatened to overwhelm him, his entire body ready to combust from the inferno of want that was Sacha Wilder. Gio dug his fingers into Sacha's slender waist as he allowed Sacha to maul his mouth. Sacha had fistfuls of Gio's hair as he held on tight. He was in control, and Gio would allow it. This time.

The sound of their heavy breathing filled the air, followed by low moans and cursing as Sacha thrust his hips down against Gio, their rock-hard erections causing the most delicious friction. Heat exploded through Gio, and he slipped his hand from Sacha's waist to his ass. Sacha gasped and pulled back, but not completely. Instead, he moved back enough to let his brow rest against Gio's. His eyes were closed, his breath ragged. He lifted his head. His pupils were blown wide, his lips beautifully wet and swollen from their kissing. He poked his tongue out and ran it over his bottom lip as if needing one last taste of Gio.

Why was Sacha so determined not to give in to his evident desire? Gio waited, and when Sacha made to get up, Gio slipped a hand around the back of Sacha's neck, bringing him in for a quick, hungry kiss. Knowing he couldn't hold on to the wild and beautiful man, he released him.

Swallowing hard, Sacha shook his head ever so slightly. He moved away, and Gio closed his eyes, hearing the soft sound of the door closing behind Sacha as he left. He was gone.

With a heavy sigh, Gio ran a hand through his hair and fell back onto the couch. Fuck. Never had he had such an intense experience in one kiss. A slow smile spread across his lips, and he touched them. Sacha had kissed him. Hope was not lost.

FIVE

HE COULD DO THIS.

"I mean, how hard can it be, right?" Joker glanced down at Chip, who stared up at him. Chip tipped his head to one side and whined. "Fuck it. Let's do this." Pressing the button, Joker waited.

And waited.

And... waited.

Hm.

"What the fuck's wrong with it? It's on." He pointed to the little red light. "See. It's on."

Chip looked from him to the machine and back, then whined again.

"Don't worry. We got this."

The machine started rumbling on the counter like it was getting ready to take off or explode. Chip bolted.

"Okay, *I* got this." Joker shook his head. "You sniff out bombs for a living, but you can't face a coffee machine? You embarrass me. Shame on you."

An argumentative bark resounded from the bedroom.

"Don't you sass me!"

Why wasn't this working? He removed his phone and did a web search. This was the first time he'd attempted to use the damned thing since he bought it last week. "Right. Let's see here." For fuck's sake. He'd spent years entering hostile territory and rigging countless explosives of varying complexities; he could work a fucking coffee machine. He probably shouldn't have thrown away the instructions.

Watching a quick online video revealed his mistake. "Oh, right. Water." In his defense, he'd never made a damned cup of coffee in his life. Someone had always made it for him. He lived in the apartment he was in because it was within walking distance of several cafes and restaurants.

In the mornings, he stumbled out of bed and zombie-walked his way to Las Palmitas Cafe just a few feet away. The owners and regulars were used to seeing him in his pajamas with his hair looking like he'd stuck his finger in an electric socket. They'd have his coffee and a breakfast sandwich ready, and he'd grunt a thanks and shuffle his way back home.

Muttering to himself, he poured the required amount of water in the designated area and tried again. This time, the weird noises led to the smell of coffee and dark liquid trickling into his mug. Grabbing the creamer from the fridge, he poured himself a generous amount and took a sip. Not cafe-quality exactly, but not bad.

He took his coffee into his bedroom and stopped in the doorway, frowning at the clothes and shoes littering the floor. Chip lay on the rumpled bed, head on his paws as he observed Joker.

"It's kind of a mess, huh?"

Chip wagged his tail as if agreeing but didn't move from his spot.

"Yeah, okay." After clearing a space on his dresser to place his coffee cup, Joker started picking up discarded clothes. Jesus, was there anything left in his dresser? "Look at that," he muttered, removing a mound of dirty work pants and T-shirts. "It's a laundry basket. I didn't know we owned one of those." Now that he thought about it, he remembered Fitz bringing over some stuff a few weeks ago. He narrowed his eyes, and his phone rang. Speak of the well-groomed devil.

"You need to stop sneaking shit into my apartment," Joker said by way of greeting. He tossed the dirty clothes into his new laundry basket.

Fitz snorted. "Joker, sweetie, I put that basket in your room three weeks ago, and you only just found it? What does that tell us?"

"It tells us I didn't have a laundry basket because I don't have a washing machine."

"I know that because we do, and your laundry is in it. As much as I love washing your underwear, it needs to be transported in something other than a garbage bag."

"Fine. And don't think I didn't notice all the new scented plug-ins." He glared at the happy little plastic succulent with some kind of lemon scent thing attached to it sticking out from one of the electrical sockets. How the hell had he not noticed Fitz plugging shit into the walls around his apartment? There were at least five more that he knew of.

"They're organic and pet friendly," Fitz informed him.

"They're a fire hazard. Also, Chip is a dog. He's supposed to smell like a dog."

"Who said anything about Chip?"

Joker laughed and grabbed his coffee mug. He sat on the end of the bed. "You're such a shit."

"I love you too."

"Why are you calling me?"

"Because I'm wondering if I need to call Jack and ask him to come home right away to start preparations for the apocalypse."

Joker shook his head in amusement. "You've been spending way too much time with Jack."

"Well, we do live together."

"Can you do it or not?" Joker asked with a grunt. It had taken him three failed attempts to send that damned text.

"Can *I*, a hairstylist with over a decade of hairstyling experience, who has styled hair for supermodels and celebrities, cut your hair? Let me think about this a moment."

"You're an ass."

Fitz chuckled. "I would very much love to get my hands on your hair."

"Now I'm terrified."

"How soon can you get here?"

"Just going to finish my coffee." He held back a smile as Chip slowly crawled down the length of bed—as if Joker couldn't see his big furry ass moving—and placed his head on Joker's lap.

"You ventured out early today."

"I, uh, made the coffee."

Silence. Then, "I'm confused."

Here we go. Joker sighed and gave Chip the scritches he wanted. "It's not a big deal."

"You *made* coffee? As in, you purchased coffee grounds and a coffee machine, put the two together, and made yourself something you're able to consume?"

"I'm perfectly capable of using a coffee machine." No

one needed to know about the water incident. Fitz hummed like he knew something. Smartass.

"I'll see you soon."

"Fine. And don't tell your stupid boyfriend. He'll just give me shit about it."

"My lips are sealed."

"I don't believe you."

Fitz's laugh was loud and made Joker smile. They hung up, and he finished his coffee. He hurried around his apartment, picking up all the shit scattered on his floor. He'd need to vacuum, but that would have to wait. Fitz had been surprised he'd owned a vacuum until Joker pointed out the big hairy black dog. Since Joker could create several more dogs from the hair Chip shed, a quality vacuum was a need, not a want. Also, King expected him to show up in a uniform not covered in dog hair, not that he could see Chip's black hair on his black uniform, so it was a win-win for everyone.

Showered and dressed in a pair of comfy, threadbare jeans, a faded Led Zeppelin T-shirt, and his beat-up old Army boots, he grabbed Chip's backpack and leash. With a whistle, Joker had Chip darting over to sit so he could clip in the leash. They headed outside. The weather was perfect for a ride in the Jeep with the top off. Opening the passenger side door, he waited for Chip to hop into the seat and settle before buckling him up in his doggie harness. He climbed behind the wheel and slipped his sunglasses on, then headed down A1A Beach Blvd.

The sun shone brightly in the cloudless blue sky, the warm breeze ruffling his hair as he drove; the heat and humidity were just about bearable at this time of day. Joker couldn't help his smile. His radio was tuned in to his favorite classic rock station; Chip sat beside him, his tongue lolling out of his mouth and his eyes closed as he enjoyed the wind in his fur. Life was good. His thoughts went to a certain dark-eyed, dark-haired someone. An image of Gio sitting in his Jeep, the wind blowing through those silky-looking curls, came to mind. Maybe he should invite Gio out for a day at the beach or something. Chip would love that.

Joker's thoughts annoyed him. Clearly he was spending too much time around the guy. The idea of being around Gio didn't bother him the way it did a few months ago. For one thing, Gio needed to learn to relax. Did he do anything other than work? So far, when he wasn't working, he'd been happy to hang with Joker, but outside of his events, he never talked about friends or meeting up with anyone who wasn't part of their little group. Okay, he needed to stop thinking about Gio.

When he'd gotten up that morning, he'd found a group text from Ace saying they were all heading to Sapphire Sands tonight. It had been a few months since they'd been, and Joker was looking forward to drinks and dancing. Getting a haircut had nothing to do with Gio's response that he'd be there. Joker's hair had started to curl around his ears, so it was time for a trim, and he wasn't about to trust just anyone. Not when his best friend's boyfriend was a fancy hairstylist.

This was his first day off after a week of working Gio's charity events, of joining him in his hotel room after and ordering room service, of eating meals with him and talking, of watching TV and watching Gio play with Chip, treating his dog like he was the most amazing thing he'd ever seen. No way did he miss having the man around. That would be stupid. Sometimes they didn't even talk. Gio would work on his laptop, and Joker would watch TV. Sure, it was nice not being alone, but it wasn't a big deal.

In no time, he was pulling into Fitz's driveway. It had taken a little while to get used to Jack living here. They'd all helped him move in a few months ago, and shortly after, Jack had rented out his apartment. He'd been the last of his brothers-in-arms to move in with his boyfriend, and at first, Joker worried it would be uncomfortable, but it hadn't been. Probably because the first to make a move had been Ace, and at the time, they'd already been treating Colton's house as a home away from home, so not much changed once Ace moved in. They simply spent even more time there, having family barbecues and get-togethers.

The door opened, and Fitz smiled brightly. "Hello, handsome."

Joker rolled his eyes while Chip did his whole-body-wiggle thing, and Fitz loved on him as if he hadn't seen Chip in years rather than a few days. An excited bark resounded from somewhere inside the house, and Chip whined, making Fitz chuckle.

"The princess awaits her prince." Fitz stepped to one side with a wide smile, and Chip lifted his pleading gaze to Joker. With an amused shake of his head, Joker unclipped Chip's leash, and Chip darted in. He hurried over to the armchair where Duchess sat in the center like a queen on her throne, a little sparkling tiara barrette clipped to the fluffy fur at the top of her head in case anyone dared to question her regalness.

Chip, however, was not content to play the submissive suitor. He jumped up onto the armchair and shoved his butt down, forcing her to move over. She let out a very put-upon sigh and made room for him, then lay down. Chip, being the gentleman he was, slid down onto his belly and shoved his nose in her face.

"There is no question he's your dog," Fitz said with a laugh.

Joker snorted. "That's for damn sure." He followed Fitz inside and locked the door behind him. With Chip's leash hung on the hook behind the door next to Duchess's, he headed for the living room.

"Want something to drink?" Fitz asked.

"No thanks."

Fitz was quiet as he entered the bedroom he'd converted into a mini-salon for friends and hair emergencies, whatever that meant. His lips were pressed together.

"Just say whatever you're bursting to say," Joker muttered.

A dainty gasp escaped Fitz, and he put a hand to his chest. "Why, whatever do you mean?" He blinked innocently, or at least attempted to. Joker arched an eyebrow at him, and he laughed. "Fine. The chair is ready; sit down and tell me everything."

"Fuck no. Besides, there's nothing to tell. If there had been, your boyfriend would've already told you." Joker dropped himself into the chair as Fitz moved around the room, gathering the supplies he needed.

"Jack doesn't tell me everything."

"Wow. You managed to say that with a straight face. Good for you."

Fitz laughed again as he draped the salon cape around him. From the moment Joker had met Fitz, before the guy had even gotten together with Jack, there'd been something different about him, something that made Joker feel protective of Fitz, like he could open up to him, have serious conversations. He'd never really had that with anyone. As much as he talked to Jack about everything, they didn't get into any touchy-feely stuff.

Despite Fitz being several inches taller than Joker, he had this air about him—a vulnerability easily targeted because of his soft heart. He had a way of creating a safe space. Joker had certainly never been the talking-about-his-feelings type, but for all his teasing, he knew anything he said to Fitz in confidence would stay between them. And it wasn't like he cared if Fitz told Jack. Other than whatever Fitz was expecting to hear, chances were Jack already knew.

Fitz ran his fingers through Joker's hair, checking the length. "I hear Gio's events are going well."

"I wouldn't know," Joker muttered.

"You're there. How much do you want me to take off?"

"I'm there working. Whatever you think, but don't leave it too short."

"Well, he's secure, so that means it's going well. Workwise anyway. Sink."

Joker stood and plopped himself down in the chair by the small black sink. He reclined back, but narrowed his eyes when Fitz loomed over him with a wide smile.

"What?"

"Nothing. Let me know if the water's too cold."

"You're a terrible liar," Joker grumbled, making Fitz laugh. He tapped a finger against his thigh as Fitz shampooed his hair, relaxing when Fitz started to massage his scalp. His eyes drifted closed, and he sighed with contentment.

"You sound like Chip when you scratch his belly."

Joker smiled. "We're simple guys with simple needs."

Fitz hummed. "And who's meeting your needs these days?" He finished washing Joker's hair. "Back to the other chair."

Joker moved, watching Fitz fuss with his hair through the mirror. "Are the scissors in your hand?"

"No. Why?"

"Just making sure you don't chop or stab anything."

Fitz met his gaze in the mirror. He was unimpressed. "Don't be silly. I'm a professional. Besides, I'm friends with Ace. Nothing surprises me anymore."

Joker considered his next words, his fingers tapping against his thigh again. Shit. Was he really going to do this? Fuck it. "I kissed Gio."

Silence.

Joker studied Fitz's frozen face through the mirror. His friend stared wide-eyed at him, mouth hanging open. Suddenly, Joker found himself spun around.

"I lied. I'm surprised. *Very* surprised." Fitz stood in front of him, eyes still huge. "Oh my God, *you* kissed *him?*"

"Isn't that what I said?"

"When? How?" He narrowed his eyes and pointed his scissors at Joker. "Spill the tea."

"You said you weren't holding the scissors!"

"I lied." Fitz waved the scissors at him. "Spill."

Why he felt the need to talk about this with Fitz—or anyone for that matter—when he hadn't even told Jack was beyond him, but the words tumbled out.

"It was after one of his charity events. He invited me to his room."

Fitz gasped, and Joker rolled his eyes.

"It wasn't like that. He invited me over for food. We'd done it before. He was too tired to go out to eat, so he ordered room service, and who am I to turn down free food?"

"Naturally." Fitz motioned for him to continue. "So he

invited you to his room for some free food, you said yes, and then...?"

"We ate and talked. He'd left his event early because he said he had some work to catch up on, and he did. I wasn't going to eat and run, you know?"

Fitz nodded and hummed. "Of course not. That would be rude, and you're never rude." His eyes twinkled with mischief.

Joker flipped him off, making him laugh. "Anyway. After we ate, he told me to make myself at home, so I did. I watched TV while he worked on his laptop. It was nice."

"Nice." Fitz seemed confused by the word.

"Yeah. Nice. At some point, he fell asleep. The guy was exhausted."

"And his sleeping form was too hard to resist?" Fitz guessed.

"Um, no. He got cold."

"How do you know?"

"How did I know he was cold?"

Fitz's amusement was not lost on him. Fucker.

"I just did, okay. You wanna hear this or not?"

Fitz pretended to zip his lips.

"He was cold, so I grabbed a blanket and went to cover him up." He ignored Fitz's little squeal. "He woke up, and we sort of stared at each other. I finished covering him up and turned to leave when he caught my wrist, and then it sort of just happened."

"Sort of just happened." Fitz nodded slowly and waited.

"Yeah, all right. I *wanted* to kiss him. I wanted to kiss him really fucking badly, so I did."

"And?"

Joker shifted in his seat. "And he kissed me back."

"And?"

"It got... heated."

"For the love of Lady Gaga, tell me!"

Joker snorted out a laugh. "Christ, I climbed him like a tree, okay? Happy? I shoved him onto the couch and climbed him, and we were both hard as fuck. We mauled each other and rubbed up against each other, and it was hot as fuck."

Fitz took a step back, one hand to his chest while he snatched the little spray bottle of water from the tray and sprayed himself, making Joker laugh. He motioned for Joker to continue.

"Then I left."

"You left." Fitz narrowed his eyes like he couldn't quite work out if Joker was telling him the truth or not.

Joker shrugged. "Yeah, I mean, nothing can happen between us."

"And why is that again?"

"Come on, Fitz. Think about it. A guy like Gio with a guy like me?"

A mist of water hit him in the face. Joker blinked up at him. "Did you just spritz me in the face?"

"I did. To wake you up. I know you're not thinking you're not good enough for him."

Joker frowned and shifted in his seat. "No, not that. We're so different. He's all tailored designer suits and private jets, and I'm faded T-shirts, jeans, and a Jeep covered in dog hair. His lint roller budget alone would be enough to fund small governments."

"You're adorable," Fitz said, making Joker frown. "Have you seen the man with your dog?" He threw a hand out and made an exploding sound. "Ovaries everywhere erupt at the sight."

Joker couldn't help his snicker. "You're such a dork."

"You know," Fitz said as he spun Joker around and went back to working on Joker's hair, "I'd thought the same about Jack. I mean, when he gets all excited about his computer stuff, I have no idea what he's talking about, but it doesn't matter because seeing his eyes light up and that big boyish smile he gets makes me so happy. And he knows I have no clue what he's saying, but he loves how attentive I am regardless. That's what relationships are, not having every little thing in common. I certainly wouldn't have fallen in love with him if he'd been just like me." Fitz snorted. "There's only room for one diva in this relationship." A bark resounded from the other room, and they both laughed. "Okay, one human and one furry diva," Fitz corrected.

Joker left Fitz's with a new haircut and some food for thought. The truth was, the differences between him and Gio didn't concern him all *that* much, at least not in the compatibility department. Joker avoided relationships for a reason, and not because he was afraid of putting in the work. There were certain things he was willing to change, but he'd gone through too much in his life to have someone come in and try to change *him*.

It always went the same. In the beginning, they loved his carefree manner. They laughed at his hijinks with his brothers-in-arms, loved how much he loved his dog, were excited he'd been a Green Beret. They expressed all the things they loved about him, and soon the newness and excitement wore off and the arguments started. He was too messy, too loud, too outspoken, cursed too much, spent too much time with his friends, cared more about his dog than them, and the list went on.

At first they'd say they were okay with him not going to birthday parties or weddings. Then they'd be arguing over why he was okay to go clubbing but wasn't comfortable going to Grandma's eighty-fifth birthday party. The arguments would escalate, the accusations of him being emotionally unavailable. So he'd stopped—stopped dating, stopped believing there was someone out there for him who might want him as he was.

With a sigh, he patted Chip's side as he drove them back to his apartment. Why was he even worried about this? He had a list of reasons a mile long why he shouldn't get involved with Gio. The guy wasn't just a friend—sort of—he was Laz's brother and Colton's best friend, two men who were in relationships with Joker's brothers. Their family had grown, and the last thing Joker wanted was to fuck up the good thing he had, and getting romantically involved with Gio was a surefire way to fuck everything up. Maybe the same went for the rest of them, but Joker had to face the fact that if someone was going to fuck up a relationship, it'd be him.

Determined not to think about it, he took Chip to the dog park near their apartment. He grabbed the Frisbee and one of the tennis balls from the floor behind his seat. They played until Chip decided he'd had enough and dropped onto his side at Joker's feet in dramatic fashion. The rest of the day went like any other day off. Soon they were home and it was time to shower and get dressed.

It really shouldn't have taken him as long as it did to pick out some fucking clothes. Since when did he ponder his wardrobe choices? He usually threw on whatever was clean, and even then, it depended on the day. Instead of grabbing jeans and a T-shirt like he would have any other night, he spent far too long picking the right pair of jeans—black—and the right shirt—a royal blue that made his eyes look more blue than gray—and his new all-black Vans.

He made sure Chip was settled and had everything he

needed before giving him love and telling him he'd be back soon. His phone buzzed, and he locked up the apartment. Downstairs, Ace and Jack waited by Ace's flashy car. Joker had no idea what time Gio would show up, but he did his best not to think about it.

"Holy fuck," Ace said, eyes wide as he smacked Jack in the arm.

"What the—"

"What?" Joker asked, stopping in front of his friends.

Ace peered at him. "Your hair... It's like you brushed it or something."

"It's been known to happen," Joker grumbled.

Jack's gasp was ridiculously dramatic. "Fitz cut your hair!"

"Holy shit! Hold on." Ace precariously leaned in and sniffed. He jolted back. "You showered."

"I fucking shower, asshole." He was going to murder his friends. Murder them dead and take Ace's fancy car.

"But you smell... good," Ace added.

"No, he doesn't." Jack leaned in and sniffed, his eyes going huge. "Holy shit, he *does* smell good." He gaped at Joker. "You showered, got a haircut, and you smell good."

"Wait." Ace ran his gaze over Joker. "You're wearing clean clothes. Clothes without holes. Going-out clothes." He gasped. "Holy fuck, you're in lo—"

"You shut your mouth," Joker growled, throwing a hand over Ace's mouth. "If you *ever* finish that sentence in my presence, I will kick your ass, you hear me? I will send Chip to shit in every pair of shoes you own and tell your mother every time you bullshit her about why you couldn't take her call."

Ace's eyes went huge, and he nodded fervently.

The fuck he was in any kind of *L*-word hell. How dare

Ace suggest such a thing! He narrowed his gaze at Jack, who stood looking like a constipated hedgehog. "Whatever you're fucking thinking in that big brain of yours, you better stop. Like, right this instant."

Jack threw his hands up in front of him. "Got it."

They climbed into the car, Joker sitting in the back. Did his friends think he didn't notice them exchanging glances? Some kind of unspoken conversation was happening in the front seats between asshole friend and asshole best friend soon-to-be-punched-in-the-face friend.

"I can see you, you know."

Ace glanced at him through the rearview mirror, a shit-eating grin coming onto his face. "We see you too, buddy."

What the fuck? Joker glared at Ace, but all that did was make him laugh. Bastard.

They picked up Fitz on the way to the club. Colton was getting dropped off a little later, since he'd had a meeting that ran over and he was still at the office in Jacksonville, so it'd take him a little longer to get there. Once they arrived at Sapphire Sands, they headed for the VIP area Frank had reserved for them and climbed into the empty huge U-shaped booth. It looked like they were the first ones to arrive.

"First round is on me," Jack said, getting out.

Joker and Ace exchanged glances, then turned their narrowed gaze on their friend. Jack wasn't fooling anyone.

"That doesn't mean you get out of it later when everyone's here," Joker said. The challenge coins would be slammed down at some point, and one of them would be buying drinks for all of them, including the boyfriends.

Jack rolled his eyes. "Yeah, yeah. Whatever. You want some booze or not?"

"You know what I like," Joker said.

Jack took Ace's order, and with his hand in Fitz's, left for the bar.

Ace snorted. "Ten bucks says they'll get distracted making out and it'll be at least half an hour before they make it to the bar."

"Do I look like a sucker to you? No bet, Sharpe."

Ace cackled. "Damn. That would have been easy money."

"Right, because you're so hard up for cash. Oh, wait. You're married to a billionaire." He fiddled with the napkin on the table. "How do you do it?"

"That's a loaded question, buddy. You might want to be a little more specific."

"Ass. I meant, how do you live in Colton's world? All those fancy parties, big spenders, investment portfolios, and stocks. It's not you."

"Oh, well, that's easy. I don't live in that world. Colton likes having me at his galas and events to support him, to keep him grounded. I never pretend to be something I'm not, and Colton never expects me to. He loves me, and he's proud to be with me. I'm not going to say it's always a blast, but it's a few hours here and there. That kind of thing doesn't bug me, and I don't let it bug Colton."

"But don't you feel... out of place?"

Ace shrugged. "Not really, but that's down to Colton. He always finds ways to include me in the conversation. A lot of the time, he introduces me to people he knows I'd have a good time talking to or someone I might have something in common with, whether it's the military or a favorite football team." He smiled knowingly. "Not everyone is an asshole."

Joker grunted.

Fitz and Jack returned with their drinks, and Joker shook

his head in shame at them. As if they wouldn't have been able to guess what the two had been up to, with Fitz's kiss-swollen lips, messy hair, and faint beard burn. What was it like to want someone so badly all the time that you couldn't keep your hands or mouth off them? The memory of his kiss with Gio flooded his brain, and he shifted uncomfortably. Great, just what he needed, to get a hard-on in front of Ace.

The music was thumping, and the dance floor was packed as usual. Their crew started arriving, with everyone there except Gio. Joker turned to Laz while the guys were giving Ace shit over something.

"Hey, was Gio getting a ride with you guys?"

Laz smiled brightly at him. "No, Saint drove him here, but they got here at the same time we did. They're at the bar getting us drinks."

The guy who didn't drink alcohol was getting the booze. Nice. Gio never mentioned why he didn't drink alcohol, only that he didn't. Not that he had to explain himself to anyone. If he said he didn't drink, they respected that, but Joker was curious. He'd heard Laz tell stories of Gio and Colton in college coming home all giggly or drunk off their asses, so at some point, Gio did consume alcohol. Knowing Gio was close by had Joker feeling restless.

"I'll go see if he needs help," Joker said to Laz, not that Gio would, considering Saint was with him, but he doubted Laz was going to give it as much thought as he was. His friends moved so he could get out of the booth, and he ignored Ace's knowing look. Joker flipped him off for good measure.

It was like Gio had a homing beacon, one Joker was tuned in to. He spotted Gio right away, his long, lean body leaning casually against the bar as he talked to Saint. The dark curls of Gio's hair were wild, as if he somehow knew how desperate it made Joker want to run his fingers through them. His expensive black dress shirt was tucked into his gray slacks, the sleeves of his shirt rolled up his toned forearms.

The air around Joker seemed to change, and he sucked in a breath when Gio straightened and turned, doing a legit double take when he saw Joker. His eyes looked black as he raked his gaze over Joker, the heat and want coming from him so palpable Joker stilled. His heart pounded in his ears, his pulse doing double time as he waited to see what Gio's next move would be.

Gio turned and murmured something to Saint, who nodded, and then he strode up to Joker and cupped his face. "Sacha..." His eyes were impossibly dark, and Joker's jeans tightened exponentially.

"Hey."

"You're all I can think about," Gio admitted.

Joker worried his bottom lip with his teeth. Was he really going to be that much of a sap? One heated look and a few sweet words and he was going to fold like a bad hand on poker night? Fuck it. He grabbed Gio's wrist and tugged him along as he hurried toward the back rooms. No overthinking, no excuses.

"If you don't want this, now's your chance to say so," Joker said over his shoulder.

Gio huffed out a small laugh. "Not a chance."

Saint appeared next to them, and Joker didn't look at Saint when he spoke.

"You can wait outside the door or at the end of the hall. We're gonna be a while."

To Saint's credit, his only break from his

professionalism was the corner of his lips pulled up in a little smile. "Got it."

They stepped through the black curtains dividing the back rooms from the club floor, and Joker led him down the door-lined corridor. He pulled Gio into the last room, closed the door behind them, and turned to face Gio.

Are you out of your fucking mind?

No matter how many times Joker asked himself that question, he came up with nothing. This had to be the worst idea in the history of bad ideas, and he knew a thing or two about bad ideas. So why was he carrying through with it? Not only could he not bring himself to stop, but he also couldn't even work out which way was up, all because of one smooth, handsome-faced motherfucker.

Instead of coming to his senses, Joker climbed Giovanni Galanos like a fucking tree, legs wrapped around the guy's waist, arms around his neck, and his tongue fighting Gio's for dominance as they kissed like it was the only thing keeping the universe from collapsing in on itself. The more Joker tasted, the more he wanted, and that was dangerous.

Gio cursed as his back hit the wall with an armful of Joker. "Sacha…"

"Don't call me that," Joker growled against Gio's lips. "Better yet, don't talk."

"Then how am I supposed to tell you how incredibly sexy you are?"

"Shut up."

Gio laughed softly, and Joker kissed him to shut him up, a hot, sloppy, *incendiary* kiss that threatened to ignite Joker from the inside out, though he was pretty sure he was already there. How was it possible to both hate and need someone so bad that he could barely breathe? Okay, maybe he didn't *hate* Gio, but he disliked what Gio brought out in him. This sense of chaos, of not being in control of himself, of his body, of needing more. Fuck, he didn't want to need this asshole. If only his fucking body would listen to his head—the one on his shoulders—maybe he could break whatever hold Gio had on him.

Joker was so hard it was painful. The heat that exploded through him was incandescent, and if he didn't get Gio inside him in the next few minutes, he'd fucking *melt*. That in and of itself terrified him. No matter his sexual encounter, *he* was in control. *Always*. Was he going to give Gio that kind of control? No. Gio might drive him out of his mind, but Joker was the one in control here. He was the one calling the shots, same as always. Gio was no different than any other hookup.

Gio's hands on his ass had Joker moaning. Damn, the man had great hands. Who knew fingers that long and delicate-looking could have such a firm grip? But then the fucker exuded strength, even with his rich-boy appearance. Everything about Gio screamed high-maintenance and expensive, from his pristine designer shirt that Joker was determined to wrinkle beyond repair to his stupidly perfect, shiny black hair, incredible cheekbone structure, sinful stubble, and that annoyingly handsome face.

"What do you want, Sacha?" Gio whispered as he moved his lips away from Joker's mouth to his neck.

"Besides you not calling me that? I want you to make me come. No questions, no overthinking, no promises, just this here right now."

Gio met his gaze, and as tempted as Joker was to avert those intense dark eyes, he didn't. He needed Gio to understand what was going on here. This wasn't a promise of anything. The most likely outcome would be that they'd get whatever this was out of their systems, and that was it. They were done.

Years of this guy getting under his skin for no fucking reason, of Joker getting annoyed by the sound of his voice, by the thought of him, it was over. The man had driven him out of his mind, and now he had Gio in front of him, he was done with all the bullshit.

"Well?"

Gio's lips quirked up in the corner, and Joker narrowed his eyes. Why did he always look like he knew some secret no one else did? So fucking annoying.

"Okay."

Joker eyed him. "Really?"

Gio nipped at Joker's jaw. "If that's what you want."

Damn skippy it's what he wanted. Joker nodded. Well, that had been easier than expected. Great! A little sex and they'd go their separate ways—though not entirely since Laz was dating Red, but whatever. Minor details. Point was, this whole thing between them could finally be put to rest. Not like Gio would want him for more than that anyway, so they might as well get a good fuck out of it and move on. Not like he wanted to *date* the guy or anything.

Gio returned his mouth to Joker's, understanding between them, meaning Joker could focus on taking his pleasure. All they had was one moment, and Joker was going to make the most of it. He allowed Gio to carry him over to the couch, ignoring the strength in the man, how easily he held Joker, and how gently he sat with Joker in his lap, despite their exploding need. Their mouths remained connected, and Joker refused to acknowledge how much he liked Gio under him.

Without moving his lips away from Gio's, he reached into his pocket and removed a packet of lube and a condom, ignoring the bowl full of lube packets and condoms on the small black coffee table next to the couch.

Gio smiled against Joker's mouth. "I see you came prepared."

"Green Beret. I'm always prepared."

Gio laughed softly, the sound going right to Joker's cock. As if he weren't hard enough. They brought their mouths together again, as if neither of them could spend more than a few seconds without breathing the other's air. Gio tasted so fucking good. Forcing himself away, Joker scrambled off Gio, his breath coming out ragged at the sight of Gio's messy state.

"I'm going to fucking wreck you," Joker told him.

Gio's eyes went wide, and before Joker knew what the hell was happening, Gio stood. He grabbed Joker's wrist, his smile turning wicked at Joker's wide eyes.

"My sweet Sacha." Gio ran a finger down Joker's jawline. He bent closer and murmured in his ear. "You're going to get on your knees for me and do everything I tell you."

Joker turned his face, his lips brushing Gio's cheek. "And why the fuck would I do that?"

"Because," Gio breathed, sliding one hand down to Joker's ass and bringing him hard against him, their erections pressing together and making Joker groan low. "We both know that deep down, you're *aching* to submit—" He nipped at Joker's jawline, making his entire body shudder. "—to me."

A quiet gasp escaped Joker, and he lifted his hands to Gio's chest, ready to push him away, but he didn't. His body was on fire at Gio's words, his dick straining painfully against his jeans.

"You've wanted to since the beginning," Gio murmured,

moving his hand to the bulge in Joker's pants. Joker pushed his erection into Gio's hand with a moan. He was practically panting. Gio licked at the corner of Joker's mouth. "I want to take care of you. Let me give you what you need."

Gio had said something similar before, back during the bachelor auction when he'd surprised the shit out of Joker.

No overthinking. No excuses.

Joker gently shoved Gio away, his gaze never moving from Gio's.

Then he did something he had never done for anyone in the whole of his adult life.

He got on his knees.

SIX

DEAR GOD.

Gio couldn't help his sharp intake of breath. His hand all but shook when he placed it on the top of Sacha's hair. He'd been dreaming of this day since they'd met, and not once had he believed it would happen. Nothing in his life had prepared him for the sight of Sacha Wilder on his knees, for *him*.

"You're going to be a very good boy for me, aren't you?"

Sacha held his gaze, his pupils blown, leaving slivers of blue-gray at the edges. He looked uncertain, and Gio knew precisely why. He brushed a finger down Sacha's cheek.

"In here, between the two of us, you do as I tell you. I'll take care of you. Out there, you do as you please, same as you always have."

Something inside Sacha seemed to click into place, and he let out a steady breath, his shoulders relaxing as if he'd been waiting to hear those words from Gio. Sacha yearned to give up control in the bedroom, but that's where his submission ended, and Gio was more than okay with that.

"Do you want to suck me off?"

Sacha's cheeks flushed the most beautiful shade of pink. He licked his lips and nodded. With a smile, Gio sat on the couch and nodded his approval. Sacha made quick work of unfastening Gio's belt, unzipping him, and exposing his rock-hard cock. A little whimper escaped Sacha as he stroked his thumb over the tip, smearing the pearl of precome. Gio sucked in a breath, groaning at the wicked smile that spread across Sacha's face as he slowly leaned in and swallowed Gio down to the root, his eyes never leaving Gio's.

Gio threw his hands out to his sides, his fingers digging into the soft couch cushions. *Jesus Christ!* The ripple of pleasure that wracked his body was something out of his wildest imagination. Never had he felt the surge of raw desire making his body tremble. He moved one hand to Sacha's hair, a smile tugging at his lips at the reminder that Sacha had gotten a haircut. Was it egotistical to believe Sacha's new hair and clothes were for his benefit? He ran his fingers through the thick, soft strands, and Sacha's eyes drifted closed, a throaty moan escaping him. The look of contentment on his face was one Gio hadn't seen before, and his heart swelled, knowing he was the cause of it.

Sacha sucked, licked, and laved at Gio from root to tip. He alternated between slow and teasing and fast and sloppy. When his other hand disappeared down in front of him, Gio put a hand on Sacha's shoulder to stop him.

"I'm afraid our first time isn't going to last very long," Gio informed him roughly. "Get up."

Sacha popped off Gio and stood, his pants unzipped. He ran a tongue over his wet bottom lip, and Gio cupped the back of his neck. He pulled him in and kissed him breathless before forcing himself away.

"Drop your pants and get on your knees facing the back of the couch."

Sacha scrambled to do as he was told. He shoved his pants and underwear down his thighs, and Gio moaned at the sight of his beautiful cock leaking precome. Everything about Sacha was breathtaking. He moved to one side so Sacha could climb onto the couch, his hands braced on the backrest and his knees spread as wide as his jeans permitted. After tearing the packet of lube Sacha had brought, Gio poured a generous amount onto his fingers and knelt on the floor between Sacha's feet.

"You're so damned beautiful," Gio murmured, caressing Sacha's left butt cheek. He had a perfect little ass, round and pert. He gave it a light smack, and Sacha jolted. Gio waited for his response, thrilled when a shiver quickly followed and Sacha arched his back with a low groan. His sweet Sacha. So responsive. Gio placed a lubed finger to Sacha's hole as he slid a hand over Sacha's ass up under his shirt to his toned back. He yearned to see Sacha's naked body under him, wanted to run his tongue over every inch of him, caress the curve of every muscle.

Pushing his finger in resulted in Sacha letting out the most delicious noises. Slowly Sacha started moving, fucking himself on Gio's finger as Gio stroked and caressed his body, purposefully ignoring his stiff erection.

When Gio added a third finger, Sacha looked about ready to shatter, his head thrown forward as he took his pleasures from Gio's fingers. Unable to take any more, Gio removed his fingers, loving Sacha's curses. He unrolled the condom onto his cock and knelt on the couch behind Sacha. Lined up with Sacha's hole, he leaned forward as he very gingerly pushed in, his lips next to Sacha's ear.

"I've dreamt of this moment for so long, of filling you, of

making you come apart in my arms. Give me all of you, your fire, your passion, your strength. I want all of you, your pain, your scars, your anger."

"*Fuck.*" Sacha thrust his ass back, impaling himself the rest of the way on Gio's cock, forcing Gio to bury his shout in Sacha's hair. He reached down to palm the steel rod that was Sacha's erection as he started with small movements. Sacha groaned and let his head fall back against Gio's shoulder. He slipped his fingers into Gio's hair and grabbed a fistful of it. Gio snapped his hips, thrusting hard into Sacha over and over, their panting breaths, grunts, and groans filling the room as Gio claimed Sacha's ass.

The sound of their bodies smacking together was wonderfully obscene, and Gio gritted his teeth to keep back the words that wanted to tumble out. He wanted to stake his claim, declare Sacha his and no one else's. The more he thought of someone else with their dick inside him or his dick in them, their arms around him, their mouths on him, the harder he fucked Sacha. He lost his rhythm, his orgasm barreling through him.

"Come for me," Gio demanded, and a heartbeat later, Sacha's hoarse shout filled the room, sending Gio over the edge. He snapped his hips as he emptied himself in the condom and growled Sacha's name. His movements slowed as the sensation became too great, and then he stopped as they caught their breaths, his chest pressed to Sacha's back. Wrapping his arms around Sacha, he peppered soft kisses over Sacha's hair, his cheek, his jawline, his heart all but ready to burst when Sacha leaned into the kisses, one arm coming to rest over Gio's.

Gio wished this would last forever. Having Sacha pliant in his arms, soft and submissive, was a heady thing, and he warned himself not to get used to it or even hope it might happen again. Sacha allowed Gio to hold his weight, his fingers absently caressing Gio's forearm. His eyes were closed, and his kiss-swollen lips were slightly parted, his expression one of pure sated bliss. But as Gio expected, the moment soon ended. Sacha dropped his arm away from Gio as Gio slipped out from inside him. He removed the condom and tossed it in the trash. With a kiss to Sacha's temple, Gio climbed off the couch and fixed his clothes while Sacha did the same.

Things became awkward with Sacha standing there, his face flushed and with a slight frown as he gazed off to the side. Gio couldn't have this. It had taken too long for Sacha to finally feel at ease around him for Gio to lose him now. He stepped in front of Sacha and slipped his arms around his waist. Sacha lifted his questioning blue-gray eyes to Gio's.

"Come home with me?" Gio asked softly. He brushed his lips over Sacha's.

Sacha shook his head and let out a shaky breath. "I can't."

Gio nodded his understanding and made to step back, but Sacha caught his arm, his brows drawn together.

"I can't go because of Chip. I can't leave him alone that long."

The weight lifted off Gio's chest, and he smiled. "Oh, of course. I understand."

Sacha worried his bottom lip. "Maybe... maybe you can come home with me?"

Gio blinked at him.

"I mean, my apartment's no mansion, but—"

Gio brought their lips together and kissed the beautiful man in his arms soundly. When he pulled back, Sacha looked dazed, making Gio chuckle. "As long as you and Chip are there, that's all I need."

Sacha's smile lit up his face, and it struck Gio, the actual danger he was in. He didn't just want Sacha, he was falling in love with him.

"You okay?" Sacha asked worriedly. "You don't have to—"

"No," Gio said quickly, his smile wide. "There's nothing I want more. Shall we?"

Sacha nodded and opened the door, music blaring and cutting through the faint sounds of men getting up to all kinds of things. Gio followed Sacha out into the corridor, where Saint joined them, following silently.

"You drove here, right?" Sacha asked Saint, who nodded. "Great. We're going to my apartment." They headed out onto the club floor, past the bar. He removed his phone and quickly tapped away at the screen before returning it to his pocket.

"Heads-up, the guys are all going to know we left together. I always text Jack to let him know when I'm leaving."

"Is that okay with you?" Gio asked. They both knew this was going to start a fire of gossip within their lovable crew of mischief-makers.

Sacha shrugged. "Ace is going to be a pain in the ass, but what else is new. It's fine."

They left the club and walked out into the parking lot behind the building, where Saint had parked the SUV. Excitement coursed through Gio. He had no idea what this night would hold, but just having Sacha invite him back to his place was more than he could have hoped for.

The hairs on the back of Gio's neck stood on end when Sacha abruptly stopped walking, his hand going to Gio's chest. Nothing looked out of the ordinary, but Gio knew better than to question Sacha's instincts. Something was wrong.

The world seemed to move in slow motion despite everything happening so fast. Tires screeched, and a black van careened forward. The side doors slid open as Sacha shouted to Saint, who shoved Gio out of the way just as a man lunged for him. Sacha spun and brought his fist with him, punching the masked man across the face as Saint grabbed Gio and hauled him to his feet.

"Go back to the club," Sacha snapped. Gio didn't hesitate. He did precisely as Sacha told him and took off toward the club while Sacha ducked under a fist and came up with his palm, striking the man under his chin and sending him reeling back. A shot fired somewhere, and Gio skidded to a halt, whirling to see Sacha on the ground kicking the knee of one of the attackers.

"Sacha!"

"Saint, get him inside!"

"You have to help him," Gio shouted at Saint, who hauled Gio toward the club.

"My job is to get you to safety. Joker will be fine."

"They have guns!" Gio was shaking now. He turned and tried to run back, only to have Saint throw his arms around him and pick him up off his feet like he didn't weigh a thing. "Goddamn it, Saint! He needs us. He needs *me*! He—"

"Needs you safe," Saint growled, throwing Gio over his shoulder and hurrying inside. "He can take care of himself."

But those men were armed! How could Saint leave his friend out there to fend for himself? Yes, Sacha had been a Green Beret, but he'd been outnumbered, facing who knew how many *armed* men. What if they shot him? What if Gio lost him…

Gio shook his head, shouting for Sacha, not caring about the commotion they were causing as Saint carried him through the packed club. Ace, Lucky, Mason, and Jack reached them just as Saint put Gio on his feet. Gio grabbed Ace.

"You have to help him!"

Jack stiffened. "Where's Joker?"

"A van showed up in the parking lot, filled with armed assailants. He was fending them off while I got Gio to safety," Saint said quickly. "Possible kidnappers."

"Where's Red?" Gio asked. If Sacha was hurt, they'd need Red there. At least that's what he thought until he saw Jack's stricken expression.

"He and Laz went home."

Ace turned to his brothers-in-arms. "Let's go. Saint, take Gio to our table. Stay with him and the others." They took off, and Saint led Gio back to the tables where Fitz and Colton sat, looking worried. The moment they saw him, they jumped out of the booth and ran to him.

"Oh my God, Gio, are you okay? What's going on?" Colton asked, putting an arm around Gio's waist and helping him sit. "We heard the alarms."

"Alarms?" Gio frowned as dizziness set in.

"Yeah," Fitz replied softly. "The guys have these special alarms. If one of them is in trouble, they have this little button on their phones that sends a notice to whoever's the closest. Since Ace, Lucky, and Jack were here, it went off."

This couldn't be happening. Not again. Gio's whole body shook. *Breathe. Remember to breathe.*

"Gio," Colton said, his hand on Gio's cheek. "Gio, what's wrong? Shit, Fitz, call 9-1-1."

Gio breathed deep through his nose, held the breath for several seconds, then released it slowly through his mouth. He repeated the technique several times in the hopes of steadying his heart rate. Darkness encroached his vision, and he shook his head. *No.* Not until he knew Sacha was safe.

"Please," Gio said to no one in particular. "Sacha." It was the last word out of his mouth before the darkness swallowed him whole.

———

WHAT WAS THAT BEEPING SOUND?

Gio stirred with a groan. Why was his head so fuzzy? He slowly opened his eyes, frowning at the dim lighting and white ceiling. Where was he?

"Hey."

Gio turned his head, and everything came back to him. "Sacha," he croaked and made to sit up, but Sacha jumped from the chair he'd been sitting in at Gio's bedside and put a hand to Gio's chest.

"Easy there, handsome. Slow your roll."

"You're okay?"

A bruise marred Sacha's cheek, but otherwise he looked unharmed.

"Of course I am. Can't say the same for the other guys." He shrugged, his expression dark. "Their first mistake was to think they could put their hands on you. Their second was to put their hands on *me*."

"I was so scared they'd hurt you," Gio murmured, covering the hand Sacha still had on Gio's chest with his own.

"Nah. I've faced worse."

"Where's Chip?"

Sacha blinked at him before letting out a soft laugh, tiny creases forming at the corners of his eyes. "This guy. He's lying in a hospital bed, and he's asking about my dog." His expression softened. "He's fine. He's over at Jack's with Fitz."

"Good."

"Jack has his team going through the club's surveillance to see what they can find out about the men who tried to kidnap you. The van was stolen and had no plates, but King's on it, so we should hopefully know something soon. Until then, did you know about this?"

No need for Sacha to specify what "this" meant. The idea of lying occurred to Gio for a split second, but he couldn't bring himself to lie to Sacha, so he nodded instead.

"Why didn't you say anything?"

"It's not a big deal," Gio muttered.

Sacha stared at him, stunned. His expression darkened, and Gio realized too late he'd answered wrong.

"Not a big deal?" Sacha pulled his hand out from under Gio's, and Gio immediately missed his touch. "Jesus Christ, Gio! You've been diagnosed with a health condition that could be fatal! You're supposed to be on medication, and instead, you're walking around like nothing's going on?"

Gio eyed him. "What exactly did the doctor tell you?"

The blush that came onto Sacha's cheeks was incredibly endearing. He cleared his throat, his gaze moving to his hands, and he shrugged. "I might have told the doctor I was, uh, your boyfriend. Not that I am," Sacha said quickly. "It was the only way they'd let me stay and tell me what the hell was going on." He moved his gaze back to Gio, his expression a mixture of anger and what almost looked like heartache. "Autonomic neuropathy?"

"*Mild* autonomic neuropathy."

Sacha was not impressed. "Right. Which includes fainting. Which stressful situations can trigger. For fuck's sake, Gio. The doctor says you're not supposed to be alone after a fainting event. You can't drive, swim alone... You're not even supposed to have a fucking bath or shower without someone being near or within earshot. Why aren't you on medication? And why don't you have a medical alert bracelet? How did this even happen?"

"I don't need medication," Gio grumbled. "I take care of myself."

"Bullshit," Sacha spat, startling Gio.

No one ever spoke to him the way Sacha did, nor did anyone call him out on anything. Not even his brother.

"Have you forgotten that I've been around for months since you got back? That I've been working around you for weeks? You take shit care of yourself. You're supposed to be hydrating, keeping cool—in fucking Florida no less—being mindful of how quickly you get up, avoiding alcohol, eating regular meals—"

"Yes, I know," Gio growled.

"Then why aren't you fucking doing it?"

"Because I prefer to ignore it. I won't let some condition dictate my life."

Sacha cursed under his breath. He wiped a hand over his face and shook his head, then crossed his arms over his chest. "Giovanni. You are not a stupid man, despite what your last statement suggests. Explain yourself."

Gio was going to say he didn't have to explain himself to anyone, but Sacha narrowed his eyes, challenging him to try it. If there was anyone who wouldn't let him get away with any bullshit, it was Sacha. Gio let out a heavy sigh.

"It was a viral infection. One that almost killed me. I

was found by villagers in the middle of the jungle, hurt and dying. They took me to their village, where, by some miracle, a small group of volunteer doctors was working out of a tent they'd converted into a makeshift hospital. I was there for months. No one knew. They wouldn't have been able to get to me anyway. Not where I was. In the end, those doctors saved my life."

"How did you end up in the middle of a jungle?"

Gio swallowed hard. He met Sacha's gaze. "I was kidnapped."

"What?" Joker slowly sank into the chair. "How? *Who*?"

"I don't know who. Not exactly. I was in a tiny village in Sri Lanka. Few people knew I was there. It was me, a translator, an assistant, and four bodyguards I'd hired through an agency. I always hired local security, and before then, I never thought twice about it. One night while I slept, I was grabbed. A black hood was thrown over my head, and I was bound and gagged. I tried to fight them and was knocked out." Gio closed his eyes, but that only made the sickness swirling in his stomach feel worse. He opened his eyes and focused on Sacha, his sweet lips, beautiful face, and expressive eyes.

"When I woke up, I was tied to a chair. I could hear quiet talking and recognized the voice of one of the men. He'd been one of my bodyguards."

"Jesus." Sacha ran a hand through his hair; his lips pressed together in a thin line. "Go on."

"I had no idea where I was or what they were going to do with me. I'd always been cautious when traveling, never fully disclosing who I was. The people I went to help would have never heard of me. I was careful. Anyway, there were always men in the room with me. I could hear them murmuring to each other. Whoever was holding me captive made sure I was given food and water, taken to relieve myself. One night I told them I had to go to the bathroom. It was the only time my hands were untied and the black hood was temporarily removed.

"While I was outside, I made my move. The guy turned away, and I barreled into him and slammed him into a tree. We struggled, and I used everything I had to win. If I didn't, I was dead. I used his knife to cut myself loose and managed to escape, found myself completely lost in a jungle, nothing to aid me. Quite frankly, I'm surprised I lasted as long as I did."

"I'm not. You're stronger than you think, Gio."

Hearing those words from Sacha meant more to Gio than Sacha could know.

"Did the authorities find the kidnappers?"

Gio shook his head. "They disappeared. I think we both know what the chances are of them being found."

Sacha let out a heavy sigh. "Right." He was quiet for a heartbeat. "Is that why you came back?"

"To be honest, I'd been thinking about it for a while. I'd been away for so long; I was missing so much of Laz's life. My work used to be fulfilling, and it still is, but traveling as much as I had been, I realized how much I missed having a home, a family." Not that he would tell Sacha, but Gio had spent many a night dreaming of him, wondering what it might be like to kiss him, hold him, make love to him, to wake up every morning with Sacha in his arms.

"I don't suppose you're talking to anyone about your PTSD?"

The question caught Gio off guard. "What? I don't have PTSD." He frowned at Sacha, whose expression turned gentle.

Sacha took hold of Gio's hand and squeezed it, his words quiet. "Baby, you have PTSD."

Tears pooled in Gio's eyes, and he shook his head. "That's not... No. I mean, everything turned out okay. Sure, it was incredibly stressful at the time—okay, terrifying, but it's over. I survived. I'm fine."

"Gio—"

"I'm fine," Gio insisted.

"It's nothing to be ashamed of. It doesn't mean you're weak." Sacha took hold of Gio's chin and turned his face so their eyes could meet. "It doesn't mean you're broken or less than. Let me help you."

"I don't..." Gio's bottom lip trembled, and he shook his head as he did his best not to give in to his tears. He was just exhausted, that was all. Was it possible? Could he have been suffering from PTSD all this time and not have known? First his diagnosis, the knowledge he'd have to take medication, and now this? What the hell was happening to his life? Sacha stroked his hair, and for the first time since his father's death, Gio couldn't hold back his emotions, and he realized he didn't want to. Not this time.

The dam broke and the tears came. Sacha didn't hesitate. He wrapped his arms around Gio, pulling him close against him. Gio buried his face against Sacha's chest and cried. He held on tight, allowing Sacha to see him as no one in his life had ever seen him, not even Laz.

After the kidnapping, when he'd mostly recovered, Gio hadn't given in to his emotions then, determined to be strong and push through it. When he was back to full strength, he continued with his life as if nothing had happened. When the nightmares started, he brushed it off as a normal side effect of his stressful experience. He figured they'd go away in their own time.

"It's going to be okay," Sacha promised, kissing the top of Gio's head. "We're going to get you through this. I swear."

Gio nodded as he clung to Sacha. He'd never felt as vulnerable as he did at that moment, but for the first time, he didn't feel as if he had to be the strongest person in the room, because he wasn't, and that was okay. Sacha was strong enough for both of them. As if sensing his thoughts, Sacha spoke up.

"Listen, I know you're used to being the tough guy, but there can only be one tough guy in this relationship, and you're looking at him."

Gio surprised himself by laughing. "Is that so?" He pulled back, smiling as Sacha wiped Gio's cheeks with the blanket.

"Yep. One of us has to be the embarrassing guy with the grandpa moves and dad jokes, and I think we both know who that is." Sacha whistled nonchalantly and wiggled a finger at Gio, making him laugh again.

No one had ever made him laugh or feel as lighthearted as the incredible man beside him. A thought struck Gio. "When you said 'in this relationship,' you mean...?"

Sacha's cheeks went pink, and he shrugged. "I'm not putting a label on it, but if you wanted to hang out and, uh, do stuff together, I wouldn't be opposed."

"By *stuff*, does that include sex?"

"Definitely wouldn't be opposed."

Gio laughed softly, then quickly sobered. "I don't share, Sacha. I especially won't share *you*."

"Then, um, we won't share. But if it doesn't work, we're cool, yeah? I'm not starting anything if it means fucking up my family."

"I agree," Gio replied. "If it doesn't work, we're cool." He laced his fingers with Sacha's. "One day at a time, yes?"

Sacha nodded. "I'd like that. Now, how about you get some rest."

"Can I have a kiss first?"

"I don't know." Sacha arched an eyebrow at him. "You going to do what the doctor tells you?"

Gio gaped at him. "Are you blackmailing me?"

"You bet your ass. Do we have a deal?"

"Deal," Gio said, his smile wide as Sacha leaned in and kissed him ever so gently, his soft lips parting for Gio. They kissed sweetly for what seemed like an eternity, and as far as Gio was concerned, he could have remained that way for the rest of his life quite happily. Sacha pulled away, and Gio groaned his protest, making Sacha chuckle.

"I need to make a phone call." Sacha removed his phone from his pocket and tapped away at his screen as he walked toward the end of the bed. "Hey, King. He's awake. No. We're good. Thanks. Can you do me a favor? Can you keep the guys away, except for Laz? Gio has some stuff he needs to discuss with his brother in private."

Gio cursed under his breath. This was not what he needed right now, but judging by the pointed look Sacha aimed his way, he wasn't being given a choice. Now was as good a time as any, he supposed. It was probably for the best. Talking to his brother would take his mind off the hot mess that was his life right now. He was certainly too exhausted to attempt wrapping his brain around a possible PTSD diagnosis.

"I will. Thanks, man." Sacha hung up and returned to Gio's side. "You've put it off long enough. Your brother deserves better."

"You're right," Gio said through a sigh.

A text came through, and Sacha winced. "Laz is on his way. I think the fact that Red felt the need to let me know says your brother is losing his shit. Do you want me to stay here with you?"

Knowing Sacha would face Laz's wrath for him made his heart skip a beat.

"Thank you, but I'll be okay. This conversation is long overdue. I deserve whatever he throws at me."

Sacha nodded and headed for the door. "I'll be outside with Saint." He opened the door, and Laz rushed through. He skidded to a halt, turned, and threw his arms around Sacha. Gio held back a laugh at Sacha's startled expression. He didn't quite know what to do with Laz's display of affection. Seeming to snap himself out of it, he awkwardly patted Laz's back.

"Thank you," Laz said, squeezing him before releasing him and stepping away.

"Sure. I'll leave you to it. Let me know if you need anything." With one last glance at Gio, he left the room and closed the door behind him.

Laz hurried over to Gio's bedside. "What happened? What's going on?"

"First, I'd like to apologize for not talking to you sooner. You know how much I hate worrying you."

"How am I not going to worry about you? You're my big brother. I hate that you've been keeping things from me." His eyes filled with a mixture of concern and hurt. "What's going on, Gio?"

The time had come. Gio told Laz everything, just as he'd told Sacha, about what happened in Sri Lanka, about the kidnapping, his almost dying, his health condition, including his refusing medication and possibly having PTSD. The silence that filled the room was almost overwhelming, but Gio waited patiently, nonetheless.

Laz dropped down onto the chair Sacha had vacated

earlier. He shook his head and moved a trembling hand to his mouth. "You almost died?" His words were barely a whisper. "I wouldn't have known until God knows when."

"I'm sorry," Gio replied quietly. "I'm so sorry."

Seeing the hurt and disappointment in his brother's big blue eyes was more painful than anything he'd experienced in his life. He'd spent so long looking after his little brother, doing everything he could to make sure Laz never wanted for anything, he never realized how much he *hadn't* been giving his brother.

"How... how could you keep all this from me?"

"It's my job to protect you." Suddenly his reasoning sounded weak. Was he protecting Laz or himself?

Anger flashed through his brother's eyes. "I'm not a child, Giovanni. I appreciate everything you've done for me, you know I do, but you need to stop treating me like that same little boy you had to raise after Dad died."

"I know."

"Jesus." Laz jumped to his feet and paced, his hands in his hair. He spun to glare at Gio. "You almost *died*!"

Gio remained silent. His brother had every reason to be livid. Would Gio have reacted all that differently had the roles been reversed?

"You almost died in some jungle in the middle of fucking nowhere!" Laz continued to pace, grumbling to himself. He shook his head, his jaw clenched tight. Turning, he opened his mouth to say something, then shut it, his jaw muscles working and eyes ablaze. "I could strangle you!"

Gio had never seen his little brother so angry, and it made him smile. Clearly, that wasn't the reaction Laz expected, and he stared incredulously at Gio.

"What on earth could you possibly be smiling about right now?"

"You. I remember a time when you would have quietly accepted whatever I said and not argued back."

Laz snorted and crossed his arms over his chest. "Yeah, well, those days are long gone."

"I know, and I'm glad." His brother had come such a long way. "You're stronger than I gave you credit for. I'm sorry. I know you don't need me to look after you anymore."

Laz's expression softened, and he placed a hand on Gio's arm. "I'll always need my big brother, but I also need you to understand that I can take care of myself. I also have a small army of former Green Berets looking out for me."

Gio laughed softly. "I see that now."

"And so do you. Maybe it's time you let someone take care of you, huh?"

Gio smiled through the wetness in his eyes and nodded. When had his little brother gotten so strong? It was going to be tough. He'd been taking care of Laz for so long. Even when he'd been abroad, he'd made sure Laz was taken care of, made sure to check in with him, to send him anything he needed. It hadn't occurred to him that his little brother was all grown up and could take care of himself. And as of a couple of years ago, he had a big strong former Green Beret to protect him as well.

"I promise I'll do better at talking to you," Gio said.

"Good." A mischievous smile came onto Laz's face as he took a seat. "You can start with telling me how things are going with Joker."

"Oh, we're, um, dating. Sort of."

Laz eyed him. "Sort of dating?"

"It's new. Like, 'five minutes before you showed up' new. We're taking it one day at a time."

"Right." Laz nodded slowly. A smile spread across his face. "Okay. If you're happy—are you happy?"

Gio's heart swelled at the thought of Sacha.

"I guess that answers that," Laz said with a laugh, and Gio realized he was smiling like a dope. "I'm happy for you."

A knock on the door stopped Gio's response, and they replied to the doctor's greeting as he stepped into the room. After reading the chart in his hand, the older man arched a disapproving eyebrow, and Gio groaned.

"Well, at least you know what you did," the doctor said with a warm smile. "Now, here's how we're going to fix it."

Gio and Laz listened intently as the doctor went over Gio's condition and the medication he'd be starting to help stabilize his heart and blood pressure, which would help with the fainting.

"Don't worry, Doctor. He's going to be following your instructions to the letter."

Gio peered at his brother.

"Because I'll be giving a copy of this," Laz said, holding up all the paperwork the doctor had given him, "to my boyfriend, who happens to be a former Green Beret and medic, and another copy to his boyfriend, also a former Green Beret."

The doctor blinked at Laz before letting out a hearty laugh. He turned to Gio with a smile. "Well then, Mr. Galanos, I expect your doctor is going to see a good deal of improvement on your follow-up visit." They exchanged a few more pleasantries before the doctor left to arrange Gio's discharge.

"Do you want me to call in Colton? Who are you going home with tonight?"

Gio cleared his throat. "I was thinking of actually sleeping in my bed tonight." Reading between the lines, Laz nodded.

"You think he'll agree?"

"I think so. If not, I promise I'll call Colton."

"Okay." Laz hugged him. "If you need anything at all, you call me."

"Absolutely."

With one more hug, Laz left the room, and a heartbeat later, Sacha stepped inside. "How did it go?"

"He was disappointed in me, naturally, but we talked it through. I should have confided in him long ago, but I was still seeing him as that scared little boy he'd once been."

"Yeah, he's less scared and a little more scary these days," Sacha said with a smile as he took a seat next to Gio's bedside. "He somewhat forcefully informed me I'd be getting a copy of your paperwork."

Gio laughed at that. "He's rather commanding, isn't he?"

"It's always the quiet ones," Sacha teased. "So, what's the plan? We won't be able to pick up your new medication tonight, but I can pick it up for you in the morning."

"Thank you." Gio met Sacha's gaze. "Would you... come home with me tonight?"

Sacha didn't hesitate. "Sure. I need to call Jack. Just to let him know, since he's got Chip."

"Do you think he'd mind dropping Chip off at mine?"

Sacha smiled warmly. "He'll be fine with it."

Not long after Gio was discharged, they stepped out into the waiting room, and Gio let out a shaky breath at the sight of all the Kings and their partners. They were all here... for *him*. Colton hurried over and brought Gio into a gentle hug.

"I'm so glad you're okay." He pulled back and narrowed his eyes. "The only reason I'm not knocking some sense into you is that you just got discharged from the hospital. If you *ever* do anything like this again, Giovanni, I'm going to be very upset with you."

Judging by the pointed look Colton gave him, Laz had brought Colton up to speed, and that was okay. If Laz hadn't, Gio would have. As calm and collected as Colton appeared—not one fair hair out of place or one wrinkle in his navy Armani suit—Gio knew the truth. He'd scared Colton.

"I'm sorry I worried you," Gio said.

Colton grumbled something unintelligible under his breath that made Gio chuckle. He smiled at Ace, who stepped forward.

"None of this suffer-in-silence lone-wolf bullshit anymore, got it? You're family, and family looks after one another."

The back of Gio's eyes stung, and he blinked back the wetness, nodding his understanding.

"All right, let's all go home," King said, patting Gio's shoulder as if to confirm Ace's words.

Colton turned to Gio. "You coming with us?"

"No, um, I'm going home."

Colton's brows drew together until Gio motioned to Sacha, who was talking to Jack. Realization dawned, and Colton smiled knowingly. "Call if you need anything."

"Will do. Thank you." While Colton headed off, Gio searched the waiting area and found Saint standing serenely to one side. Even in the hospital waiting room, he was on the job, vigilant as he assessed everyone in the place. Gio headed over.

"Thank you for everything, Saint. I'm sorry for giving you a hard time earlier tonight. I know you were just doing your job."

"Don't worry about it. You were scared for him. I

understand that, believe me. It wasn't easy to do, but you're my priority, and he understands that. Pretty sure he would kick my ass if I let anything happen to you." Saint's eyes widened. "He's kinda scary for a little guy."

"Don't worry." Gio patted Saint's bicep. "I'll protect you."

Saint snorted and resumed his seat to wait for them. It couldn't have been easy for him to walk away from Sacha, from that situation. It was a testament to Saint's professionalism that he'd done what he had to, despite the dangers they faced.

Sacha stepped up to Gio, hands in his pockets, and his lips quirked in a little smile. "Jack's gonna pick up Chip and drop him off. Ready?"

With Sacha at his side, Gio was pretty confident he was ready for anything.

SEVEN

IT WAS LATE when they got in, and Gio looked about ready to collapse, but first, he wanted a shower. Joker couldn't blame him. It had been one hell of a night.

Jack was on his way with Chip, so Joker ignored Gio's griping and instructed Saint to stand outside Gio's bathroom suite door while he showered in case he got dizzy or passed out. Since he'd had a bad episode, the doctor insisted Gio not do anything alone that might leave him in a vulnerable position or without someone within hearing distance.

Tomorrow Joker would pick up Gio's new medication and make damn sure he started taking it, though after tonight, with everyone on his ass, Joker would guess Gio wasn't going to be taking any more stupid risks with his health.

Since Gio was occupied and Jack hadn't arrived yet, Joker took the opportunity to do a quick scan of the perimeter. For possible threats, not because he was nosy and wanted to have a good look at the house. He planned on making a closer inspection in the morning when he could see everything properly.

Gio didn't spend a lot of time at his house, and Joker couldn't figure out why. The place was amazing and huge, as Joker had expected. The guy was obscenely wealthy, after all. However, Joker hadn't expected Gio's house to be smaller than Colton's.

"What the—" Joker stood outside on the patio and stared up at the house. "It's fucking pink." Not just any pink. He squinted at the wall next to the bright wall sconce. Salmon pink. "Of course it is." Joker shook his head, amused. It should have been tacky, but instead it was charming, with its white shutters, white windows, white trim, and a pale gray roof.

The house was a three-story luxury oceanfront property with two garages, a pool, spa, and firepit. A private walkway led down to the quiet beach. Everything about the house screamed Gio, from the property's pristine landscaping and impeccable paint job to the interior's eclectic decor and comfortable-looking mismatched furniture.

This was the house of a man who'd traveled far and wide and brought back with him a little piece of his experience. Each room was painted a different color—the dining room a pale salmon pink, one guest room a light blue, another a light yellow. The only white rooms were the living room, foyer, and halls.

Artwork from various parts of the world hung in each room, along with framed photos of Gio smiling wide with the many people he'd helped. The entire house burst with color, inside and out. Anyone who didn't know Gio and went on outward appearances might be confused, but it all made perfect sense to Joker. For Gio, the places he'd visited, the people he'd met and those he'd helped were more than a job; they were a part of his life.

Joker had discovered a small elevator inside the house on the main floor, but the doorbell rang, interrupting his exploration. After checking who it was, Joker opened the door for Jack and Chip.

"Here's your rotten brat. He wouldn't shut up the entire ride over here. You didn't come pick him up like you were supposed to, so he made his displeasure known."

"Aw." Joker knelt to give Chip some love. "Were you a pain in the ass for your uncle Jack? Who's my good boy?"

Chip howled and barked, letting Joker know he was mad and he had words for him about it. After an acceptable amount of scritches had been given, Chip turned his nose up at Joker and trotted off to explore.

"Good luck with that," Jack said, laughing. "Your dog is such a diva."

"He's fine. He'll ignore me and give me the side-eye for the rest of the night. I'll give him his you-know-what in the morning and all will be forgiven."

Jack nodded and handed Joker Chip's bag, along with Joker's beat-up Army backpack. "What about you?"

"What about me?" Joker peered at his best friend. He looked a little smug for some reason. Jack shrugged and glanced around the expansive living room.

"So... pink house."

Joker shoved his hands into his pockets with a heavy sigh. "Salmon pink, yes."

"It's nice."

"Why are you telling *me*?"

Another shrug. "Chip's gonna love running on the beach."

"What's with the shrugging? You got a tic or something?

Cut it out." And of course Chip would love running on the beach. It wasn't exactly a new experience for him. Why did Jack make it sound so weird?

"Hi, Jack." Gio appeared, and Joker almost swallowed his tongue. He must have made some kind of noise, because his asshole best friend laughed while Gio looked at Joker with concern. "You okay?"

"Yep. Just, uh, feeling a bit parched. Need some water."

"*Parched*?" Jack mouthed, and Joker flipped him off when Gio had turned away.

"There are bottles of cold water in the fridge," Gio informed him, his smile huge as Chip barked, howled, and danced excitedly around his feet.

Joker headed for the kitchen, ignoring the thin white pajama bottoms hanging low on Gio's hips, the fabric of which left *nothing* to the imagination. His hair was wet from the shower, his feet bare, and the white V-neck tee he wore accentuated every muscle of his strong arms, chest, and flat stomach.

"I better get going," Jack said, his lips quirked in a smile. "Call me if you need anything."

"Thank you." Gio walked him out, Chip on his heels like he was afraid Gio was going somewhere. Gio locked up after Jack, then headed back into the living room. He dropped down onto the end of the gray L-shaped sectional. Chip didn't waste any time jumping up to sit next to Gio, making him laugh.

"Just tell him to get down if you don't want him on your furniture." Joker shook his head at Chip as he came around the counter of the open-plan kitchen. "He knows better."

"Furniture is meant to be used," Gio replied cheerfully as he scratched Chip behind his ears.

"He sheds," Joker warned him. "A lot."

Gio shrugged. "That's what lint rollers are for."

"Mind if I use your shower?" Joker asked. He wasn't about to ask where he'd be sleeping, but he assumed it was one of Gio's many guest rooms. "Where's Saint?"

"Of course you can use my shower. And Saint's in his room. I told him I'd be heading off to bed soon and would let him know if I needed him." Gio sighed. "It's strange, having a bodyguard around all the time."

At some point, Gio would have a whole team around him. The time for him to decide on live-in protection was coming up fast. He was simply too much of a target not to have a small team watching his six at all times, and he knew it. Someone out there wanted to get their hands on Gio, and whether it was the same men who'd kidnapped him in Sri Lanka or someone entirely different, Gio was in danger. He couldn't afford to act like a regular guy anymore.

"Let me show you to the bathroom." Gio stood, and Chip jumped off the couch to trail after Gio like his furry shadow.

Joker followed Gio up two flights of stairs to the third story with the master suite. Good God, his entire apartment could fit in here. The room was terrific, with the far wall made up of three floor-to-ceiling windows offering a breathtaking view of the ocean. The room was painted a soft blue with white accents and looked incredibly inviting, from its lush white-and-blue bedding to the plush couch and footrest in front of the windows.

"This is my bedroom." Gio shifted awkwardly, his gaze on the vast king-sized bed. "I haven't slept a full night in my bed since I bought it."

Joker knew the feeling well, and it squeezed his heart. "How about we sleep in it tonight?" He waited with bated breath as Gio turned to him, his eyes searching Joker's.

"What if I wake you up with one of my nightmares?"

"Then you wake me up."

Gio looked uncertain, and Joker gently placed a hand on his arm.

"Nothing is going to happen to you while I'm here, Gio."

"You'll protect me?" Gio's smile reached his dark eyes as he brought Joker into his embrace.

"Pft. What do you think?"

"I think you'd do almost anything for me."

Joker barked out a laugh. "Whoa, hey now. Someone's feeling bold." He wasn't about to tell Gio how stupidly happy his words made him, because, yeah, he would. As terrifying as the thought was, Joker realized he was okay with it. Gio was nothing like Joker had first imagined.

"Tell me you wouldn't do almost anything for me."

Joker pretended to think about it. "I'm not eating okra for you. That's a dealbreaker. Or eggplant. I might consider beets if the incentive is good enough."

"Oh, well, I mean, okra. That's understandable. Pretty sure I can make you come around on the eggplant."

"You keep telling yourself that."

Gio brushed his lips over Joker's. "Face it. You like me."

"Hm. I find you tolerable at best."

"Well, that's okay, because I only want you for your dog."

Joker gasped. "Oh, you fucker!" He laughed. "I see how it is."

"I mean, you're cute, but not Chip-cute."

"Ass." Joker couldn't help his stupidly happy smile. How could he resist a guy who seemed to love his dog almost as much as he did? Speaking of, Chip trotted past them like he owned the joint and jumped up onto the bed.

"Excuse you," Joker said, gaping at Chip as he circled several times in the center of the bed, then dropped down all curled up in a ball. He lifted his head and stared at Joker like, "What?"

Gio laughed and kissed Joker's cheek. "Well, now you *have* to sleep in my bed."

"Unbelievable." Joker shook his head at Chip as he headed for the bathroom. "Make yourself comfortable. People are going to think I didn't teach you any manners." Chip laid his head on his paws, his big eyes looking up at Joker. "Don't you give me that I'm-just-a-cute-puppy face. I'm immune to that face."

"But I'm not," Gio said, throwing himself on the bed and laughing when Chip rolled over onto his back and wriggled so he could attack Gio with his tongue.

"You two are ridiculous." Joker held back a smile. They were also going to make his heart explode. Seeing Gio rolling around the bed laughing with Chip barking and wagging his tail happily as he lavished Gio with doggie kisses was something Joker had no idea he'd been missing in his life. If he wasn't careful, he could quickly get used to having Gio around.

Leaving the two dorks to it, he walked into the enormous en-suite bathroom. He closed the door behind him, then dropped his bag onto the marble counter. The bathroom had a fancy shower big enough for two with one of those giant rainfall showerheads he'd seen in Colton's house. Next to it sat a jacuzzi-style bathtub, also big enough for two, not that he was getting any ideas. Probably best not to look at it too much.

After turning on the shower, he reached into his backpack and grabbed the toiletry bag that Jack had packed for him. Was he actually here in Gio's house using his shower? How the hell had that happened? More importantly, had he just started a relationship with the guy? Getting into the shower, he dropped the toiletry bag onto the shelf at the far end, then stilled. *Holy fuck*, he was in a relationship!

With Gio.

He had a boyfriend. As in, he was seeing one person, sleeping with one person, and having sex with one person. *Oh fuck.*

Sticking his head under the hot spray, he let the water sluice over him, relaxing his muscles. He leaned against the expensive tiled wall and willed himself to breathe. What the hell had gotten into him? Dumb question. He knew exactly what had gotten into him.

When those masked men had shown up, a fear he'd not felt in a long time took charge. Knowing they were there to take Gio, to hurt him, sent rage flaring through him, and he'd beaten the shit out of those guys. They'd been lucky to get away from him.

Seeing Gio taken away on a gurney, then sped away in an ambulance had his heart trying to beat out of him, so when he showed up at the hospital, and the nurse asked who Joker was to Gio, he'd said the first thing that had come to mind—that he was Gio's boyfriend. The rest of the guys, including Laz, hadn't arrived, and there was no way he was going to leave Gio in there all alone. The hospital didn't care for bodyguards, so Saint had to wait outside.

"Fuck." Joker grabbed his shampoo and started washing his hair. The terrifying part of all this was how declaring himself in a relationship hadn't scared him as much as it should have. He loved kissing Gio, loved the taste of him, the feel of his body against Joker's. Loved...

Nope. Enjoyed. He *enjoyed* kissing Gio. *Enjoyed* the taste of him and the feel of his body. No *L* words involved.

Images of him on his knees for Gio flooded his mind, and he quickly pushed them down. How the hell was he supposed to sleep in the same bed with Gio after what they'd done in the club?

"Easy," Joker told himself. "Tonight isn't about you, so you do whatever he needs you to do."

Finishing up his hair, he quickly washed and got out. After drying himself with one of the soft, fluffy white towels, he dressed in the checkered blue-and-green pajama pants and blue tee Jack had stuffed in the backpack for him.

It was oddly quiet out in the bedroom. Could Gio have fallen asleep? Stepping out of the bathroom, Joker stilled. Gio lay on his side facing Chip, who lay stretched out on his back tucked against Gio, his face against Gio's shoulder as Gio murmured at him and slowly rubbed his belly. Chip wasn't just out for the count; he was snoring.

Sensing he was there, Gio lifted his gaze, his smile stealing Joker's breath away. This man was hazardous to his heart. He looked so soft and comfortable, so damned happy, like there was nowhere else in the world he would rather be than right here with Joker and his dog.

"I can tell him to get off the bed," Joker said quietly as he dropped his bag off on the couch by the window before heading toward the bed.

Gio stared at him. "Where would he sleep?"

"Um, the floor?" Joker tried not to laugh at Gio's scandalized expression, as if he'd suggested Chip sleep out in the cold rain or something.

"Absolutely not. He'll sleep here with us. I'm assuming he sleeps with you on your bed?"

"Yeah, though I need to warn you to be careful when

you go to the bathroom, because if he gets hot, he likes to lie down on the tiles to cool off, so just look for the big hairy black blob on the floor."

Gio chuckled, and Chip wriggled, twisting his body so he could see Joker approaching the bed, some of his teeth visible, making Joker laugh.

"You're such a butt."

Chip's tail thumped against the comforter in response.

"All right, move your big furry ass. This is my spot." Joker tugged at the covers, and Chip grumbled his displeasure. "Don't make me move you." With a huff, Chip rolled over and pushed himself to his paws, then gave himself a good shake, nearly whacking Joker in the face with his tail. He took his sweet-ass time on his way to the foot of the bed, then dropped himself down with the most dramatic sigh to ever come from a dog. Gio pouted at Joker.

"Oh my God, you're such a sucker." Joker climbed into bed with a laugh. "He's got you smitten."

"He's not the only one," Gio said softly, his dark eyes filled with affection and... something else as he met Joker's gaze. Thankfully, Gio didn't wait for a reply. Instead, he got up to turn off the bedroom lights. "Will that bother you? Because I can close the blinds." He motioned to the windows at the end of the room overlooking the beach where the ocean and night sky seemed to stretch on forever. "You can't see in from outside. I made sure to have a special film installed for privacy."

"I'm good with it if you are. It's quite the view."

"I love the ocean," Gio admitted, climbing into bed. "There's something so calming about it; even when a storm is raging, it's soothing somehow."

"I get that. It's why we all decided to move to St. Augustine Beach, to be near the water. Well, Red's therapist suggested it, so the rest of us joined him. It definitely helps."

Gio turned onto his side, facing Joker. "Thank you for staying here with me."

"It's not exactly a hardship."

"Have you always been so brutally honest?"

"Yep." Joker thought about it. "Actually, not always." He rubbed at his chest over his heart. Fuck. He was *not* going to get all sentimental and sappy.

"Oh?"

"I used to be quiet and shy."

Gio stared at him, and Joker laughed.

"I'm serious. When I was little, I barely spoke." His smile faded at the hazy memory. It was a lifetime ago. "I was too scared to talk."

"Why?"

"Because I couldn't speak English."

"What?"

Joker nodded. "I spoke Russian. I was told no parents would ever want a Commie kid. If I wanted to get adopted, I needed to speak English without an accent." His heart warmed at Gio's horrified expression.

"That's outrageous!"

"Yeah, well, it was the eighties, and I was an orphan, so..." Joker shrugged. "Anyway, for some reason, they kept Sacha, but they changed my last name. They taught me to speak English, had me work on getting rid of the accent. It took a while, but I did it." No trace of his heritage remained, but then what heritage could he have salvaged when he'd been so young and had no idea where he'd come from?

"How old were you?"

"Almost four. All I know is that my mother fled to the US when I was a baby. I barely remember her. When I was old enough to ask about my parents, they told me my mother was dead and they had no idea who my father was. Years later, I found out my father had died in some Russian prison, and an asshole boyfriend had killed my mother. The neighbors heard a kid screaming nonstop and called the cops." Joker wrinkled his nose. "He was long gone by then."

"He just left you there?"

"Yeah, but then again, he was a murderer, so, you know, probably not the best babysitter."

Gio brushed his fingers down Joker's jaw. "I'm sorry."

"It was a long time ago. I remember being alone in a tiny room, maybe a closet? There was a lot of screaming somewhere, then silence. I don't remember much of it, which is probably a good thing."

"Did you get adopted?"

Joker shook his head. "I spent a lot of time in foster homes. By the time I was seven, I wasn't all that quiet and shy anymore. My accent was long gone, and I was angry. I was a cute kid but small, so I got picked on a lot. Plus, my name was Sacha. You can imagine how well that went down with the other kids."

"Is that why you don't like to be called by your name?"

Joker shrugged. "It reminds me of who I used to be, as opposed to who I became when I found my real family."

"I didn't know that. I'm sorry. I can stop calling you Sacha."

Joker thought about it. At first it had bugged him, but now it was different. He didn't mind it so much. And it wasn't all bad. Jack still occasionally called him by his real name. "No, don't stop." It occurred to him that he liked Gio calling him by his name. Like he was somehow helping Joker reclaim something of his that had been lost. "I like it when you say it."

Gio's smile was beautiful. "Okay. Back to you being shy."

"Yeah, well, that didn't last long. I learned real quick how to hold my own, but I hated everyone, so I got into a lot of fights. Then when I was eleven, I ended up with the perfect family. They were like one of those TV families from back in the day. Everyone was good-looking with perfect hair and perfect smiles. They dressed in fancy labeled polo shirts and drove expensive cars. Magnolia was a former beauty queen; Thatcher was a college professor." His jaw muscles tightened, and he sighed. Jack was the only one he'd ever talked to about his past. Jack and the therapist Joker had seen when he and what was left of his brothers-in-arms came home for good.

"I'm not going to like this, am I?" Gio whispered, his eyes filled with heartache for Joker. The moonlight that filtered in from the wall of windows was enough to cast an ethereal glow across the bed, making it easy for Joker to make out the softness of Gio's face.

"When I started high school, I was the smallest kid in school. I thought my foster parents would yell at me, hit me, whatever, for all the fights I got into, but they never did. I couldn't help but be suspicious. No one could be that perfect, certainly no one who wanted *me*.

"But the more I tried to find something wrong, the more I couldn't. I had my own room with my own stuff. They fed me, bought me clothes, equipment, gadgets, took me to the movies and county fairs, introduced me to all their country club friends. I started wondering if it felt too good to be true because I'd never had a real family. When I met Jack's family, I realized there *were* good people out there. His family wasn't perfect by any means, but they loved one another. Maybe if I stopped trying to find what was wrong with my foster parents, I'd discover I'd found a good thing."

Joker rolled onto his back and stared at the ceiling. "I thought I'd put them to the test, so I came out to them when I was thirteen. I told them I didn't just like girls and boys, but everyone. They hugged me and said they didn't care. For the first time in my life, I started thinking maybe I'd finally found a home and people who loved me." He felt Gio's hand in his hair, and Joker closed his eyes. "When I turned sixteen, I discovered I'd been right the first time."

"What happened?" Gio's voice was hushed and shaky, as if he wasn't sure he wanted to know.

"When I was sixteen, Magnolia climbed into bed with me one night and tried to have sex with me while Thatcher masturbated. I managed to shove her off the bed, grab my backpack, and run the hell out of there. It wasn't until I got to Jack's house that I realized I wasn't wearing any shoes."

The room filled with silence, and Joker opened his eyes. He turned his head, staring at Gio, who was deadly still. He opened his mouth to say something when Gio shot up out of bed. Joker bolted upright.

"Gio?"

"Where are they now? I will fucking murder them!"

"As sweet as your offer to commit homicide on my behalf is, they got what they deserved. Someone hacked into a storage facility where they happened to have a unit. It was shortly broken into, and that very night the cops got an anonymous tip about the child porn Magnolia and Thatcher were hiding."

Gio turned, his fists balled at his sides and his eyes narrowed. "I have connections, you know. Accidents happen."

"All right there, Punisher." Joker patted the mattress. "Get back here."

With a grumble, Gio climbed back under the covers. He was practically thrumming with unsettled energy. Considering how calm and collected Gio always was, Joker was pretty positive that if he asked Gio to rain down retribution on his behalf, Gio wouldn't so much as hesitate. He'd be on his fancy phone, calling in all kinds of favors like he was some kind of mafia don. Who knew Gio had a dark side to him? Wanting to ease Gio's anger, Joker tugged him close, smiling when Gio shifted and moved down so he could lay his head on Joker's shoulder.

"Before they went to prison, I spent every minute I could with Jack. His mother got suspicious and even dropped by the house on the pretense of meeting the foster parents of her son's best friend. I could tell she was confused, but my guess is some kind of real motherly instinct kicked in, and when she got back, she told me I could stay over whenever I wanted. I moved in with them after that."

"What did those monsters say?"

"They couldn't say a word, and they knew it. I just wanted to be as far away from them as possible. When the Army recruiters came to our school, I talked at length with them. I thought real hard about it. Jack had the chance to do something great with his life, but what the hell was I going to do? My grades weren't good enough for any kind of scholarship. I had no support system other than Jack and his family, and there was only so much they could do when they weren't my legal guardians. I wanted to do something with my life, get away from all the shit I'd grown up around. So I talked about it with Jack and told him I was going to join the Army. I never expected him to join up with me. His family wasn't happy, but they accepted his decision."

The room went silent again, but this time it was a comfortable silence. Joker rubbed his cheek against Gio's hair, wondering how the hell he'd ended up here. When had this happened? When had he gone from disliking the guy purely on principle to lying in bed with him smelling his shampoo while Chip snored at their feet?

"I just want you to know that I'm in awe of you."

"Of me?" Joker frowned. "What for?"

"You've been through so much hardship in your life, and you could have given up, but you didn't. You kept going; you found yourself a new family, one worthy of you. You pushed yourself and became a Green Beret, risked your life for others, for your country, and even after everything you lost, you came home and built an amazing career for yourself. You're an inspiration, Sacha Wilder."

Joker didn't know what to say. No one had ever said anything like that to him. Yeah, life had dealt him a shit hand, but he'd done what he'd always done—survive. Though now, with Gio in his arms, he wanted more than survival, more than his career. When had he gone from being perfectly happy with sex to wanting a happy ever after?

"Thank you for trusting me. I understand now why it's so difficult for you to put your trust in others."

"It's why I struggled with trusting you," Joker admitted. "You seemed too good to be true."

"And now?"

"Now I know you're not perfect. Far from perfect. Very imperfect."

Gio chuckled. "I could have told you that."

"In case you haven't noticed, I'm a bit stubborn. I needed to see for myself."

"And now that you have?"

"I guess I'm not totally opposed to you."

"Oh good," Gio said, sounding amused. He shifted onto his side and propped himself on his elbow, his expression filled with affection. "Thank you for everything. For sharing your heart with me, for looking after me, for letting me be a part of your life."

What the hell was he supposed to say to that? Nothing. And with Gio, he didn't feel like he *had* to say anything. At least not with words. Instead, he cupped Gio's cheek and kissed him.

Their kiss was sweet and slow, with Joker savoring the taste of him, the softness of his lips, the warmth of his mouth. He took his time in a way he never had with anyone else. With Gio, Joker was content to simply let himself get swept away by everything Gio made him feel, by the multitude of emotions coursing through him. Never had he felt like he'd go out of his mind if he didn't touch someone, breathe in their scent, or put his mouth on them. And Gio seemed as content to just kiss Joker as if he couldn't get enough of him.

The distant crashing of waves provided a soothing soundtrack as they kissed unhurriedly. Joker caressed the smooth skin of Gio's neck, his fingers trailing down to his collar while Gio's fingers found Joker's skin beneath his T-shirt. When was the last time he'd done anything like this? Had he ever done anything like this? No. In the past, his sexual encounters had been about that, sex, about getting off and finding release, not about taking the time to enjoy every dip and curve of his partner.

Gio moved his lips from Joker's, brushing them over his

cheek and peppering the softest butterfly kisses over Joker's skin. Then he lay down, his head on the same pillow as Joker. He slipped his arm around Joker and held him tight.

"Get some rest. We're right here," Joker murmured, kissing Gio's forehead. "You're safe."

Gio hummed softly, and within several heartbeats, his breath evened out. He had a peaceful expression on his face, the lines on his forehead smoothed out, his lips slightly parted. Joker's thoughts went back to their conversation in the hospital, and a low, thrumming white-hot rage flowed through him at the knowledge someone had kidnapped him. Gio had been extremely lucky. Joker guessed they'd been after money. They'd discovered who Gio was, and most people in Gio's position had some kind of kidnap insurance. They would have collected the money, and Gio would have ended up dead.

For all of Gio's talk of being in awe of Joker, he had no idea how inspiring *he* was. Gio wasn't a Green Beret. He had no training, not even self-defense training, and yet he'd fought for his life. Twice. The man had no fear, going off into unknown territories to help others have a better life. After the death of their father, he'd raised his little brother and worked several jobs to send his brother to college and provide for him. He'd made smart investments, worked damn hard for his fortune, and what did he do with it? He gave it away. The more money he made, the more he gave away.

For years Joker had heard about Gio from Laz, Red, and the others, but Joker had made up his mind about the guy without even meeting him, believing no one could be so selfless or perfect. He'd been convinced something was up, and technically, he'd been right. Gio wasn't perfect. No one was. But Gio's imperfections didn't make him sinister; they made him human. He was a regular guy who happened to have a shit ton of money and wanted to do something good with it.

One of these days, he'd ask Gio why. That was one question he'd yet to figure out—why Gio did what he did. For now, he'd enjoy the man. Enjoy the warm closeness that came from being with someone he trusted.

Not long after Joker fell asleep, he was woken up by a jolt in the bed. Gio was having another nightmare. It didn't appear to be as bad as the one he'd had the night at Colton's, but his brow was beaded with sweat, his eyebrows drawn together, and his lips pressed tight. He shivered and moaned. Joker didn't move. He didn't have to.

Chip crawled up the bed and stuck his nose against Gio's cheek. When Gio didn't wake up, Chip licked his face and nudged him under his chin. Gio groaned and opened his eyes; he blinked at Chip, and then a slow smile spread across his face. With a soft chuckle, he scratched Chip behind the ear. Another doggie kiss later and Chip wedged himself between Gio and Joker, closed his eyes, and went back to sleep. Gio met Joker's gaze, his smile reaching his eyes. He mouthed, "Thank you," and Joker nodded. When Gio closed his eyes and fell back asleep, Joker knew what he needed to do. It scared the hell out of him, but it was the right thing to do, and he couldn't think of anyone else more deserving.

EIGHT

HE COULD GET USED to this.

Gio lay on his side, his gaze on the beautifully sleep-rumpled man in front of him. Sacha was still asleep, Chip snoring softly on his back between them. Last night Gio had another nightmare, and instead of being woken up by Joker, he'd woken up to doggie kisses. The moment he'd opened his eyes, he'd smiled. His heart rate slowed far quicker than it had in the past, and a sense of safety and peace he'd never felt before washed over him. He'd never fallen asleep so quickly after one of his nightmares before, and usually when he did end up falling asleep, another nightmare often followed, but not this time.

For the first time in forever, Gio almost felt... rested.

Chip was the first to wake up. He stretched his neck out and licked at Sacha's chin. Gio was forced to press his lips together to keep from laughing at Sacha's scrunched-up nose. He moved his face, but every time he moved, Chip managed to get him somewhere else.

"Ah fuck," Sacha groaned when Chip got him in the nose. "Stop trying to shove your tongue up my nose."

Gio couldn't help it, he laughed. Sacha opened his eyes, then narrowed them at Gio.

"Laugh it up. Wait until he does it to you. That thing has terrifying accuracy. He's gotten me in the ear, the eyeball, inside my mouth, and up my nose."

Gio rolled onto his back and laughed some more. He could just imagine the cursing Sacha had done after getting tongued by his dog.

"Chip, kiss Gio."

Chip rolled onto his belly and launched himself at Gio, who yelped as he was assaulted by a doggie tongue, Chip's heavy weight crawling all over him.

"I give!" Gio laughed. The more he tried to cover his face, the more determined Chip was. Suddenly he found himself flailing, and he let out a very manly yelp as he hit the carpet with a *thud*. Chip, of course, landed on his feet and continued his assault while Gio curled up in a ball as he attempted to fend off the slobbery attack. Above him on the bed, Sacha was in tears from laughing so hard. "I'm up! I'm up!" Gio pushed himself to his feet. He shook his head at Sacha. "Thanks for not saving me."

Sacha let out an indelicate snort. "I'd say I was sorry, but I'm not. That was the funniest shit I've ever seen."

"I'm glad I amuse you. How about some breakfast? I usually go for a run after."

"Sounds perfect." Sacha rolled out of bed and grabbed his phone before they headed downstairs with Chip.

Saint was already up and in the living room, working on his laptop.

"Hey, man," Joker said, nodding at Saint. "Any word from HQ about last night?"

Saint shook his head. "Jack's team has been scraping

surveillance all over the place. King said to call him when you got up."

"I'll get breakfast going," Gio said while Sacha put in a call to King.

"You're on speaker," Sacha said. "Gio and Saint are here."

"Good. I've got an update, but it's not much. We've established that the men sent to kidnap Gio last night were professionals."

"Can't be that professional if I kicked their asses," Sacha replied, taking a seat on one of the chairs at the kitchen counter.

"Yeah, well, my guess is they didn't expect to come up against someone like you. Whoever sent them didn't do their homework. After what happened, Jack's team found someone trying to hack into our system. They were looking for information on you and Saint. The team traced the hack, but when our team got there, they were gone. They underestimated us once. It's unlikely they're going to do so again."

"Any connection between these guys and the ones from Sri Lanka?"

Gio jolted. "You think it's the same people?"

"We don't know. Jack's team is still gathering intel on the kidnappers from Sri Lanka. The team's looking into kidnap activity in the area, as well as any possible witnesses, but so far, no luck. It's been a little over a year since the incident, so it's going to take time. We'll keep you posted. In the meantime, I'm putting a second team on you, Gio. I'm also going to send someone else to back up Saint. These guys aren't just going to walk away from this. They're going to regroup and try again."

Sacha glanced up, and Gio nodded. He let out a shaky

breath. As much as he hated the idea of more security, it was the right thing to do.

"Okay. Thanks," Sacha said before hanging up. He got up and sat next to Saint on the couch.

While the two discussed King's idea to up Gio's security, Gio got to work on cooking the three of them breakfast. It was nice having people over. His big house didn't seem so empty. Maybe he should think about having a barbecue or something, let everyone know they were always welcome in his home. His thoughts went back to Sri Lanka. He still couldn't wrap his head around the idea that what happened back then could be connected to all of this. If it was, why now? Why wait almost a year to make another attempt? He needed to stop thinking about this. Without any real information, he'd just be grasping at straws.

Gio made plenty of scrambled eggs for the three of them, along with bacon. Chip stared up at him with those big brown eyes, his tail wagging. Darting a glance at Sacha, Gio slipped Chip a piece of bacon, whispering, "Don't tell Daddy."

"I like that you think I don't know what you're up to."

Gio startled, a hand flying to his chest. "Christ!" He turned to glare at Sacha. "Where the hell did you come from?"

Sacha laughed. "You were too busy conspiring with the furry troublemaker to realize I'd gotten up." He arched an eyebrow at Gio. "Did you think you were going to cook bacon and get away with him not trying to fleece you?"

"It was just one little piece." One little piece that Chip seemed to have swallowed whole. "I'm not sure he chewed, though."

"Yeah, bacon isn't meant to be chewed, only sucked in

like a vacuum. Also, you're a pushover, so I'm here to make surc you don't give him any more."

Chip whined, and Gio looked from Sacha to Chip and back. Sacha planted his hands on his hips.

"Listen here, you two. This is not a democracy. You're not cute, and you're not as sneaky as you think you are."

Gio batted his lashes at Sacha and pointed at Chip, who licked Gio's finger. "But that face."

Unimpressed, Sacha pointed at his face. "*This* face. This is the face you need to be concerned about. I know he's got you wrapped around his paw, but you need to be stronger than this. Give him an inch and he'll—"

Chip barked, spun around, then dropped onto his side in the middle of the kitchen. Gio gasped.

"Oh my God, what happened? What's wrong with him?"

Chip barked and howled as he twisted and turned, paws waving as he flopped about.

"What happened is he sensed your weakness, and now he's throwing a temper tantrum."

Gio stared down at Chip. He'd never seen a dog throw a temper tantrum before. "That's hilarious."

"Yeah, real fun when you're in the middle of the supermarket."

"Should I—"

"Ignore him? Yes. This will be a common occurrence if you give in, so just step over him and carry on. When he sees you're not going to give in, he'll get up."

So much personality. Somehow Gio wasn't surprised. He was Sacha's dog, after all. Doing his best to resist Chip and his epic side-eye, Gio placed plates filled with breakfast on the counter. The three of them ate, and as Sacha predicted, when Chip saw he wasn't going to be given any extra bacon, he got up and headed into the living room; his huff when he lay on the couch could be heard several counties over. They laughed, much to Chip's displeasure.

Once they'd eaten and the dishes were in the dishwasher, they went to change into running clothes. Saint would be accompanying them. It was still before seven in the morning, so there was still a nice breeze, and the humidity wasn't so bad when they got outside. Chip trotted alongside Sacha as they headed for the beach.

"A pink house?" Sacha asked, one thick brow poking up from behind his sunglasses.

Gio shrugged. "I like the color. Plus, it had a very soothing quality to it. You don't like it?"

"I didn't say that," Sacha grumbled, making Gio smile.

Once they were on firmer sand, they started jogging. Chip bolted off ahead to chase the waves as they crashed against the shore. A flock of seagulls screeched their displeasure at being run off the beach by the big black fur ball. Tongue lolling, Chip trotted back toward them, head lifted proudly, as if he'd just defeated a great threat for them.

"Why do you do it?"

"Do what?" Gio asked.

"The charity stuff. Did you wake up one morning and say, 'I think I'm gonna be rich and give away loads of money'?"

"Exactly that," Gio teased, earning himself a playful shove from Sacha. "My father inspired me. I always wanted to help people, but what happened to my father changed my life."

"He died of cancer, right?"

"Yes. Lung cancer."

"I'm sorry."

"Thank you." Gio slowed to a walk, Sacha following his lead. "When I came out as bisexual, my parents' families were outraged, but when Laz came out as gay, they turned against my father, blaming him for our 'perversion.'"

"What? That's fucking stupid."

"Agreed. When my father was diagnosed, I called my grandmother for help. She wouldn't even take my call. Even while he lay in that hospital bed dying, they refused to acknowledge we existed. I applied for as much financial help as I could, but the best treatments, the ones that might give him at least a bit more time with us, were out of our reach."

Sacha stopped and turned to him, his eyes filled with heartache. "His family just let him die?"

"Laz and I were the only ones at his funeral." Gio swallowed hard, his gaze focused on the horizon. The water seemed to stretch on forever. "I promised I would do everything I could to make sure those I loved would never be denied treatment or anything essential because of a lack of funds. I studied and researched my ass off, made good investments, and decided I would help those who had nowhere else to turn. Good people who deserved better."

The ocean breeze felt good against his skin, but not nearly as amazing as Sacha's arms wrapping around him and squeezing him tight.

"You're a good guy," Sacha said, his voice rough.

"Thank you."

They continued to jog, and Gio smiled. He could get used to this. He enjoyed early morning jogs, though he tended to get up earlier for his runs. Having Sacha at his side made all the difference, and of course, having Chip as well. Gio couldn't remember the last time he laughed so much.

"When we get back, I'll shower and pick up your prescription for you. What's your afternoon look like?" Sacha asked. "I'm not scheduled to work anything of yours today."

Gio wiped the sweat from his brow. "Thank you for doing that for me. I've got some work I can do from home, but nothing else going on. My next event is on Saturday. I have a charity gala."

"Another gala?"

"Yes." Did Sacha sound disappointed? Gio would certainly rather spend the time with him, but Gio had made a commitment, and as one of the evening's benefactors, he could hardly cancel. "Would you like to join me? As my date?"

Sacha stopped jogging, and Gio did the same. "Your date?"

"I know it's short notice."

"No, um, it's fine. I've still got my tux from Colton's wedding. Will that work?"

"Of course."

"Okay, good. Let's head back. I have some stuff I need to take care of."

They jogged back to the house, Saint trailing close behind Gio and Chip ahead of them. The silence wasn't exactly uncomfortable, but it wasn't as easy as it usually was. He hoped Sacha wasn't nervous about this weekend. As far as events went, it was mostly mingling and listening to the host's speech about the charity and thanking everyone for donating. It was only a few hours of conversing, drinking, and dancing. Would Sacha want to go with him to his events? He supposed it was one of those things they'd eventually have to discuss.

When they got back inside, Saint went to his room to

shower while Sacha and Chip followed Gio into his room. A wicked little smile curled Sacha's lips.

"You know, we should probably shower together. That way I don't have to wait until you're done. Save time."

Gio hummed. "That does sound like a very smart idea." He took hold of Sacha's hand and led him toward his bathroom. "I'd much rather have you inside the shower with me than standing outside it."

Sacha told Chip to lie down, and Chip happily trotted over to the window and jumped up on the armchair, curling up and staring out the window. Gio shut the door behind them and got the water running. When he turned around, Sacha was down to just his boxer briefs. A groan left Gio's lips.

"You're wearing far too many clothes for a shower, Galanos."

Gio quickly undressed, tossing his clothes to one side.

"Fuck, you're gorgeous," Sacha said, his gaze raking over every inch of Gio. He ushered Gio into the shower, closing the glass door. Then he stood in front of Gio, his face lifted, and their eyes locked on each other. He was waiting. A delicious shiver went through Gio. He brushed his fingers down Sacha's jaw.

"Hand me the shower gel and sponge," Gio told him.

Sacha quickly did as Gio asked, handing him both. He stood patiently as Gio poured a generous amount of gel onto the luxurious sponge.

"Turn around."

Sacha turned to face away, and Gio stepped close, one hand caressing Sacha while he lathered Sacha up with the other, slowly running the soft sponge over his smooth skin, taking note of every freckle and every faint scar. Sacha trembled as Gio brought the sponge up between his legs.

"I've never done this before," Sacha admitted, his voice rough.

"Have someone bathe you?"

Sacha shook his head, and Gio was sure there were going to be plenty of firsts for both of them. It didn't surprise him that Sacha had never let anyone take care of him in the bedroom, just as Gio had never had anyone take care of him outside it.

"Step under the water," Gio instructed, and Sacha did, allowing Gio to rinse him off. Then he turned Sacha around and brushed his lips over Sacha's cheek. "Wash me."

Sacha let out a shaky breath as he diligently and slowly washed every inch of Gio's body, the sight of him on his knees again getting Gio hard. Sacha slid his strong fingers up Gio's thighs, the sponge in one hand. His eyes stayed on Gio's as he lathered Gio up, fingers slipping between Gio's crease to tease his hole.

"Get up," Gio growled.

Sacha quickly complied, and Gio rinsed off. He moved Sacha against the shower wall and got on his knees, smiling at the curse Sacha let out. Geo wrapped his hand around Sacha's rock-hard length.

"I want you to fuck my mouth," Gio ordered. He swirled his tongue around the head of Sacha's cock, lapping up the pearls of precome, humming at the way Sacha's entire body trembled. He swallowed Sacha down to the root, moaning when Sacha cried out. He grabbed fistfuls of Gio's hair and started rocking his hips, small thrusts at first. Gio slipped one finger between Sacha's ass cheeks to tease his hole as he alternated between sucking and licking Sacha's cock.

"Oh fuck! Gio." Sacha held on tight to Gio's hair, his hips picking up speed as he thrust into Gio's mouth over and over, fucking his lips the way Gio had demanded of him.

Gio kept his gaze on Sacha, his own leaking cock painfully hard just from the expression of pure bliss on Sacha's face. His cheeks were flushed, his lips parted, and his pupils blown.

Sacha gasped, then moaned, his hips losing their steady rhythm as he pumped himself faster and faster. "Gio," Sacha warned, but Gio simply doubled his efforts until he felt warm salty come shoot down his throat. He took all of Sacha, sucking until Sacha was spent.

Standing, Gio brought Sacha against him and kissed him so he could taste himself, smiling when Sacha melted against him, soft and pliant. When they pulled apart, Sacha let out a shaky laugh.

"Holy fuck. That was... wow."

Gio kissed him again before turning them both back to the shower. They finished washing up, and Gio stepped out with Sacha. He wrapped Sacha in a fluffy towel, his heart overflowing with joy, even at Sacha's little grunt. His grumpy man. Leaving Sacha to finish drying himself, Gio wrapped a towel around his waist. They walked into the bedroom to get dressed for the day.

"I shouldn't be too long," Sacha said as he finished tying the laces on his boots.

"Are you leaving Chip here or taking him with you?"

"Do you mind if I leave him here with you?" Sacha stood and chuckled. "I have a sneaking suspicion he's made his choice."

Gio looked down and found a pair of big brown eyes staring up at him. "Well, hello there."

"Be back in a bit." Sacha popped a quick kiss on Gio's

lips, making his heart flutter. Did Sacha have any idea how sweet he could be?

"See you soon." Gio went into his walk-in closet to get dressed, and pulled on a white pair of boxer briefs, some comfy chinos, and a blue button-down shirt with the sleeves rolled up to the elbows. He smiled as Chip padded alongside him as he made his way downstairs. Saint was in the living room on the couch reading a book. He nodded a greeting at Gio and went back to his book.

While Sacha was gone, Gio stretched out on the long couch with his laptop to check his emails and do some work; Chip curled up at his feet, his soft snores filling the room. Every so often, Chip would hear something and lift his head, cocking it to one side to listen. Hilariously, Saint would then do the same, and Gio had to make the very serious effort to not laugh. Chip was a furry alarm and a good indicator of whether they needed to be concerned with the sound or not. He'd shot up off the couch a couple of times and darted to the door to bark, which had Saint leaping into action, only to find it had been the mail truck down the block on one occasion and the UPS truck on the other.

About an hour later, Chip barked and hopped off the couch, tail wagging happily. He pranced by the door, and Gio sat up. Considering how excited Chip was as he barked and whined, Gio figured it was either someone they knew, or Sacha had to be back. Saint answered the door, and Sacha walked in, laughing as Chip jumped excitedly.

"I hope you were a good boy for Gio," Sacha said, scratching Chip behind the ear.

"He was a very good boy. Warned us when the mailperson was approaching."

Sacha laughed at that. "Ah, his arch-nemesis. That's

because our mailman lives on our block and has a cat that was spawned by Satan. Chip is terrified of it."

"Are you serious?" Gio looked at Chip, who sat staring up at him as if he knew what they were talking about. His doggie eyebrows were up, making him look very concerned.

"Yep. When I take Chip out to do his business, if he gets too close to the guy's lawn, the hellspawn shoots out from his hidey-hole and divebombs Chip. Chip's a good boy, though, and he knows when not to attack, so he just runs away or hides behind me. I mean, all he has to do is bare his teeth or give that fur ball a growl and it would rethink its life choices, but my boy is a good boy." Sacha loved on Chip, who soaked it up with happy butt wiggles. "Here you go." Sacha handed Gio his prescription. "Also, when you're done reading through that and taking your first dose, put your shoes on. We're taking a little road trip."

Gio's curiosity was piqued. "Where are we going?"

"You'll see when we get there."

Why was Sacha being so mysterious? "Is it a surprise?"

"Sort of. I'm going to take Chip out to potty real quick while you do that."

At the mention of "potty," Chip howled and barked. Sacha led him outside, and Gio looked over his new medication information. Seemed pretty straightforward. He frowned at the little white pill. Was this really going to help?

"What are you thinking?" Sacha asked softly as he came to stand next to Gio.

"Is this going to make that much of a difference?"

"You won't know unless you try. What about it bothers you?"

Gio sighed. "It's going to sound awful, but I've never wanted to be dependent on a pill for anything. It makes me think of my father. All the treatments and medications, some of which made things worse, none of it helping in the end..."

"Understandable, but this isn't the same thing, Gio. I get that there's still a good deal of stigma around medication, but if this can help you feel better and improve the chances of your condition not hurting you, isn't it worth a try?"

"What if it makes me feel worse?"

"Then we'll talk to your doctor and go from there. One day at a time, yeah?"

Gio nodded. Sacha was right. He couldn't keep going the way he was. How many episodes had he had in the last month alone? Gio hadn't been taking care of himself, and that needed to stop. He took the pill with some water, then kissed Sacha's cheek. "Thank you." Knowing Sacha was at his side, helping him navigate this new journey, made it all seem less daunting. He could do this.

"Ready?"

"My shoes are by the door." Gio slipped into his pull-on sneakers, then grabbed his wallet and keys. "Ready."

Saint stood to one side. He opened the front door and scanned the area outside, nodded to Sacha, who stepped out after him, with Chip on his heels. Chip sniffed the air but remained quietly at his side.

"Okay," Saint said, motioning for Gio to come outside. This was his life now; he might as well get used to it. He stood next to Saint, who set the alarm and locked up the house, and then they walked to the SUV. Gio climbed into the back, followed by Chip and then Sacha. Once Saint was behind the wheel, Sacha leaned in between the seats and showed him his phone.

"This is where we're going."

Saint typed it into the GPS. "Got it."

Wherever they were going, it was just over twenty minutes away and off US-1. Sacha was tight-lipped, giving absolutely nothing away.

"You must be really good at poker," Gio grumbled, making Sacha laugh.

"You bet. Note of warning, don't play poker with the Kings. Between Lucky and Ace, they will take all your money and not feel even the least bit bad about it."

"Duly noted."

Chip climbed over Sacha so he could stick his nose against the window. He whined, and Sacha shook his head. "Sorry, bud. I can't put the window down. We'll be there soon enough."

There wasn't much traffic where they were headed, so they got there quickly. The area was sparse. Mostly a few buildings scattered here and there, with lots of trees and shrubbery. They turned right and drove up a concrete driveaway flanked by magnolia trees, then stopped at an iron gate at the end. Sacha tapped away at his phone, then put it to his ear.

"Hi, it's Sacha Wilder. I'm at the gate in the black SUV. Thanks."

Soon after, the electronic gate opened and they drove through. There seemed to be quite a bit of security here. Gio had no idea what was going on, but he was wildly intrigued. Saint parked, and they got out. They were surrounded by greenery and fencing, with a couple of buildings and a house.

"Where are we?" Gio looked around, but it was hard to tell. It was some kind of facility for something.

"You'll see. And listen, no pressure, okay? This is about what feels right to you."

"Um, okay?" Just what was going on?

The door to the house opened, and a blond woman with a messy bun dressed in dirt-stained jeans and a dirty black T-shirt walked out, her smile wide.

"Mr. Wilder?"

Sacha crossed the gravel courtyard, his smile friendly. "Kendra, so good to finally meet you. This is Giovanni, who I told you about." He turned and motioned to Gio.

Sacha had told her about him? What exactly had he told her? Gio was so confused, but he smiled politely at the woman. "It's lovely to meet you, Kendra. Please, call me Gio."

"Great to meet you, Gio." She opened the door wide and motioned them to come through until she noticed Chip. "And who is this handsome boy?"

"This is Chip," Sacha said.

"Chip, I've heard all about you." She waited as Chip sniffed her, then barked happily. "Can I give him a treat?"

"Sure."

She reached into her pocket and removed a treat. "Sit."

Chip sat and waited patiently, then caught the treat in midair when she tossed it at him.

"Gio, if you go out to the back, we'll be right with you," Kendra said, then turned to Sacha. "If you wait in here with Chip, I'll call you when we're ready."

"Sounds good."

We? Gio followed Sacha through the house toward the back to a sliding glass door that led to a huge fenced-in yard. Outside there were several pieces of equipment and what looked like some kind of obstacle course.

"Wait out there," Sacha instructed, opening the door for him. "Saint will be here inside."

"Um, okay." Gio shoved his hands into his pockets and waited as Sacha disappeared back inside. It was a beautiful day, a light breeze rustling the leaves of the magnolia trees as the sun shone in the bright blue sky. It was quiet out here, peaceful. He heard the glass door slide open and turned in time to see a golden retriever trotting toward him. He stopped at Gio's feet and lifted a paw, making Gio laugh. He kneeled to take the offered paw.

"Well, hello. Aren't you a happy puppy."

The dog wiggled excitedly, tail wagging and tongue lolling from his sweet face.

"I see you two are getting along," Kendra said as she stepped outside.

"Who wouldn't get along with this sweet boy." Gio ruffled the dog's fur. "That's right, you're a sweet boy."

"This is Cookie. He's two years old."

Cookie lavished Gio with kisses, and Gio laughed, petting his soft fur.

"Aw, hello, Cookie. You're a good boy. Yes, you are."

"What do you think of him?"

Gio's smile couldn't get any wider. "I think he's the sweetest thing I've ever seen."

"How'd you like to be his new person?"

Gio's head shot up, and he stared at Kendra. "What?"

"Sadly, Cookie's person passed away. She had a very similar condition to yours, among some other serious health issues. He's a service dog."

Gio snapped his head to the glass door, where Sacha stood. He waved at Gio, a shy smile on his face. Sacha had arranged all this. For him.

"Your boyfriend and I had a long chat, and he came to see Cookie. He thought you two would make a good pair, and I have to agree."

His boyfriend.

"Would you like to see how he gets on with Chip? I know that's important to you both."

Gio nodded, too choked up to reply. He stood, waiting as Kendra nodded to Sacha. He opened the sliding glass door, and Chip trotted out. He went straight to Cookie. The two of them sniffed each other excitedly, tails wagging, and then they were off playing together, chasing each other, jumping and rolling around in the grass.

Sacha came to stand next to Gio. "He's yours if you want him."

"You want to get me a service dog?"

"I think you two need each other."

Gio's heart was all but ready to explode. He surprised Sacha by bringing him into a hug right there in front of Kendra. "Thank you," he murmured, his lips close to Sacha's ear. He closed his eyes, basking in the sensation of Sacha returning his embrace and holding him tight, his words quiet when he spoke.

"You're welcome."

Gio stepped back, his heart skipping a beat at the flush on Sacha's cheeks. He cleared his throat and shoved his hands into his pockets. "We'll take him."

"Hold on. Before you agree," Sacha said, turning Gio toward him. "I need you to be sure about this. Cookie isn't a pet or an emotional support animal. He's a service dog. That means getting used to doing things a certain way. He's going to go with you everywhere; that includes your events and when you travel."

Gio hadn't thought of that. He got to experience the joy and fun of having Chip around, but he never really considered the work Sacha had to put in, and Chip wasn't a service dog, at least not the way Cookie would be to Gio.

"It also means educating people who approach you,

colleagues and strangers. Having Cookie changes things. This is a decision only you can make."

"You can take your time and think about it," Kendra said. "Cookie's not going anywhere just yet."

Gio thought about it. He'd wanted to cut back on his events and travel for a while. Spend more time at home with his family. But taking on a service dog also meant admitting to the world that he needed help. That there was something wrong with his health, something severe enough to warrant a service dog. He'd barely accepted that his life had changed, and the next step would likely be therapy for the PTSD. Maybe it was time he faced the truth and took control of his own life rather than letting aspects of his life control him.

"I want him," Gio said, determined. It was time for a change. For too long, he'd felt like he was losing his grip on his own life, and he'd had enough.

"Wonderful!" Kendra motioned toward the house. "If you'll both just follow me to my office, I'll get the adoption paperwork ready and work out a training schedule."

"Training schedule?" Gio asked.

"Before you can take Cookie home, we need you to come in for some time with him, show you how he's been trained, the commands he's familiar with, what he'll be looking out for with your condition, and how you can help him better serve you. I'll also give you some paperwork and a training video we did with Cookie."

Cookie and Chip followed them inside, the two making Gio's heart swell when they cuddled up together on the giant dog bed in the office.

It took a couple of hours to go through everything, and although Gio was nervous, by the end, he knew he'd made the right decision. When they were done, he said goodbye to Cookie and promised they'd see each other real soon. He was scheduled to come in over the weekend to spend some time with Cookie and go over his training.

Inside the car, Gio could barely contain his smile. "I can't believe you got me a service dog."

Sacha shrugged, his cheeks turning a lovely shade of pink. "The way you are with Chip, and with everything going on, it made sense. I know they can be a lot of work, but it's worth it."

Chip poked his nose into Sacha's cheek, making him chuckle.

"Even when they're a furry pain in the ass. But I can give you some tips."

"Thank you. What are your plans for the rest of the day?"

"I've got the day off so..."

Gio held back a smile at the way Sacha left the rest of the sentence hanging. "Spend the day with me? We can swim in the pool or go to the beach."

"Wait, are you saying you're going to..." Sacha gasped dramatically, making Chip tilt his head. "Take the day off?"

Gio rolled his eyes. "Yes, I'm going to take the day off."

"Who are you, and what have you done with Gio?" Sacha demanded.

"Ass." Gio shook his head, loving Sacha's amused smile. He seemed to smile easier these days, and Gio loved it. He lived to hear Sacha laugh, to see the little wrinkles appear at the corners of his sparkling blue-gray eyes when he laughed.

They got home and climbed out of the car, Saint scanning the half-circle driveway and the greenery around them. They headed up to the house, and Gio unlocked the door, then stepped quickly to one side so Saint could disarm the alarm. He scrolled through the security feed like he always did after they came home from somewhere, a quick browse, and then he'd get on his laptop and check through the footage.

"Pool or beach?" Gio asked.

"Let's go with the pool," Sacha replied.

They headed upstairs to Gio's bedroom and both changed into swim trunks, then slathered each other with sunscreen. Gio made sure to stop by the kitchen and grab them some bottled water. Outside, Saint took a seat in one of the shaded lounge chairs, and Chip lay on the concrete floor in the shade as close to the pool as he could get so he could keep an eye on his people, a bone Sacha had given him between his paws.

The water was the perfect temperature, not too warm but not cold, thanks to the sun. Gio took the stairs into the pool while Sacha jumped into the deep end, water splashing everywhere. Chip had been smart to lay toward the shallow end. He lifted his head from his bone, tail wagging as he waited for Sacha to resurface. Once he did, Chip went back to gnawing on his bone.

With a relaxed sigh, Gio swam to Sacha and pulled him into his arms. He worried Sacha might not be comfortable showing affection in front of one of his coworkers, but to his relief, Sacha didn't seem to care at all. Then again, he'd been fully aware of Saint standing outside the back room in Sapphire Sands, knowing they were having sex.

"This is nice," Gio said, brushing his lips over Sacha's. "I should take time off more often."

Sacha hummed. "Quite the incentive, huh?" He kissed Gio, the two of them wading together, enjoying the feel of each other, in no hurry to be anywhere or do anything.

"I could get used to this," Gio murmured against Sacha's lips, their hardening cocks pressed together. Sex in the pool was out of the question at the moment, but that didn't mean they couldn't get intimate. A thought occurred to him, and he laughed.

"What's so funny?"

"I have a Cookie, and you have a Chip."

Sacha blinked at him. "What?"

"Our dogs."

"You're such a dork," Sacha said, shaking his head at Gio, his eyes alight with amusement.

"Imagine if Cookie's name had been Salsa. Then we'd have had Salsa and Chip."

Sacha didn't look impressed. "That was an Ace-level joke right there."

"Or Banana. Banana Chip."

"No one in their right mind would name their dog banana."

"What about Potato?"

Sacha arched an eyebrow at him. "I'm done with you now. We're done." He made to get away from Gio, who only held on tighter.

"Wait, don't go! I'm very serious about our relation-*Chip*."

"Nope. There's a line, Gio, and you just crossed it."

Gio threw his head back and laughed. Oh, having Sacha for a boyfriend was going to be even better than he expected.

NINE

THE MOMENT JOKER STEPPED OUTSIDE, he knew he should have declined the invite. What the hell had made him think he could play this part? Already his collar and bow tie were too tight, but he refrained from tugging at it. Thank God the weather was still cool enough in the evenings where wearing a tuxedo outdoors wasn't a recipe for heatstroke, especially since he was already sweating, and not because of the heat.

A live orchestra played some kind of jazzy music beneath the huge white canopy decorated in twinkling white lights, while people dressed in expensive designer tuxedoes and gowns laughed and chatted with champagne glasses in their hands.

When Gio had asked him to be his date, Joker had been reluctant, but he hadn't wanted to let Gio down. Everything with them was still so new, and he cared about Gio. A lot. He wanted to show his support, so he'd agreed to the date. Fancy parties were nothing new to Joker, but most of the time, he was at an event as part of the security, not as a guest. His job was to keep people secure, not make conversation with them. Usually, they had no idea he was there.

"Ready?" Gio asked, holding his arm out to Joker, who took it.

"Yep."

Nope. So much nope. A big fat nope. But he'd do this. Maybe if he thought about the week they'd had before this, he'd keep in mind what things were like for them outside these events.

This past week had been fun, and Joker couldn't remember the last time he'd laughed so much. Gio and Chip were a hoot together, and as much as Joker pretended their antics were ridiculous, he couldn't help how stupidly happy it made him.

Gio had taken time off, and even on the days he worked, he finished what he was doing to spend time together. He'd asked Joker to stay with him, and Joker had packed a bag and stayed pretty much every night over at Gio's with Chip. At first he worried they'd get on Gio's nerves, but the guy genuinely *wanted* to hang out with him *and* his dog. It seemed like the more time he spent with Joker, the more he wanted him around.

Somehow Joker wasn't surprised Gio was a bit of a homebody. He enjoyed spending time with their friends, but he seemed to enjoy lounging around the house watching movies, streaming TV shows, swimming in the pool, or going down to the beach just as much.

They'd gone to two training sessions with Cookie where Gio took to working with the happy golden retriever as if they'd been together for years. Cookie would be coming home with Gio tomorrow, and after half an hour at this shindig, Joker knew he'd made the right choice. Gio needed Cookie. As much as Joker cared about Gio, the chances of their relationship working out was pretty slim. Love had never been in the cards for Joker, and he didn't see that changing anytime soon. Not that he wouldn't enjoy their time together while he could. Joker ignored the pain in his heart but accepted it for what it was. If Joker wasn't around, he'd feel better knowing Gio had Cookie to take care of him.

"Are you okay?" Gio asked quietly as they made their way through the crowd, Saint trailing close behind in his tuxedo so he wouldn't stand out as much. Blending in at these events could be challenging when you were over six feet tall and built like a brick wall. Tonight's party required security to be discreet, so most of the bodyguards Joker had spotted wore tuxedos with clear earpieces in their ears.

"Yeah, I'm good. Don't worry. You just do your thing."

Gio nodded, but he didn't look convinced. To his credit, he did his best to include Joker, introducing him as his boyfriend. He never volunteered information about Joker, letting Joker decide what he wanted to share. Everyone wanted to know what he did. It was usually the first question out of their mouth. *"Nice to meet you. And what do you do?"*

"I'm a silent partner for Four Kings Security," Joker said in response to the man's question. He was the owner of some country club Gio was a member of but never seemed to visit. The guy was interested in having Gio donate to a project he was putting together. Joker had already forgotten the name of the club because he didn't give a shit. There was a reason Gio had his polite and tolerant smile on for the man, and that was all Joker needed to know.

"And what does that entail?"

"I work security for entertainment and events. Sometimes we do military contracts. I have a K9 I work with."

Someone called Gio's name, and he excused himself, promising he'd be back in just a moment before turning to greet a woman Joker recognized. She'd been at one of his previous events. A gorgeous woman with dark skin and a dazzling smile. The way they talked made it clear they'd known each other for a while.

"Security. That's... interesting," Mr. Country Club said. What the fuck did he say his name was? Joker should have been paying more attention. In his defense, he couldn't give two fucks about Mr. Country Club.

No one ever expects security. Those who'd heard of Four Kings Security tended to offer praise and share their positive experience with the Kings. Some nodded politely, then changed the subject to something more interesting, and some people looked at him like this asshole.

"What did you do before that?"

"I was a Green Beret. Special Forces."

"The military. I see."

Joker didn't like the way the guy's mouth twisted with distaste when he said the words. *Don't ask. For fuck's sake, don't ask.* "What do you see?" Fuck, he asked.

"I suppose you feel that the government owes people like you."

Joker's hackles went up, but he told himself to chill. "People like me? Soldiers? Military veterans? What exactly do I feel the government owes me?" *Go on, Mr. Country Club. Why don't you tell me how I feel.*

The guy shrugged and waved a hand. "Financial support for the rest of your life. Paid medical bills, rent, free education for your kids."

Wow. Joker blinked at him. He opened his mouth, but Country Club cut him off.

"I mean, you all knew what you were getting into. You signed up for that."

Joker balled his right hand into a fist and quickly shoved it into his pocket. Punching the douchenozzle in the middle of a high-society party and getting arrested was not a good idea. "I didn't sign up to have half my unit—good men—blown up in front of me. Their families didn't sign up for that." The people around them whispered nervously to one another. One guy even tugged discreetly at his friend's sleeve, as if trying to get him to shut up, but Country Club was just getting comfortable on his high horse.

"That's the risk."

"Risk is involved," Joker agreed.

"But you believe you should be compensated for the rest of your life for the few years you *voluntarily* served. The government provided you with training, room and board, food, and medical treatment."

Joker let out a humorless laugh. "Are you kidding me? How about I send *you* into the middle of a warzone in some godforsaken place where everyone wants to kill you, make you stay awake for days on end, with no food, minimal water, a seventy-pound dog strapped to you, and we'll see how you do."

"My point is, you signed up for it. You shouldn't expect to be supported the rest of your life for it."

"I don't expect shit from our government. Would I like for them to treat those who fight for our country with the respect and care they deserve? Yes, I would. If you think a soldier who's wounded in service to his country doesn't deserve to be taken care of by said country, then I don't know what the fuck you're doing at a charity event. I got news for you, pal. If you think Gio is going to give *you* money, you're barking up the wrong tree. Excuse me."

Fuck that guy. He had no idea what he was talking about, but then again, there were many people like that asshole. Usually he didn't let that sort of thing get to him. What bugged him was that the guy was here at a charity event, pretending he gave a shit and wanting Gio to give him money for his project. Un-fucking-believable.

Joker went to the bar and ordered a whiskey. He downed the expensive liquid in one gulp as Gio appeared next to him.

"I'm so sorry I left you alone with Lawrence. I'd promised Ada I'd have lunch with her and had to cancel, so I wanted to apologize to her and let her know I'd make it up to her." Gio studied him. "What's wrong?"

"Nothing," Sacha growled. "It's fine."

"Yes, clearly. That was obviously a happy growl."

"The guy's an asshole. Not a big deal."

"Sacha—"

Joker turned to Gio and sighed. He reined in his temper. This was exactly what he'd been afraid of. The last thing he wanted was to ruin Gio's good time or his reputation. Everyone loved and respected Gio. Joker didn't want to fuck up any more than he had.

"Please, it's fine," Joker assured him, kissing his cheek. "Go on and mingle. Please."

"Okay. Let me introduce you to Ada. She's been dying to meet you."

Joker arched an eyebrow but didn't ask. He joined Gio, following him back to the woman Gio had been talking to earlier.

"Ada, this is Sacha. Sacha, this is Ada, a good friend."

Joker took Ada's hand in his and placed a kiss on the back of it. "It's a pleasure to meet you, Ada."

Ada's hazel eyes glinted with delight. "Oh, you're a keeper."

Joker chuckled. "I certainly hope so."

"Definitely a keeper," Gio replied, winking at Joker.

Talking with Ada was the highlight of his evening. Joker liked her, and he was glad Gio had a friend like that in a world where so many people wanted a piece of him. From the few people Joker had been around, it was sickening how many were only interested in Gio because of his wealth. Several didn't even attempt to hide that all they cared about was getting Gio to donate funds. Joker had never heard so many elevator pitches for projects and charities in his life. Everyone wanted something from Gio, whether it was his money, attention, connections, or time. There wasn't one person Gio spoke to who didn't have an agenda. Actually, there had been *one*. Ada.

Joker had no idea how Gio did this over and over again. He listened to everyone, asked questions, or politely referred them to other people who he thought would be a better fit for them. He handed out his business cards to those he was genuinely interested in hearing from, and those like Country Club Guy got a polite "call my office" type answer.

Gio tried hard to include Joker in conversations, but there wasn't much for Joker to say. Not many people here were interested in talking about private security, dogs, or the military, and he doubted they'd be interested in learning anything about explosions, weapons, or office pranks. He got into a couple of conversations about football, but that didn't last long. These people had about as much in common with him as Chip did with Satan's cat.

It wasn't that he couldn't have an adult conversation; he

just didn't know the first thing about hedge funds, portfolios, brokers, vintage wine, or European chalets. He had no idea who was who or what they did, couldn't care less about any scandals, and didn't have opinions on foreign policies he knew nothing about. He wasn't one to talk out of his ass. If he didn't know something, he wasn't going to pretend he did. His job was security. That's what he knew. Even now, he found himself watching the exits and scanning the crowd for anything out of the ordinary. He made sure Gio stayed hydrated and ate, because when Gio was mingling, he tended to forget silly things like his health. They were going to have another serious conversation about that soon.

A couple of excruciating hours later, Gio pulled him discreetly to one side. "Are you sure you're okay?"

"Yeah."

"You don't sound okay."

Joker averted his gaze and tried to play it cool. "How long do these things usually go on for?"

"Ready to go?"

"No, no. You do your thing."

"I never knew you were such a terrible liar," Gio said, amused. "Come on. Let's go home."

"Gio, you don't have to."

"I want to," Gio promised.

Saint brought the SUV around while Gio said his goodbyes to a few people. The moment they got in the car, Joker removed his tie and unbuttoned the top two buttons of his shirt. Finally, he could breathe.

The ride back to the house was silent and awkward. So much so that Saint felt the need to run interference by talking about Cookie and how Gio must be excited to be bringing him home finally.

Joker was in a foul mood, and now he kind of wished he

hadn't agreed to stay at Gio's tonight, but he'd promised to go with Gio in the morning to pick up Cookie. He needed to chill. Tonight hadn't been Gio's fault. When they got inside, Joker headed to the fridge and grabbed a bottle of water, then chugged half of it down in seconds.

"I'm going to do a perimeter check," Joker said roughly, but Gio pulled him into his arms and kissed him. Damn it, all of Joker's anger melted the moment Gio's lips touched his. The softness of them, his taste, all distracting him to the point where the only thing his brain could process was Gio. Fuck, he smelled so good.

Man, he was such a sucker.

"Let Saint go," Gio murmured against Joker's temple. "Come upstairs with me."

Joker nodded. How could he say no to the unspoken promises in that quiet request? He asked Saint to do the check instead and text him as soon as he was back inside. The alarm would be set afterward. Joker let Gio lead him upstairs to his bedroom, the door closing behind them. Joker waited until Saint had texted him that he was back inside and everything was as it should be. He walked over to the wall of windows, his gaze on the ocean sparkling beneath the moonlight. It was a beautiful night.

Turning, he stilled. Gio sat on the couch facing the windows, but his eyes were on Joker. The bright moonlight was enough for Joker to see every sinful, sexy inch of him. His eyes were impossibly dark, his lips slightly parted, and a curl of his pitch-black hair had fallen over his brow. The air in the room changed around them, crackling with the need and heat between them. Gio spread his legs, and Joker stepped in between them. He slowly lowered himself to his knees, his eyes never leaving Gio's as he slid his hands up Gio's legs to his thighs toward the bulge straining against his dress pants. He was so fucking gorgeous, Joker was getting hard just looking at him.

Gio reached out to cup Joker's cheek. He ran a thumb over Joker's bottom lip, the touch sending a current of need through Joker, unlike anything he'd ever experienced. Never had he wanted anyone so desperately, and for more than a fuck. He wanted to keep Gio, wanted to mean something to him. If Joker knew what was good for him, he wouldn't let himself get caught up in the fantasy of Gio loving him. It would only lead to heartache. Instead, he'd focus on their pleasure, on the moment. Joker waited patiently for Gio to tell him what to do, knowing Gio would make the wait worth it.

"I want to feel these lips around my cock," Gio said, his voice low and husky.

Joker sucked in a sharp breath, his pulse racing with anticipation. He kept his gaze locked on Gio's as he removed Gio's shoes, then his socks. He unfastened Gio's pants, then unzipped him, a shiver going through Joker at the sight of Gio's hard cock straining against his white boxer briefs.

Taking hold of Gio's underwear and pants, Joker moaned when Gio lifted his hips so Joker could slide his pants and boxer briefs down, leaving him in his dress shirt and tuxedo jacket, his tie undone and hanging haphazard around his neck. Fuck, he was the sexiest thing Joker had ever seen. He dropped Gio's pants to one side, then returned his hands to Gio's thighs, the fine hair soft against Joker's palms as he slid them up again, his eye on the prize, that thick, gorgeous length.

Joker wrapped a hand around the base of Gio's cock, loving Gio's sharp intake of breath. With a wicked grin, Joker leaned in and lapped at the pearls of precome on the rosy tip of Gio's cock, enjoying the way Gio groaned. He stroked Joker's hair, murmuring sinful words of encouragement as Joker licked at Gio's length, alternating between swirling his tongue around the head and sucking on it. Gio's fingers tightened around a fistful of Joker's hair, tugging when Joker swallowed Gio down to the root.

"Fuck!" Gio brought his right hand to join his left, and Joker hummed with pleasure as he sucked Gio off and fondled his balls, giving the best blow job he'd ever given to please the man he was coming to see as his. Reaching down, he unfastened his pants and hastily shoved his hand into his underwear to palm his own erection. He was painfully hard, and if he wasn't careful, he wasn't going to last long. Gio gasped and put a hand on Joker's shoulder to stop him. It would seem Joker wasn't the only one in danger of blowing his load too soon.

"I want you naked and on the bed, on your stomach."

Joker scrambled to do as he was told. Quickly he got naked, then climbed onto the bed and lay on his stomach. Behind him, Gio moaned.

"You have no idea how stunning you are."

Joker heard rustling behind him, and then the bed dipped. He shivered at Gio's warm hands caressing his thighs just before Gio shoved Joker's legs open. A deep, throaty moan came from Gio, and Joker thrust his hips against the comforter in response. He was so hard it hurt. Gio's hands on his ass had Joker arching his back. He'd been about to beg Gio to do something when Gio parted Joker's ass cheeks and his tongue pierced his hole.

"Holy shit!" Whatever Joker had been expecting from Gio, it hadn't been that. "Oh God, yes. Fuck!" Gio rimmed him like a pro, using his tongue and fingers to wreck Joker and turn him into a quivering mess, begging and moaning like a porn star. Joker made noises he'd never fucking made in his life. His toes curled, and he grabbed fistfuls of the covers as Gio took him apart. Just when Joker thought he couldn't take anymore, Gio stopped.

Sweat beaded Joker's brow, his breath coming out in pants as Gio went to the nightstand to grab a condom and lube.

"Turn around. Head on the pillow."

Joker got onto his back and moved up until his head was on the pillow. He drew his knees up and opened his legs wide, smiling wickedly when Gio froze in the middle of tearing through the condom packet. Gio's eyes were so dark, it was like he could see into Joker's soul. Removing the condom, he rolled it down his cock and kneeled between Joker's knees. He looked like he wanted to say something, his lips parting, and Joker's heart threatened to beat out of his chest. Whatever it was, Gio seemed to decide against it. Instead, he leaned in to kiss Joker, stealing the breath from him. He lined himself up and slowly pushed against Joker's hole.

The burn soon gave way to delicious fullness, and Gio continued to kiss Joker as he started to move. Joker had expected Gio to pound his ass, but Gio appeared to have other ideas, moving at an unhurried pace as he made love to Joker's mouth, their tongues dancing, embracing, savoring. Joker slipped his fingers into Gio's hair, loving the silky softness of it. He'd never felt this raw, this open, and he didn't know what to do with it. Holding on to Gio, praying he wouldn't let Joker go, wouldn't let him fall, was all he could do.

As if sensing his thoughts, Gio moved his lips to Joker's cheek, peppering kisses along his jawline. His hips maintained a slow, steady rhythm as he brushed feathery light kisses over Joker's face as if he were sending Joker a message, one Joker wasn't sure he was ready to hear. Needing to feel more of him, Joker moved his hands down to Gio's shoulders, his fingers digging into the firm muscles of his back. He thrust his hips up to meet Gio's movement.

"Please," Joker breathed.

Gio thrust in deep, making Joker cry out. He brushed his lips against Joker's temples, his words so quiet Joker nearly missed them.

"Take everything. Anything you want, anything you need, is yours."

Joker swallowed hard. If only it were that easy. Could it be that easy? Would it be so terrible if he laid himself bare to Gio? If he opened his heart and presented it to him?

"I want it all," Joker whispered, his heart beating in his ears and his pulse racing. He pressed his lips to Gio's shoulder, smiling when Gio cursed under his breath and snapped his hips forward, his thrusts growing deeper and quicker. Joker threw his head back, his eyes closed, and pleasure rippled through him as an incendiary heat flared, threatening to set him ablaze. The more Gio gave him, the more he wanted.

"Sacha..."

Joker's name was a whispered plea on Gio's lips.

"Yes," Joker said through a moan. "For you... yes. The answer is always yes." He didn't know what the fuck had gotten into him. Bullshit, he did know. Opening his eyes, he met Gio's gaze. He wrapped his arms around Gio's neck and met every one of his thrusts with a thrust of his own until the bed moved beneath them. Their panting breaths, moans, and curses filled the room, sweat beading both their brows as they moved together as one, their thrusts growing more erratic as they chased their orgasms.

Gio reached down between them and wrapped a hand around Joker's leaking cock. "Come for me, baby."

"Oh fuck!" The endearment caught Joker off guard, and his orgasm slammed into him, his body shaking from head to toe as he cried out Gio's name, hot come spurting onto his stomach and all over Gio's hand. Gio growled and cried out, his muscles tensing, glorious heat filling Joker as Gio came inside the condom. He thrust his hips erratically as he chased the last of his release, then collapsed on Joker, arms around Joker's head, fingers in his hair. Joker smiled softly as he held Gio to him. He placed a sweet kiss on Gio's bare shoulder, wincing briefly as Gio reached between them to hold the condom and carefully pull out of him.

Gio tossed the condom into the little wastebasket to the side of the bed, then returned to lay half sprawled on Joker, one arm thrown over his chest and one leg around Joker's, as if he were afraid Joker might try to slip away.

Joker had no intention of going anywhere. At least not this very second.

Thoughts of earlier in the evening attempted to invade his bliss, and Joker quickly pushed them aside. He was going to enjoy this right here, right now. With a kiss to Gio's brow, Joker closed his eyes and basked in the moment, squirreling away every detail. He brushed his fingers through Gio's hair, cataloging how soft it was, inhaling the intoxicating scent of Gio's musk mixed with his shower gel and their sex.

With a quiet sigh, Joker stroked Gio's arm, taking note of the soft hair on his arm, the firm corded muscles, the weight of Gio's leg on his, the warmth of his body pressed against his side. It shouldn't have felt as right as it did. As if they'd been doing this for so much longer when their relationship had been so different only a few months ago.

Then again, even during the times when Joker had been grumbling about Gio, the guy had been on his mind. Was it possible his head had been raging one war and his heart another?

When Joker woke the following day, it was in Gio's arms. At some point in the night, he must have plastered himself against Gio. It struck him then that Gio hadn't woken up. Was it possible he hadn't had any nightmares last night? Not that Joker believed Gio had been cured, but it was a good sign. Gio had agreed to talk to Red's therapist, and they had an appointment for a chat to see if they'd make a good fit. At least Gio was on the road to healing.

Gio stirred and turned with a hum, his arm tightening around Joker and a smile spreading on his face. He opened his eyes and brushed a kiss over Joker's brow.

"Good morning, sunshine."

"That's me," Joker mumbled through a grunt. "A bright little ray of sunshine." This guy.

Gio chuckled and rolled him onto his back. He pressed his lips to Joker's, not in the least bit concerned about morning breath. Joker shook his head.

"I need to brush my teeth."

"Sweetheart, you've kissed me after I've come in your mouth. You think a little morning breath is going to bother me?"

"Charming."

Gio got up and playfully smacked Joker's flank. "Come on. Let's shower. We're picking up my new furry partner in crime today."

Joker laughed at Gio's excitement. He was like a little kid at Christmas who'd just gotten a new puppy. They kissed in the shower but didn't get to fool around. Gio was too excited about bringing Cookie home, and Joker couldn't blame him. His life was about to change.

Jack had dropped Chip off on his way to work. Since they'd been in the shower, Chip had settled on the couch with Saint, which was where they found him when they came downstairs. Chip barked excitedly, his butt wiggling as he pranced around Gio and Joker.

"We're going to pick up your new friend," Gio told Chip. He grinned at Joker. "So you know, there's an epic level of boxes arriving. I've pretty much bought stock in lint rollers since I'm now buying them in bulk."

Joker snickered. "Did some research on golden retrievers, huh?"

"Yep."

"Welcome to the wonderful world of dog glitter."

"Oh, by the way," Saint said, turning to Joker, "Jack brought your Jeep over."

"Great. Thanks. I need to stop by the apartment later and pick up a few things," Joker said as he headed for the front door, Chip at his heels.

They got into the SUV and headed over to Kendra's place. When they got there and she brought Cookie out, Joker couldn't tell who was more excited, the dog or Gio. They were ridiculously adorable together. Gio had already ordered more dog stuff than any dog needed. Cookie was going to be spoiled rotten. When they got back to the house, Gio took Cookie on a tour, showing him his new luxury dog bed inside Gio's bedroom, though Joker had no idea who Gio was trying to kid. The only place Cookie would be sleeping was on the bed with Gio.

Joker left Chip with Saint and Gio so he could quickly drop by his place and pick up some more clothes and drop off his dirty laundry. He'd taken the day off today but had to check some emails and put through a few invoices. It had been a while since he'd worked overtime, preferring to be with Gio. He was looking forward to the first whole weekend they had together. Maybe they could take the dogs somewhere.

It was nice, sitting in Gio's living room with his laptop, doing some work while Gio played with Cookie and Chip. Never in a million years would Joker have believed he'd enjoy just lounging around doing close to nothing with someone else. He'd always wondered how Jack and Fitz did it, spent so much time at home together. What did they do when they weren't having sex? Not that he thought about his brother and Fitz having sex, because yikes, but he wondered how the hell they cohabited. Sounded boring as fuck.

Gio's loud laugh made Joker smile, and he glanced up to find him on the floor with the two furry beasts attacking him with their tongues. Joker shook his head at them.

"Oh, I have a meeting with King on Thursday to discuss a permanent security team," Gio said, sitting up.

"That's great." Joker reminded himself he needed to talk to King about that. Until the threat to Gio's life was over, he wanted to be working those events, but he wasn't sure how King would feel about that, considering Joker and Gio were now involved.

Joker's email client pinged, and an email came through with what looked like an updated schedule. Gio's updated schedule. Was it terrible that Joker hoped Gio had canceled an event or two? He opened the attached spreadsheet and frowned. "I thought you said you were cutting back on the number of events you were doing?"

"I am."

Joker's heart thundered as he looked over the schedule.

Chill. Do not overreact. But the more he studied the schedule, the more pissed off he got. "You added seven new events to your schedule, Gio. And that's just across the next two weeks." He glowered at the sheet in front of him. "You're working the whole weekend, and you don't have a day off next week."

"I know it's a little tight, but I'd forgotten a couple of commitments I'd made and had to move things around. Next week was the only week I could fit them in that worked for the organizers."

"Gio, you can't work seven days a week." He pointed at the screen. "For fuck's sake. You have three days of back-to-back meetings. You didn't even schedule time for lunch."

"I'll grab something quick in between." Gio took a seat on the couch across from him, his brows drawn together in a scowl. "It'll be fine."

"Really? Is that supposed to happen in the five minutes between your morning and afternoon meetings?"

"I've done it before."

"Yeah, and that's worked out so well for your health." As soon as the words were out, Joker regretted them.

Gio folded his arms over his chest. "Now, wait a minute. That's not fair."

"You're right. It's not. I'll give you that."

"Not exactly an apology," Gio muttered, one eyebrow arched.

Joker closed his laptop a little more forcefully than he'd meant to. "Fair enough. I'm sorry for the dick comment, but I'm not sorry for calling you on your bullshit. You promised you'd start taking better care of your health. I don't know what you think that looks like, but it's not this."

"Connecting with people at events is part of my job."

"And you can't do that without going to a party?" When

would it end? They'd talked about this. For fuck's sake, did Gio not realize the changes he'd have to make were permanent?

"Of course I can, but it's not the same as connecting with someone in person in that kind of setting. It's more than champagne and tuxedos. It's looking people in the eye, hearing their stories, and working through solutions. I can't do that through an email or a phone call."

"Can't or won't? What happens next month when someone approaches you with more commitments you can't let pass. You can't save everyone, Gio."

Gio jumped to his feet. "I know that," he growled. "You think I don't know that?"

"I don't think you do," Joker said, standing. He loved that Gio helped people, loved how selfless he was, always giving, but when did it become too much? "When will it be enough?"

"I've been doing this for far longer than I've known you. I know what I'm doing."

Joker narrowed his eyes at Gio. "If you did, you wouldn't have ended up in the hospital."

"Again, you're going to throw that in my face?"

"No, I'm reminding you. I can't be at all your events making sure you stay hydrated and eat."

Gio lifted his chin, his haughty expression getting Joker's hackles up. He'd never looked at Joker that way. "From your display last night, it's obvious you can't even make it through one."

The words bore like a punch to the gut, and Joker stared at Gio, regret written all over Gio's expression. His eyes were wide, his face flushed. When he spoke, his words were a whisper.

"I'm sorry."

Joker shook his head. "No, it's the truth. Let's face it. You don't want me. You never did."

"How can you say that?" Gio took a step forward, and Joker took one back.

"You had an idea of me. You clearly know what you want, and I can tell you right now, I don't fit that mold. I'm not Ace. I'm not the guy who hangs on your arm and makes polite conversation over finger foods. Even if I was, I won't stand on the sidelines and watch you work yourself into the ground. We were kidding ourselves."

"Stop," Gio snapped. He shook his head. "Don't do this."

"Do what? Speak the truth?" Joker shook his head. "We were just kidding ourselves, Gio, and you know it as much as I do. We don't fit. Better to walk away now than down the line."

"I can't believe you're not even going to give us a chance." Gio shook his head in disbelief. "There are so many things I've thought about where you're concerned, but the one thing I never thought was that you were a coward."

Joker flinched. "Fuck you, Gio." He grabbed his laptop and shoved it into his backpack. Then he called Chip and stormed out of the house, slamming the door behind him.

Fuck this, and fuck Giovanni Galanos. He threw his shit into the back of the Jeep, then opened the door for Chip, who whined. He sat on his haunches, his big brown eyes staring worriedly up at Joker.

"Get in the fucking car!"

Chip's ears flattened, and Joker cursed under his breath. Great. Now he was being an asshole to his dog. He leaned in and kissed the top of Chip's head. He scratched him behind the ears, murmuring at him.

"I'm sorry." He patted the passenger seat, and Chip jumped in. Joker got in behind the wheel, then closed the door and hesitated. Glancing up at the house, his heart splintered into hundreds of tiny pieces. He wasn't a coward; he was a realist. The truth had come out. As sorry as Gio was, or as much as he regretted his words, the truth had been there. Joker couldn't be what Gio needed him to be, and neither could change who they were deep down.

After turning the engine on, Joker hesitated for another heartbeat, then drove off. He wrinkled his nose, refusing to give in to his emotions. Yeah, it hurt like a son of a bitch, but somewhere between Gio returning home for good and now, Joker had invested far more of his heart than he'd planned to in them. He hadn't meant for his heart to get involved. It was supposed to have been a little fun, some hot sex, fooling around, and an eventual progression to being friends. It wasn't supposed to *hurt*.

Chip whined again, and Joker shook his head. "We're gonna be fine. Just you and me, buddy. We don't need him." Chip gave him the side-eye, and Joker couldn't help his chuckle. "Yeah, I know."

This was better for both of them, and maybe in time, they *could* be friends. When he got home, Chip sensed something was off, and he was having none of it. He howled and barked at Joker until Joker was forced to tell him to lie down, which Chip did, with his back to Joker.

"Oh, so now you're going to be pissed at me too?"

Chip huffed but didn't so much as look at him—little shit.

The doorbell rang, and with a grunt, Joker got up, his heart pounding with stupid hope. He opened the door, his heart sinking when he found a package instead. Picking it

up, he frowned at the label. An auction? He hadn't bought
anything—

Oh, wait.

Heading back inside, he locked the door behind him
and hurried into the kitchen. The box was extremely well
packaged, and inside was another box, this one made of
wood and old-looking. There was a little card on top of it
dated the night of the auction. The night they'd first kissed.
Joker opened the note and read.

IT DOESN'T MATTER *what it cost. You're both worth every*
penny.

Love, Gio.

OPENING THE BOX, Joker let out a watery laugh, tears in
his eyes. "That fucker."

What had Gio spent an obscene amount of money on at
the auction? Jewelry? No. An old firearm or celebrity
trinket? No. Furniture? Nope. A fucking dog food bowl
from the late 1920s that belonged to Rin Tin Tin, the
famous German shepherd. Fucking Gio had paid who knew
how many thousands of dollars on a food bowl for Joker's
dog.

"You bastard."

He was *not* going to be one of those assholes who cried
after a breakup. No fucking way. Son of a bitch, he *was* one
of those assholes. The tears sprung free, and Joker quickly
wiped them away. He returned the stainless-steel bowl to
its box and carried it into his bedroom. Chip followed him
in, whining at him, and Joker dropped onto the end of
the bed.

"You and I both knew we'd end up here one way or another," Joker told Chip. "His life isn't our life."

Chip disappeared under the bed, and a heartbeat later, crawled back out, Jack's baseball cap in his mouth.

"Guess we know who's the real brains around here," Joker muttered. "Come on. Let's go see Uncle Jack."

A few minutes later, they stood outside Jack and Fitz's door. When had he turned into such a sucker? Fuck it. He hated this. Hated feeling like shit, hated the fact he missed Gio already, that he didn't want to go home to his empty bed tonight. He laughed without humor. When had he become such a clingy, needy fuck?

The door swung open, and Jack stood there, a huge grin on his face and his mouth open, ready to say something teasing until he took in the sight of Joker. His smile fell away.

"What happened?"

"It's over," Joker replied quietly just as Fitz appeared beside Jack.

Fitz gasped softly and grabbed him, pulling him into a tight hug. As much as Joker wanted to fight Fitz on this, he didn't have the energy, so he just wrapped his arms around Fitz and sighed heavily.

"What happened?" Fitz asked softly, leading Joker inside toward the living room. He pulled Joker down with him as he folded himself onto the couch.

"What was always going to happen. He wanted me to be something I wasn't."

"I don't understand." Jack took a seat in the armchair.

Was he really going to sit here bitching and moaning about his failed relationship? Not like it hadn't happened before. Of course, it never hurt this fucking much before.

"He asked me to be his date to one of his fancy galas. It

was fucking excruciating. I got into an argument with some asshole. I've never felt so shit in all my life. Then today, his updated schedule came through, and he'd added all these events. He promised me he'd take better care of himself, but obviously, that was bullshit, or he was just placating me. We got into an argument over it, and we both said some shitty things. I can't be what he wants me to be."

"What did he say he wanted you to be?"

Joker blinked at Jack. "What do you mean?"

"What exactly did he say he wanted from you?"

"Well, he didn't *literally* say he wanted me to be anything, but he did. He said I couldn't even make it through one event. It obviously bothered him since he threw it in my face. Why else would he ask me to go with him?"

Fitz shrugged. "There are a million reasons he might have asked you. Maybe he thought you'd feel left out if he didn't invite you, or that you'd think he was embarrassed by you, or that you'd want to go because you were dating, or that you might enjoy a party since you work entertainment events, or—"

"Okay, yeah, smarty-pants, I get it." Fuck. Was it possible Gio had asked him for a completely different reason than Joker had thought? What if he'd told Gio he didn't want to go to his events?

"What exactly did you think he wanted from you?" Jack asked.

"I thought he wanted what Colton has. You know, how Ace goes with him to all his parties and events, charms the pants off the guests, shows his support."

"And you thought the only way to show your support was to force yourself to be Ace?" Fitz patted his arm. "Oh, honey, think about that. No one in their right mind expects *anyone* to be Ace. I'm pretty sure Ace doesn't expect half the shit he does or says."

Joker snickered. "You're not wrong." Was it possible he'd gotten it all wrong? "Maybe he doesn't expect me to be Ace or go to all his events; I'll give you that. But that doesn't change the fact that he's not serious about taking care of his health, and I can't be at every event to make sure he does. He's not taking his health seriously despite the fact he's on medication now and has a fucking service dog."

"He got a service dog?" Fitz asked, a hand going to his chest.

"I, uh, well, I got him a service dog. Cookie. He was trained for Gio's type of condition but lost his owner a while back. He's a two-year-old golden retriever." Joker couldn't stop himself from smiling. "The two of them are a couple of big dorks together. They really hit it off."

Jack stared at him. "You got Gio a service dog?"

Heat crawled into Joker's cheeks, and he nodded.

Jack's expression softened, his words quiet when he spoke. "You're in love with him."

No fucking way. Joker was ready to deny everything. He opened his mouth to tell his best friend to fuck off, but instead something else came out.

"Yeah, I think I am."

Fuck. He was in love with Gio.

Joker met his friend's gaze, his heart in his throat. "I love him."

TEN

THIS COULDN'T BE HAPPENING.

Gio sat on his couch with Cookie, his head on Gio's lap as he stared up at Gio with big brown eyes.

"I'm a fucking idiot," Gio said to no one in particular. A glass of water appeared before him, and Gio blinked up at Saint. He'd forgotten Saint was there. Good God, he'd witnessed the whole awful ordeal. Taking the glass from Saint, he thanked him and took several sips. His phone rang, and his pulse sped up. He answered without checking the ID.

"Hello?"

"Hey," Colton said cheerfully.

"Oh, hi."

"Um, okay. I'm sorry to disappoint you. Clearly, you were hoping it was someone else."

"I'm sorry," Gio replied with a sigh. "You know I'm always happy to hear from you."

"Right. I was calling to see if you and Joker wanted to join me and Ace for lunch, but it sounds like you've got something else going on."

The back of Gio's eyes stung, and he cleared his throat. He petted the soft fur on Cookie's head. "Sacha's not here. He... um, likely won't be coming back."

There was a long silence before Colton spoke up. "We'll be there in ten minutes."

"Colt—"

"We'll be there in ten minutes," Colton repeated.

"Okay." Gio hung up and slumped back against the couch. He took another couple of sips before placing the glass on the coffee table next to him. "Colton and Ace are dropping by," he told Saint, who merely nodded.

When the doorbell rang exactly ten minutes later, Saint went to open the door. He greeted Colton and Ace. The three of them entered the living room, and Cookie lifted his head, his tail wagging happily at their guests.

"Oh my goodness, who is this?" Colton asked excitedly.

"This is Cookie. He's my new best boy."

Colton's eyes all but sparkled. "Can I pet him?"

"Go ahead."

Ace's smile for his husband as he cooed and loved all over Cookie squeezed at Gio's heart. The love between those two was palpable, and it reminded Gio of what he might have just possibly lost. How could he have been so foolish?

"You got a dog?" Ace asked, taking a seat on the couch next to Saint and playfully smacking his leg in greeting.

"Sort of. Sacha got him for me. He's a service dog."

Ace's mouth dropped open. "Joker got you a dog?"

Why was that such a surprise? "Yes. He thought with my condition I could use someone to look after me."

Ace promptly shut his mouth and didn't say another word, which was very unlike him. Instead, he glanced around the room. "Where's Joker?"

"We had an argument," Gio said, his voice coming out rough. "He left. For good."

Colton and Ace exchanged glances before Colton took a seat on the couch next to Gio. "What happened?"

"Everything was going great, and then that stupid party happened. I know that's what started all this." He ran his fingers through his hair. The signs had been there. Why hadn't he pressed Sacha to open up and talk to him? Something had clearly been bothering him, and Gio knew it, no matter how much Sacha denied it. Something had happened. Fuck, it was probably Lawrence. Gio shouldn't have left Sacha alone with him. What had he been thinking?

"What party?"

Colton's words brought Gio out of his thoughts.

"I asked him to go with me to a charity gala as my date. He agreed."

Ace held up a hand. "Wait. Joker wore a tux and went to one of your charity galas with you, as your date?"

"Yes. Isn't that what I said?" It wasn't like Sacha had never worn a suit or tuxedo before. Sometimes his job required it based on the assignment, so it couldn't have been that much of a big deal.

"You do realize I can count on one hand the number of times that man has worn a tuxedo for something that wasn't a work requirement."

"Then why agree? If he was going to be so damned miserable, why say yes?"

Ace arched an eyebrow at him like he was indeed the biggest dork on the planet. "Really? You don't know why he would put himself through that? Why he'd get dressed up in fancy clothes that make him uncomfortable, attend a huge glitzy party filled with rich strangers, and force himself to have awkward conversations?"

"I would have never asked him if I thought he'd be uncomfortable. I'd never want to make him feel uncomfortable. I thought maybe he might be upset if I never asked him. Like maybe I didn't want him there or something."

"Did you tell him that?" Colton asked gently.

"No, but he could have just told me he'd rather not do that again, that he was uncomfortable, and I would have happily accepted. Then my updated schedule was sent to him, and he lost his shit over that. Granted, I might have packed in a little more than I should, but it's nothing I can't handle. He threw my health issues in my face and accused me of not really wanting him. How can he think I never wanted him when he's all I've wanted from the moment I heard his voice? But how can I give up my events? That's part of what I do. I love my job; I love helping people. I won't give that up for anyone, and I can't believe he expects that of me."

Ace peered at him. "Joker told you he wanted you to give up your charity work?"

"Well, not in so many words, no. He demanded to know why I had to go to so many events."

"So he didn't say, 'I want you to give up your charity events'?"

"No."

"How many charity events have you had in the last month? How many meals with clients and colleagues, how many meetings, video conferences, phone calls?" Ace gave him a pointed look. "Here's an easier question. How much free time have you had in the last month, and with everything new you've added, how much free time do you have coming up?"

Gio swallowed hard. "It's nothing I can't handle."

"Really? Because you were in the hospital, Gio. You have a service dog because of your condition. Things aren't the same as they've always been."

"I know that," Gio muttered, picking at some invisible lint on his pants.

"Weren't you the one who said you were going to slow down?" Colton asked. "Weren't you also the one who promised to take better care of himself?"

Gio frowned but didn't reply. That was pretty much what Sacha had asked him.

Colton folded his arms over his chest. "So what you're saying is, you planned to keep going, working yourself to death, expecting Joker to just stand by and watch as someone he clearly cares a lot about ends up in a hospital or worse."

Gio opened his mouth, then closed it, his best friend's words taking hold of something inside him. If the roles were reversed, would Gio have stood by while Sacha needlessly put himself in danger, risking his health and his life?

"He came to me for advice, you know," Ace said.

Gio met Ace's gaze, his heart skipping a beat. "He did?"

"Yeah. He wanted to ask me how I did it. How I navigated Colton's world. Why do you think he wanted to know that? My guess is he thought you wanted him to be for you what I am for Colton."

"I never asked him to be that. I don't *need* him to be that for me. In fact, he distracts me when he's there because I'd rather be with him than working."

"Did you tell him that?" Colton asked.

Gio stared at him. "No." He'd never asked Sacha to be anything he wasn't, and he never would.

With a heavy sigh, Ace motioned to Cookie. "Gio, the guy got you a dog. Not just any dog, a service dog trained for your condition. None of us got a dog from him. I didn't get a dog. Red didn't get a dog. Shit, not even Jack got a dog. Do you have any idea what that means? For him to share that part of himself with you after what happened with Echo?"

The name was familiar. "Echo. That was his dog back in Special Forces, right?"

"Yep. Echo was his best girl. When she wasn't strapped to him or he wasn't carrying her on his shoulders, she was at his feet. She was his pillow, his confidant, his best friend. Facing the shit we faced, having each other made all the difference, but having that dog..." Ace shook his head. "She didn't just keep us safe; she kept us sane."

"What happened to her? Sacha doesn't talk about her."

"When we were ambushed and half our unit was killed, Echo..." Ace swallowed hard and blinked back the wetness in his eyes. "They never found the body. To this day, Joker's haunted by the fact he couldn't bring her body back home, but the most heartbreaking part? That's the narrative he's chosen to believe because the truth is too painful for him to accept."

"What truth?"

Ace met his gaze, his eyes glassy. "She took the brunt of the explosion. There wasn't enough of her to bring back."

"Jesus." Gio put a hand to his chest over his heart and rubbed the spot, tears welling in his eyes. He couldn't begin to imagine the pain Sacha must have felt. Losing his brothers-in-arms and Echo.

"Yeah. It took him a long time to heal, and when he was

ready, Chip helped with the rest. So you see, him gifting you Cookie, someone to love you, look after you, and enrich your life... That right there is Sacha Wilder proclaiming his love to you, and let me tell you, that guy has never, *ever* given such a gift to anyone in his life."

Gio closed his eyes and let his head drop into his hands. "I fucked up."

"I think you both did. Do you know why Colton and I work? Because we don't assume, we talk. I don't pretend to know what he's thinking. If I'm not sure, I ask. He does the same. Do we still have arguments? Of course. But it doesn't break us. Are we different? Fuck yeah, but like I said, we talk, work through things." He took Colton's hand in his, adoration in his eyes as he gazed at his husband. "There's nothing I wouldn't do for him."

"Thank you," Gio told his friends. He didn't know what he would have done without them. "You're right." He picked up his phone.

"What are you going to do?" Colton asked, getting up.

"Talk to him," Gio replied, sending Sacha a text. He knew exactly what to say. Three little words were all he sent.

"I need you."

Colton and Ace said their goodbyes, and Gio promised to call Colton later to let him know how things went. That was, if Sacha showed up. Gio never knew what the man was going to do. He was unpredictable at the best of times. It was one of the many things Gio loved about him.

As Gio sat there stroking Cookie's soft fur, he thought about everything Colton and Ace had said, what Sacha had said to him. They were right. Gio kept going on about how he'd do better, take better care, and it had been bullshit. At the very first opportunity to prove he meant to keep his promises, he hadn't even tried.

For fuck's sake, he had a service dog. His life had changed. When was he going to face the truth? He *had* to make changes. Sacha had every right to expect better of him. God, he hoped it wasn't too late.

The wait was excruciating. Gio's phone showed that Sacha had read the text, but he hadn't replied. He looked up at Saint, sitting serenely on the couch across from him.

"Have you ever been in love?" he asked Saint.

Saint scrunched up his nose. "Yeah."

"Didn't go well?"

"At first it did. Married my high school sweetheart. Everything was great until I joined the Navy. She knew I'd always wanted to join. We're a military family. My dad and brothers all served. Uncles, cousins, and so on. Anyway, knowing I was going to serve and experiencing it were two different things. She hated picking up and leaving everything behind to start over again somewhere else. In the end, it was too much for her. By the time I came home for good, she'd fallen for someone else. I started at Four Kings Security, and we got divorced."

"I'm sorry."

Saint shrugged. "We've been divorced three years now and were separated for two, so it's been a while."

"And there hasn't been anyone since? No special person?"

The flush that spread across Saint's cheek was absolutely charming on the big man and said all Gio needed to know. Saint shifted uncomfortably in his seat. "No, there's been no one. No special woman." He cleared his throat. "I'm not gay."

Gio pressed his lips together to keep himself from

smiling. Interesting, considering he hadn't asked Saint about his sexuality. Frankly, it was none of Gio's business. He nodded his understanding, though he couldn't help but note the way Saint kept avoiding his gaze.

"Not that it would matter if I was, just, if I were gay, bi, pan, whatever, I'd know that about myself, wouldn't? I sure as hell would have known a long time ago, right?" Saint frowned as he gazed out the sliding glass doors toward the beach.

"Not necessarily," Gio replied gently. "Everyone's experience is different. Some people know from early on in their lives, while others might not discover that part about themselves until much later in life. As humans, we're always evolving, changing, learning, adapting."

Saint cocked his head to one side. "That's true." He smiled shyly at Gio. "You've given me something to think about. Thank you."

"Of course. And if you need to talk, I'm always here."

"Thanks."

Gio needed to take his own advice and accept that he was a different person now than he had been before the kidnapping in Sri Lanka. He also had to accept that it was *okay*. His life had changed, and he'd been fighting it, whether consciously or not. Everything Sacha had said to him had been the truth, which was why it had hurt so much to hear. He kept telling Sacha he was changing, but he hadn't actually planned to until Sacha once again called him out on his bullshit. He'd promised Sacha he'd call Red's therapist, then put it off. He'd told Sacha, King, Colton, Laz, all his friends that he planned to cut back on his schedule and yet continued to add to it. Why? Because he couldn't accept things had changed? And what had his broken promises cost him? The man he loved.

Gio dropped his head into his hands with a groan.

"What's wrong?" Saint asked worriedly.

Gio lifted his head. "I love him. I love him, and I let him go."

Saint's expression softened. "For all his blustering, Joker's a smart guy. I have a feeling he'll be back."

"God, I hope you're right." If he didn't hear back from Sacha soon, he'd call Jack and find out where he was. He needed to fix this, to tell Sacha how he felt and apologize for being such an asshole.

The doorbell rang, and Gio's heart leaped into his throat. He jumped to his feet, and Saint held out a hand to stop him from going to the door. Gio was practically vibrating. Cookie whined, so Gio gave him a reassuring scratch behind his ears.

"It's okay."

Gio waited with bated breath, his heart doing a flip when Sacha came into view, his hands shoved into his pockets. His eyes were a little red, and Gio wanted nothing more than to gather him up in his arms and kiss the hell out of him.

"You said you needed me," Sacha said, his voice low and rough.

"Always." The word was almost a whisper. "Can we talk?"

Sacha nodded, and Gio turned to Saint. "Do you mind if Cookie stays here with you for a bit?"

"Of course not."

Gio told Cookie to stay, then headed for his bedroom, glancing over his shoulder to make sure Sacha was following him. Once they were in the room, he closed the door behind them. He couldn't believe he'd fucked things up with this beautiful man.

"I'm so sorry." Gio stepped up to him and brushed his hair away from his brow. "I can't believe how shortsighted I was. You are incredible, Sacha, and my life is better with you in it. I promise I'll try harder at communicating properly. You were right about everything, about calling me out on my bullshit. I promised you I'd take care of myself, and I wasn't even making the effort to keep that promise. I also never want you to do anything you're not comfortable with. I don't expect you to be Ace. Quite frankly, having you there is kind of distracting because all I can think about is you and wanting to be with you. Sacha, I love you just the way you are."

Sacha stared up at him. "Say that again."

"Which part?"

"You know which part."

Gio wrapped his arms around Sacha's waist, a thrill going through him when Sacha leaned into him. He met Sacha's gaze. "I love you. All of you. And I don't ever want to be without you."

"You... love me?"

Gio smiled warmly. He placed a kiss on Sacha's cheek. "Yes. You. Every inch of you."

"I love you too."

Gio froze. He moved his gaze back to Sacha, whose blue-gray eyes were filled with uncertainty and something else, something big. The words sank in, and Gio could barely contain his smile, his heart swelling in his chest. "You do?"

"Yeah. I don't know when it happened, but I know that leaving you, being without you, was fucking shit."

Gio chuckled at Sacha's glower, because Sacha wasn't glowering at Gio, but at himself.

"It sucked. It fucking hurt like nothing has hurt in a

long time, and I didn't like it." Sacha wrapped his arms around Gio. "I don't want either of us to do that again. No walking away. I know I'm kinda shit at talking about my feelings and what I'm thinking, but I promise you I'll try harder too. I won't assume. Maybe we can help each other out with that, huh?"

"It's a deal," Gio promised. "You're stuck with me now, Sacha Wilder. I'm going to hug you, kiss you, love on you, and when you and Chip are ready, I want you to move in with me."

Sacha looked around him. "You mean that?"

"I wouldn't say it if I didn't."

"What if I were ready sooner than you thought? Like, this week ready."

The joy that filled Gio threatened to overflow. "Really?"

Sacha shrugged. "I'm all in, Gio. Why would I want to stay in my shitty little apartment where you aren't when I can stay with you in your very salmon-pink house?"

Gio threw his head back and laughed. "You have a deal. How about we seal it with a kiss?"

"Baby, whatever you want, it's yours." Sacha wrapped his arms around Gio's neck and lifted up to bring their lips together. The moment he had his mouth on Sacha, Gio was a goner. There was nothing he wouldn't do for this man. His man. Sacha Wilder had no idea what an absolute gem he was. He might be grumpy and curse like a sailor, but no one had a bigger heart.

Sacha drew back suddenly and glared at him. "I got your gift, or should I say Chip got your gift."

It took Gio a second to realize what Sacha was talking about. "Oh! Did he like it?"

"We're going to have to set some expense boundaries, aren't we?"

Gio hummed and nibbled on Sacha's ear. "But do we really?"

"Yes, we do, because certain individuals are suckers and don't seem to have any kind of self-control where the furry ones are concerned."

"But they're so cute."

"You know what's not cute?" Sacha said as Gio pulled him toward the bed. "Your whining."

"I call bullshit. You love everything about me, including my whining."

"Fine, but we're still setting limits."

"For the dogs." Gio sat on the edge of the bed and pulled Sacha in between his spread knees.

Sacha eyed him. "Yes?"

"Why do you look so suspicious?" Gio asked with a laugh.

"Because you're trying to put one over on me, and it's not going to work. You're not spending a fortune on me."

"What if I want to sweep you away to some private beach on a tropical island where we can make love all day and night?"

Sacha ran his hands up Gio's thighs. "I might be willing to negotiate on certain things."

"Done. I think we need a little something more than a kiss to seal this deal."

"I like how you think, Giovanni." Sacha tugged Gio's shirt out of his waistband and kissed him. He pulled back suddenly, his eyes filled with concern. "Are you sure about this, Gio? About me? I'm not the easiest guy to get along with. I'm messy, loud, curse a lot, and I've been told I can drive a nun to drink."

Gio ran his fingers through Sacha's hair. "I wouldn't change a thing. Neither of us is perfect, and I wouldn't want that. I love your fiery spirit, that no one can impose their will on you. You're so damned strong. It's why I feel so safe around you. Like I don't have to carry the weight of the world on my shoulders."

"And you don't," Sacha said, brushing his fingers down Gio's jaw. "You've got me, and I can take some of that weight. I can take care of you."

"I never knew how much I needed that until you," Gio admitted. For all his capable ways, for all his life experiences, Gio needed someone to care for him, love him, look out for him. And in return, he had so much love to give, love he wanted to give to Sacha.

With a sweet smile, Sacha leaned in, slowly undoing the buttons on Gio's shirt as their tongues tangled. A moan escaped Gio as Sacha brushed his fingers down Gio's chest, stopping over his nipples to give them a tweak. How could he have been so foolish to let this man go, even if they'd only been apart a short time? The thought of not having Sacha was too painful to think about. Despite everything that had happened between them, the words that they'd thrown at each other, when Gio had texted Sacha that he needed him, Sacha showed up, for Gio.

"I want to go to bed every night with you in my arms," Gio said, breathless. "And wake up to you every morning."

Sacha's eyes filled with affection. "I want that too."

They undressed each other, hurriedly removing their clothes. But once they were naked, they slowed their pace. Gio wanted to show Sacha that he meant every word, that he planned to cherish him and love him for as long as Sacha would let him. He climbed onto the bed, arranging the pillows so he could sit back against the headboard, his eyes never leaving Sacha's. With a wicked smile, Sacha got onto the bed and crawled over to him. He sat back on his heels, and Gio drank in the glorious sight of Sacha's tight, sinful body.

"Tell me," Sacha said.

Gio ran his tongue over his bottom lip. He knew exactly what Sacha wanted. From the moment he'd heard Sacha speak, something about him had given Gio the crazy idea that Sacha was desperate to submit, but only in the bedroom, and to the right person.

Gio leaned over to the nightstand and pulled the drawer open. Removing the lube and condoms, he stilled when Sacha spoke up.

"I'm good to leave off the condoms if you are. I get tested for work every few months, and I'm negative."

"Me too." Gio tossed the condom back into the drawer, his body thrumming with need. The thought of being inside Sacha without a condom was almost too much, and he was forced to calm himself. He held the lube out to Sacha. "Get yourself ready."

Sacha's eyes were dark, leaving only a sliver of blue-gray. He flipped the cap open and poured a generous amount on his fingers, then closed the bottle and tossed it to one side on the bed. Positioning himself between Gio's spread legs, Sacha turned, then lowered himself onto one arm, his ass in the air within Gio's reach. He spread his knees, opening himself and making Gio groan. Sacha started with one finger, giving Gio one hell of a show as he fucked himself, then added another. Gio sat up and placed a hand on Sacha's ass cheek. He couldn't help it. Rubbing the smooth globe, he bit down on his bottom lip as he delivered a light smack. Sacha arched his back, a deep moan filling the room.

"You like that?"

"Yes," Sacha replied, breathless. He added another

finger to his hole, his movement a little quicker now. Another curse escaped him when Gio smacked his ass cheek again, making sure to rub the pink spot. He added his finger to Sacha's, joining him in stretching him.

"You're so beautiful," Gio murmured, loving the way Sacha shivered.

"Gio. Please."

"Come here." Gio sat back against the headboard again. "Ride me."

Sacha straddled Gio's lap, and Gio groaned as Sacha took hold of Gio's rock-hard cock and pressed the tip to his entrance. Carefully he pushed back, and Gio's eyes all but rolled into the back of his head as he breached Sacha's hole. The tightness was heavenly, and not having anything between them filled Gio with an overwhelming need to bring Sacha into his arms and never let him go. He placed his hands on Sacha's hips as Sacha lowered himself until he was seated against Gio.

"You feel so good," Gio said, his toes curling when Sacha started to move, rolling his hips.

"I've never wanted anyone as badly as I want you, and I want you all the damn time." Sacha slid his hands up Gio's chest, his movements picking up speed when Gio palmed his leaking erection. He matched his strokes to Sacha's movements. They'd started out slow but were quickly picking up speed as Sacha fucked himself on Gio's cock.

Sweat beaded Gio's brow as he pumped Sacha's dick, a gorgeous flush spreading up Sacha's neck to his face, his hair sticking up wildly. How had Gio gotten so lucky? Unable to help himself, he shot forward and grabbed hold of Sacha's ass cheeks, spreading them so he could take control, thrusting into him over and over.

"Fuck, Gio, that feels so good." Sacha slipped his fingers into Gio's hair, grabbing fistfuls of it.

"That's it, sweetheart. Let me take care of you." Gio pumped himself into Sacha, deep, hard thrusts. The sound of their bodies smacking into each other filled the room in wonderfully obscene fashion, soon joined by their panting breaths and sinful moans. Gio's muscles tensed as he pounded Sacha's ass. "Jerk yourself," Gio growled.

Sacha took himself in hand, his strokes matching Gio's now frantic pace. Never again would he take the man in his arms for granted. Sacha was a gift, and Gio would do well to remember that. His orgasm swept through him like a tsunami, and he crushed his mouth to Sacha's as he came undone, his heart and soul laid bare. He shouted Sacha's name as he came, filling Sacha with liquid heat, leaving his mark. A heartbeat later, Sacha cried out, his hot come hitting Gio's chest.

"Holy fuck," Sacha said through a gasp, collapsing against Gio. "What were you saying about that tropical island?"

Gio laughed softly as he lay back against the pillows, holding Sacha against him. He ran his fingers down Sacha's spine, caressing his soft skin. "Anytime you want. I know you don't want me to spend a lot of money on you, but..." He turned Sacha's face so he could gaze into his eyes. "What's the point of having all that money if I can't use it to take care of the people I love?"

Sacha seemed to think about it. "I asked Ace about that once. About why he's okay to let Colton buy him an expensive sports car or fly him to Europe for a weekend. All the money Colton spends on him. He said it was how Colton showed his love."

"Because Ace knows it's not about the money. It's about the thought behind it, the physical expression of his love."

"That makes sense. So is it the same for you?"

Gio thought about it. "I think it's a little different for me. I much prefer to show my love by doing something for someone. I think that's how you show love as well."

Sacha blinked at him. "Me?"

"Yes. You're always doing things for others, whether you realize it or not. Think about it. You make sure I eat, stay hydrated, got me a service dog."

"I never thought about it that way."

"I think it's the same for all your brothers-in-arms. It's why you opened Four Kings Security. With your military background, it makes sense. You all show you care through acts of service."

Sacha delivered a kiss to Gio's jaw. "You're a pretty smart guy, ain'tcha?"

Gio laughed at that. "Sometimes. We should probably get up and shower before we get stuck together, huh?"

Sacha's grunt made Gio laugh. Reluctantly they got up and went to shower, which led to more kissing and touching, which was certainly *not* regrettable. Gio loved that they could laugh together, and no one made him laugh like Sacha. Knowing Sacha and Chip would be moving into his house had Gio almost giddy with happiness. He'd never expected Sacha to be ready so quickly, but then again it didn't surprise him. Sacha was the kind of guy who knew what he wanted, and he didn't see the point in wasting time.

They finished their shower and got dressed, then headed downstairs, Sacha's hand in Gio's. He kissed the back of Sacha's hand, enjoying the subtle blush that came onto Sacha's cheeks. One thing for certain, his life with Sacha would be anything but mundane and predictable, and he couldn't wait. The first thing Gio was going to do was look at his schedule and make some calls. As much as he loved what he did, his family had grown, and though there would be times he let Sacha or Laz down, it wouldn't be because he was putting his job before them. His family meant the world to him; it was time he proved it.

ELEVEN

"EVERYONE IN POSITION?"

Joker waited for confirmation from their team. As soon as he got it, he pressed his PTT button. "Remain vigilant, and if you get even the slightest hint those assholes are here, I want to know about it." He went back to scanning the field, keeping an eye for anything or anyone out of place.

Intel had come in the early morning hours from Jack and his team. With the help of Leo and his hacking skills, they'd managed to track down the bodyguards who'd betrayed Gio in Sri Lanka. Unfortunately, those guys were dead, which explained why Jack had been having trouble tracking them down, but the team managed to find their old bank accounts with wire transfers from an offshore dummy corporation. The same corporation had also wire-transferred twenty-five thousand dollars to each of the five men hired to kidnap Gio. Always follow the money.

Although Jack and his team were still jumping through hoops to find out who owned the dummy corporation, they'd found their kidnappers holed up in some tiny motel near St. Augustine Beach. Even more disturbing was the private plane that had been booked under one of their names. Seven passengers were scheduled to depart for Costa Rica this afternoon. Joker was under no illusion the sixth seat wasn't reserved for Gio. They were going to make another run at kidnapping him. The big question was, who was the seventh seat for?

If those assholes were going to make their move, this was where they'd do it. Gio had made good on his promise and shifted his schedule around, limiting the number of events he'd be attending throughout the month, but today's was one he hadn't been able to cancel, as he was one of the three hosts. Joker hadn't been happy about it, but he understood. It just sucked that of all his events, this one provided the perfect opportunity for someone to grab him.

The Children's Charity Fair was hosted in the city's biggest park because of its vast grassy fields and more than thirty acres of dense trees and shrubbery. There were walking trails, biking trails, and picnic areas. Tents and vendor booths littered the fields, with food trucks parked along the trail. The place was packed with adults, children, and pets, eating, playing games, and enjoying the festivities. Although plenty of law enforcement was around, as well as a considerable team provided by Four Kings Security, it could quickly turn into a logistical nightmare if they weren't careful.

Joker had no intention of letting any of those assholes near Gio, who was judging some pie contest where young children had baked the pies. He then had a speech scheduled that he'd make from the main stage, currently occupied by a live band playing cheerful pop music. The day was sunny and bright, a subtle breeze ruffling Joker's hair. His eyes were on Gio, who laughed at something a little girl told him. She was clearly talking about Cookie, who sat at Gio's heel, tongue lolling from his happy face.

If Joker had only made one right decision in his life, it was introducing Cookie and Gio. In the short time the two had spent together, they'd formed a special bond. Gio had quickly adapted to Cookie's commands and what he could and couldn't do with a service dog. He was still spoiling the damned dogs rotten, but Joker couldn't really be mad. Gio didn't just have a lot of love to give; he needed to express that love. Whether it was buying two stupidly expensive dog beds for every damned room in the house or booking a dog-friendly tropical vacation, Joker wasn't about to change that.

The air filled with the sound of laughter and children shrieking as they ran around, high on sugary treats. Chip stood at Joker's side, sniffing the air, his body language and ears stating he was on high alert. He had his work vest on, and it almost seemed as if he knew what was at stake, because Joker had never seen Chip look as focused or fierce as he did right now.

They moved around their assigned perimeter, and Joker kept in constant communication with his team. Saint and a small army of bodyguards were dressed in civilian clothes, blending into the crowd but close enough to Gio that they could quickly intervene if anyone tried anything. If the kidnappers thought they would get their hands on Gio, they were in for a painful awakening. Gio was clearly worried and trying not to show it, but he had faith in Joker and their family to protect him.

When Joker had spoken to him about it that morning, Gio had smiled at him, kissed him, and said, *"I know you and the team will keep me safe. I love you."*

Jack's voice came through Joker's earpiece, interrupting

his thoughts. "We've got eyes on our five kidnappers. They just went through security. They're not armed, but my guess is they stashed weapons and equipment somewhere in the park before this morning."

"Any idea about our seventh guest?" Joker asked.

"Not with the five that arrived, but that doesn't mean they won't show up."

"We can't let these guys get those weapons," King growled. "Ace, Lucky, Mason, Joker, and I will take them down. Red, have the authorities on standby. I don't want any incidents."

"Copy that," Joker said along with the others. "Jack, where am I going?" Like with any op this size, Jack was nearby in the surveillance truck with his team, and each one would guide one of his brothers-in-arms. They were going to find these assholes and make them regret their life choices.

"Three o'clock. Jett Clark. The Sugar Puff booth. Clark is buying cotton candy. White male, black baseball cap, olive-green polo shirt, black shorts. Shit, the cotton candy dude just handed Clark a gun. He's tucked it into the waistband of his shorts under his shirt."

"Copy that. Red?"

"Soon as Clark's out of the way, I'll introduce our cotton candy guy to one of St. Augustine's finest."

Joker gave Chip the command, and they both slipped into the crowd. It was time to go hunting. Chip stayed close to Joker as they stalked their prey, moving with the groups of people. With Joker's height and Chip being a black dog with a black vest, it was easy for them to stay hidden. The challenge was keeping Chip between him and adults so the smaller kids wouldn't scream about the "doggie." Not that Clark would be able to hear them over the noise of the fair.

Between the music, speaker announcements, and kids shrieking as they played, not being heard wasn't much of a challenge.

Joker kept his eyes on Clark as he moved. The guy was discreetly talking into his wrist, most likely a microphone he had hidden there. He didn't see Joker because he was too busy watching Gio.

"Talk to me, Jack," Joker murmured. "What are they saying?"

"Ace, Lucky, your guys are going to go around the back of the judges' booth. There's a small trailer parked back there. Mason, your guy will strike up a conversation with Gio to distract him and get him behind the booth. They'll ambush him and drag him behind the trailer. King, your guy is going to get their stash and bring the van around. Joker, your guy is—shit. Your guy is talking to someone else. They're using a voice scrambler. Whoever it is, they're being careful. Clark is going to meet them as soon as Gio is in the van."

"That's our mystery guest," Joker hissed. "The moment anyone spots them, I want to know."

"Copy that," Ace replied, followed by confirmation from the others.

"I'm moving in on Clark," Joker said. He kept his gaze on his target, maintaining enough distance between them so the guy didn't see him coming. Clark still had his eye on Gio, but he was moving toward the back of the cotton candy stall. Joker went one stall over with Chip at his heels. He stopped at the end of the stall and carefully peeked around. The guy was sneaking toward the trailer behind the pie booth, cotton candy tossed to the ground.

The back of the stalls and booths were filled with boxes, packing equipment, and generators to run the electric equipment, with more than one small trailer parked in the grass, all of it hidden from guest view unless you ventured back here. The mess provided plenty of places for someone to hide. The scent of food filled the air—popcorn, funnel cakes, pizza, you name it. No one paid any attention to the sinister thugs preparing to kidnap a man.

Joker murmured a quiet command to Chip, and his furry companion darted off, head lowered as he became one with the shadows, using boxes and anything else he came across to dart behind as he hunted.

Clark reached the trailer and slipped around the back of it. Joker moved in quickly and silently. He stopped at the end, checked around the opposite corner in time to see Chip duck under the trailer. With a wicked grin, Joker rounded the corner. As he'd suspected, the guy was waiting for him. He took a swing at Joker, but Joker ducked.

"He said you'd be here," the guy snarled, taking another swing that Joker dodged.

"Yeah? Did he tell you who else would be here?"

The guy looked confused for a second before Joker jumped out of the way, and the big man hit the grass with a loud curse.

"What the fuck?" He rolled onto his back, yelping at the loud growl as Chip stood over him, ears flattened against his head, sharp teeth bare as he snarled, brown eyes glowing. "Holy shit!"

Removing the zip ties from his pocket, Joker ordered Chip to stand down, then grabbed the asshole, rolling him over to secure his hands behind his back. He tapped his PTT button, when the door to the trailer flew open. A black blur that Joker realized was Chip soared past him just as a shot rang out. For a second, his heart stopped when Chip yelped and rolled across the dirt. Joker scrambled to his feet, barreling into the masked man who stood on the steps to the trailer, his gun aimed at Chip. They crashed to the ground and fought over the gun. Joker searched for Chip, relief flooding him when he saw Chip scramble to his paws and shake himself before he was back in work mode.

"Did you just try to shoot my dog?" Joker growled, landing a fierce punch across the guy's face. Whoever the fuck this guy was, he was officially on Joker's shit list.

Their masked guest punched Joker in the ribs, making him grunt at the pain. Chip lost his damned mind and charged, but Joker couldn't have that. He shouted the German command for Chip to stay. They were still fighting for the gun, and it was swinging wildly.

Enough of this bullshit. Joker punched the guy in the throat and knocked the gun away from him. It went bouncing in the grass. Before Joker could grab for the guy's mask, something slammed into him hard, and Joker went tumbling. He quickly got to his feet, Chip at his heel barking and spitting from how worked up he was. Clark thrust his hands down over his ass, snapping the zip tie. The plastic fell to the ground, and he rubbed his wrist, his glare on Joker.

"You're not getting your hands on him," Joker promised.

"You think I'm scared of you?" The masked man spat out a mouthful of blood and saliva.

Joker froze. He knew that voice. No fucking way. "William." He shook his head in disbelief. "You son of a bitch."

"*What?*" Jack cursed in Joker's ear. "Fuck. This explains so much. I'm on it."

William pulled the black mask off and sneered. "Well, what do you know? Not just a boot polisher after all."

Joker ignored the remark, his thoughts immediately

going to Gio. He was going to be devastated. As much as Gio had been hurt by the way his relationship with William had ended, to find out the man he'd been with for years, had shared his life and his bed with, had paid to kidnap him? Joker had already hated the guy, now he wouldn't piss on him if he was on fire.

"Oh, I'm going to enjoy this." Joker charged the two men, ducking under Clark's right hook and delivering a left hook into his ribs, then kicking at the back of his leg, sending him onto his knees. He lifted the guy's shirt, swiped the gun, and pointed it at William.

"You're not going to shoot me," William said with a laugh.

"You betrayed Gio *twice. And* you shot at my dog."

William shrugged. "I kicked your dog. I was going to shoot him after. Then you. Two dogs down."

"Oh, I'm going to fucking love sending you to prison," Joker said. William's gaze darted to his gun on the grass, and Joker shook his head. "Don't do anything stupid."

Not only did William do something stupid, but he was also even more of an asshole than Joker first thought. The guy shoved Clark at Joker, then took off running.

"Are you fucking kidding me?" Joker punched Clark in the throat and then the solar plexus, putting him out of commission. Clark dropped onto his knees, gasping for breath, his eyes rolling into the back of his head. Joker shouted at Chip, who took off after William while Joker swiftly grabbed several zip ties. He secured Clark's wrists and ankles. "Let's see you break out of that, you prick." He got to his feet, snatched up William's discarded gun, and sped off. He tapped his PTT button. "Target is down and by the trailer. Pick him up. In case you hadn't heard,

William is the fucker behind everything. Chip and I are in pursuit."

William threw everything he could in Chip's path, not seeming to understand how shepherd dogs worked. Chip could turn on a fucking dime. He could leap ten feet into the air and climb a fucking wall. Did the guy think a wooden crate was going to stop the furry bullet? Shepherds weren't just fast as fuck; they were smart and calculating. They didn't run in straight lines after their prey, they figured out the best shortcut to get to their targets faster, and nothing got in their way.

Joker had no idea where William thought he was going, but it was cute that the guy believed he would escape. Chip flew out from behind a stall, and William yelped, swerving at the very last second and missing Chip's jaws by a hair's breadth. The guy discovered some newfound adrenaline and sped up, Chip on his heels. William made a sharp turn, darting into the woods. Where the hell he was going was anyone's guess. The guy was unarmed, had a dog and a Green Beret on his ass.

William stormed down the pier that led to the river, shoving people out of his way, at least those who didn't dive out of his path when they saw Chip barreling after the guy.

Joker pressed his PTT button. "Jack, I need to know where William is going."

"There's a small speedboat parked below to the right side of the deck."

"Fucker's going to jump." Joker couldn't let the asshole get away. Firing a shot was out of the question; there were too many people on the pier. Joker shouted a command, and Chip leaped onto the guardrail and propelled himself off it, slamming into William and sending him rolling. Chip was on him in a heartbeat, standing over him, teeth and gums bare. William took a swipe at Chip, something in his hand, but Chip jumped out of the way. Just as Joker neared, William shot to his feet and grabbed a woman who tried to run past him.

Fuck. Joker tapped his PTT button. "I've got a hostage situation here."

"We're notifying the police and are en route," King replied.

"William, let her go," Joker said, gun pointed at William.

"Call off your mutt," William spat.

Joker called Chip to him, but he didn't put his gun down. Tears streaked down the woman's cheeks as William held the small switchblade to her throat. He dragged her with him as he edged slowly toward the end of the pier.

"It's over," Joker told him. "Let her go."

"Fuck you. I'm getting out of here."

What did William plan to do, jump over the side with his hostage in tow?

"We're going for a little swim," he growled at the woman.

Well, that answered that question.

Ace's voice came through the line, and he sounded breathy. He was running. "I'm almost in position."

Joker didn't respond. He didn't need to. His steady aim remained on William. He didn't have a clear shot, and the last thing he wanted was to shoot the hostage, even if it would be a flesh wound. The poor woman was going to have enough nightmares as it was. Whatever happened, William wasn't getting away from him. This man hadn't just threatened Gio, he'd had him kidnapped, was responsible for Gio almost dying all alone in the middle of some jungle, of giving him nightmares and PTSD. Yeah, William was going away for the foreseeable future. Joker would make sure of it.

"Please," the woman whimpered, her big brown eyes on Joker.

"It's going to be okay," Joker promised. He just needed to buy Ace a little time. "William, think about what you're doing."

"Oh, I am. Do you think you can keep him safe from me? I already got him once; I'll get him again."

Joker's heart slammed in his chest. Knowing William had been behind the kidnapping then was one thing, having him confirm it was another. "Sri Lanka. That *was* you."

"If those idiots hadn't underestimated him, none of this would have happened."

"And Gio would be six feet under in some remote jungle somewhere."

William shrugged. "No loose ends."

Joker gritted his teeth, clenching his jaw so tight he was in danger of hurting something. Fucking asshole. "It's. Over," he said between his teeth.

"I don't think so. My men probably have Gio in custody right now, so if you ever want to see him again, alive, you'll let me go."

"You think so, huh?" Joker tapped his PTT button. "Sitrep?"

"All targets in custody," King replied. "I'm on my way."

"I'm in position," Ace murmured. "Take a step to the right."

"Copy that." Joker smiled at William. "Well, what do you know? It looks like your friends are going for a little ride with the local law enforcement." He widened his stance, discreetly taking a step to the right. "You're going to be joining them soon."

William's grin was smug. "You might as well put the gun down, Wilder. You don't have a clean shot, and you're not going to risk hurting the hostage." He started edging closer to the end of the pier. They were only a couple of yards away.

"You're right. I don't have a clean shot, but I don't need to have one." He barked out a command, and Chip lunged forward, barking and snarling, startling William, who thrust the knife out in Chip's direction. What followed happened in the blink of an eye.

A shot exploded through the air, the bullet from Ace's sniper rifle hitting William in the shoulder and flinging him back. The woman in his grasp screamed, dropping to the wooden boards and covering her head just as Joker tackled William to the ground, knocking the knife out of his hand. He rolled William onto his stomach and pulled his arms behind his back, ignoring his growl of pain.

William turned to look at him over his shoulder, eyes huge. "You don't understand! I owe some very dangerous people a lot of money, and if I don't come up with the cash, I'm a dead man. There's nowhere they won't be able to get to me, not even prison."

"Should have thought about that before you made a deal you couldn't deliver on." Joker removed a couple of zip ties from his pocket and secured them around William's wrists. He gave the command to Chip to stand down, then dragged William to his feet just as King arrived and rushed over to help the woman. King wrapped an arm around her and gently steered her away.

"You son of a bitch!"

Joker turned in time to watch Gio punch William in the face.

GIO HADN'T WANTED to believe it.

When Jack told him William had been behind everything, Gio had hoped he was wrong, even if deep down inside he knew it to be true. Despite the Kings advising against it, Gio had insisted on seeing for himself, and they'd reluctantly given in, but only if their small army of bodyguards escorted him, and *only* after King had personally confirmed William had been restrained.

As much of an asshole as William had been at the end of their relationship, Gio never thought him capable of kidnapping. Three years. They'd been together for three years—dating, traveling, sleeping together, and all that time, William had only been after one thing.

"How could you?" Gio demanded as he faced William. "Do you have any idea the hell you've put me through?"

William clenched his jaw but said nothing.

"You don't care, do you? You never did." Gio swallowed hard. "You only ever wanted my money." He thought about everything William had done and what it resulted in. The nightmares, his PTSD, his medical condition, the medication... His head was ready to explode, but his heart reminded him of what he'd also gained. Coming home, his family, Cookie, Sacha. Gio moved his gaze to the man he loved. Sacha stood watching him, heartache written all over his face for Gio. If it hadn't been for William, would Gio have found his way home to Sacha?

With a small smile, Gio moved his attention back to William. "You took so much from me, William, but you also gave me more than I could have imagined. Because of you, I came home. Maybe my life isn't perfect or how I expected it to be." He moved his eyes back to Sacha, his heart full at seeing the love in those beautiful blue-gray eyes. "But that's fine. I'm happy now. Truly happy, and I know I'll be okay."

The police arrived, and Sacha handed William over, informing the officers how William confessed to kidnapping Gio over a year ago, and now his attempted kidnapping and hiring of kidnappers. Gio briefly explained his experience and agreed to come down to the station to give his full statement. King left the young woman William had taken hostage in the care of a medic and a pair of female officers, then stepped forward to put a hand on Gio's shoulder.

"Are you okay?"

"I will be," Gio replied. He might have just acquired something else to discuss with his therapist, but he felt the truth in his words. He'd face these challenges the same way he faced everything else in his life, head-on. Only this time, he wouldn't be too stubborn to ask for help.

King nodded and turned to Sacha. "Well done."

"Thanks," Sacha said, and it was clear from his posture that the compliment on a job well done from King made him proud. Old habits died hard. The Kings might not be serving as part of a unit anymore, but Gio had no doubt certain feelings were still there. The camaraderie, the hierarchy. From what Gio knew of King, the man didn't hand out praise easily. Like with all things King, it had to be earned.

While the guys talked to the police, Sacha pulled Gio to one side. The day was beautiful, the ocean sparkling like diamonds beneath the bright sky.

"Talk to me," Sacha said quietly, his hand on Gio's waist.

"It's a lot to take in," Gio admitted. "I'm still trying to wrap my head around the fact I spent three years of my life with a man as ruthless as William. He left me to die." The backs of his eyes stung, and he wrinkled his nose. "And for what? Money? The time we spent together meant nothing to him. My life meant nothing to him."

Sacha brought Gio into his arms and kissed his cheek. "I'm so sorry that bastard hurt you the way he did, but he's going to be paying for his crimes for a very long time. He won't ever hurt you or anyone else again. I'm here for you. Every step of the way."

"Thank you," Gio murmured, wrapping his arms around Sacha. "And thank you for loving me." Unlike William, Sacha was a man who wore his heart on his sleeve. Whatever emotion he was feeling, you'd know it. No hidden agendas, no games, no lies. Sacha wasn't just an amazing man, he was a safe place for Gio, and Gio had a feeling his heart had known that before he had.

Ace approached them with a huge grin on his face, and Sacha took a step back, rolling his eyes, making Gio chuckle. These two.

"Still got it," Ace said, making a gun with his fingers and blowing on it.

"You got something all right," Sacha teased. "Thanks for having my back."

"Always," Ace replied, winking at him before walking off. A loud whine met Gio's ears, and he lifted his gaze to find Saint holding on to Cookie and Chip's leashes. The two were prancing excitedly around Saint's feet. The big man just shook his head in amusement.

"You better go to them before their butts fall off," Sacha said.

Gio didn't have to be told twice. He hurried over to his favorite furry boys and dropped down to one knee, laughing as the two lavished him with doggie kisses. Some of the police officers came over to greet Chip. The Kings seemed to be familiar with all the officers from St. Augustine PD. King said it was in everyone's best interest to get along. It made their jobs easier. Chip got some love, and once the scene was clear, Sacha knelt to love on his best boy too for doing such a good job.

As Gio watched Sacha with Chip, he acknowledged that his life had changed in drastic ways. Yes, he had a lot to work through, but he was surrounded by people who loved him, by family. Because family wasn't just bound by blood, but by love, and Gio was never going to take that for granted again.

TWELVE

WHAT A DAY, and his shift wasn't even over.

Joker headed back to the festivities with Gio and the dogs. Everything was back underway, despite the disturbances caused by their team apprehending William's crew. Thankfully, the pier had been far enough away that guests had no idea what had gone down until the police arrived on scene. None of them had expected a hostage situation, and it wasn't the type of thing they usually had to deal with, but they managed it. For all the crazy they'd experienced over the last few years, most jobs tended to go pretty smoothly. They were good at what they did.

Gio gave his speech, and Joker's heart swelled with love as he watched Gio up on that stage, thanking everyone for coming. The man was adorable, and he was all Joker's. Had someone told him a year ago that he'd end up falling for Gio, he'd have told them to fuck off. In fact, he'd done that on several occasions to his matchmaking friends. Or rather Ace.

Gio finished his speech, and everyone cheered. He waved at the crowd and left the stage, Cookie trotting alongside him. When he searched the crowd and caught sight of Joker, his smile stole Joker's breath away. Gio headed toward him, shaking hands with a few people along the way. For the first time in a long time, he looked rested, like a weight had been lifted off his shoulders.

"Hey, sweetheart." Gio stopped in front of Joker and brought him into his arms. He kissed him, a brief but passionate kiss, and Joker melted against him.

"Hey, baby." Joker led Gio to the other side of one of the tents so they could have a little privacy, the dogs at their sides. He stepped behind a large tree and brought Gio against him, kissing him, letting all his love and desire for this amazing man come through in his kiss. He loved the way Gio hummed in pleasure, how he soaked in everything Joker had to give.

When they were forced to get some air, Gio brushed his lips over Joker's temple. "You're off the clock in an hour. How about I buy you some funnel cake?"

"Ooh, now we're talking. I might even let you buy me a soda too."

Gio threw his head back and laughed. "Big spender."

The rest of the day went quickly. There were a few incidents, but nothing out of the ordinary for this kind of event. A couple of kids got separated from their parents and were promptly found and returned. Some teenagers got a little too rowdy and had to be given a talking-to—that sort of thing. Joker changed out of his uniform when his shift ended, and he locked it away in the trunk of his car, along with Chip's vest, before returning to the fair to enjoy the day with his boyfriend.

Gio bought Joker a funnel cake bigger than his head and a soda. There was a stall that sold organic treats for dogs. It stunk to high heaven, but Chip and Cookie gobbled those things up so fast, Joker wondered if they'd even bothered to chew.

Then Gio stopped by a water gun game and gasped, then turned to Joker.

"There's a stuffed dog toy that looks like Cookie." Gio's eyes widened innocently. "If only I had someone who was a great marksman who might procure said adorable stuffed toy."

Joker pressed his lips together to keep from laughing. His boyfriend was ridiculous. "Would you like me to win you that toy?"

"I would very much like that. Yes."

"Okay." Joker popped a kiss on Gio's lips. He removed five bucks from his wallet and handed it over. "I remember when these things used to cost a quarter." The teen behind the booth blinked at him.

"Was that, like, in the 1940s or something?"

Joker peered at him. "What? No, it wasn't in the forties. How old do you think I am?"

The kid opened his mouth, and Joker waved the water gun at him.

"Never mind. Step aside, freckles." Joker positioned himself, closed one eye, and aimed. He hit every target that tried to dart past him, a satisfying ding going off with each shot until a siren sounded and a red light flashed. Joker twirled the water gun and returned it to the plastic holster. "And that's how you do it." He arched an eyebrow at the kid and pointed to the stuffed dog. Rolling his eyes, the kid grabbed the dog and handed it over. "1940s, my ass." He turned to Gio, who had the happiest, sappiest expression on his face. "Your prize."

"Aw, you do love me," Gio teased, taking the toy from Joker. Never mind that the guy could buy out the contents of every toy store in the city several times over; he was thrilled about this one.

Joker shook his head at his boyfriend. Jesus, would he ever get used to that? As he strolled through the fairgrounds, he couldn't remember the last time he'd done anything like this. Probably because he never dated. He was more interested in hookups and sex than getting to know anyone or spending any alone time together. It was nice. Despite everything that happened earlier, it was a great day. So this was what life with Gio would be like.

"Oh my God." Gio stopped abruptly and threw a hand out across Joker's chest. Instantly, Joker went into high alert mode, and he scanned the area for threats.

"What? What is it?"

"Fried snack cakes."

Joker slowly turned his head to stare at Gio. "I'm sorry, *what?*"

"Fried snack cakes," Gio said excitedly. "I've always wanted to try it." His dark eyes glittered with pure joy, and Joker couldn't even be mad.

"Come on," Joker grumbled. "I'll get you a fried snack cake." Was there anything he wouldn't do for Gio? Probably not. Well, the okra was still not happening, but everything else was fair game. After he bought Gio his fried Twinkie, they sat together beneath one of the large trees, the dogs settling into the grass beside them. "This is nice."

Gio hummed in agreement. He held a finger out to Joker, talking around a mouthful of deep-fried cake. "Want to lick my cream?"

Joker barked out a laugh. When he sobered up, he took hold of Gio's finger, their eyes meeting. "I always want your cream," Joker said, his voice low and husky. Thankfully Gio had swallowed his food by then because he broke into laughter. He started laughing so hard he was in tears.

"Okay, that was bad," Gio said with a snicker.

"Really? And 'want to lick my cream' wasn't?" He popped Gio's finger into his mouth and sucked it clean. Gio's eyes went dark, and he licked his lips.

"I didn't think this through, did I?" Gio grumbled, shifting uncomfortably.

"Nope," Joker said, popping the *p*.

"Maybe we should go home and—"

Joker covered Gio's mouth. "The next words out of your mouth better not be an innuendo or bad pun involving the word *cream*."

The laugh that reverberated behind Joker's hand was infectious, but Joker remained firm. He could not let Gio believe that sort of humor was acceptable. These kinds of boundaries had to be set early on in a relationship or he could end up like poor Colton, doomed to a life of terrible puns. Eyes narrowed at Gio, he slowly moved his hand away.

"What I was going to say was that we should go home." He leaned in to nibble on Joker's ear before whispering, "I want to get you sticky."

Heat flared through Joker, and he got to his feet so quick he startled Chip. His dog scrambled to his paws and barked at Joker.

"I'm sorry," Joker said through a laugh. "But a guy's got needs."

Chip let his displeasure be known until Joker promised to give him a piece of bacon when they got home.

Home.

Joker liked the sound of that.

As he walked hand in hand with Gio out of the park,

their furry companions at their sides, Joker couldn't remember the last time he felt so at peace. The man next to him loved him. Yes, his brothers-in-arms loved him, but it was a different love. Gio wanted him, loved him, every surly inch of him. He didn't want to change Joker, didn't expect him to be someone he wasn't. Arguments were sure to happen, but Joker was confident if they talked it out, they could get through anything because there was no one he wanted to try for more than Gio.

JOKER HAD BEEN wrong about Gio. Well, sort of.

Gio might not be perfect, but in Joker's eyes, he was as close to it as someone could get. Nothing else explained the absolute goodness of the man's heart. The two of them shouldn't have worked, but the more Joker got to know Gio, the more he realized no other man would have been good enough. There had been a time when he'd believed he wasn't meant for love. He'd spent years doing everything to avoid it, only to have a bunch of troublemakers worm their way into his heart. Then he'd let few more people in. Bibi, Nash, their sweet daughter, Lily. Colton, Mason, Leo, Fitz, and Laz. Every year, someone new seemed to join their family, and for a while, it had scared the shit out of him. Especially when his brothers started falling in love. He'd braced himself for the day he'd be left out in the cold, just him and Chip, but that day never came, and whatever happened with Gio, Joker knew that day would never come, *because* of love.

Chip whined, and Joker scratched the top of his head. "Don't be jealous. You know Daddy still loves you and Cookie best." Joker smiled from his position along the side of the huge white tent. It was muggy as balls out here, but at least there were plenty of fans blowing icy air. Gio knelt on the ground, not caring one lick if he got grass stains on his expensive cream-colored linen suit. He was in doggie heaven petting a German shepherd puppy. Cookie sat happily at his person's side.

"He's something, isn't he?" King said, appearing next to Joker.

Joker nodded, pride filling him. "Yeah, he is."

Helping people was what Gio did, but his life had taken a new path, and with it, so had his charity work. For days after William's arrest, Gio had been thinking about his work, about what he loved. Then, like with all things, he made up his mind and made it happen. Gio had been in talks with Ada for a long time about having her join him in his organization since she did the same type of charity work, just on a smaller scale. He'd known Ada for years and trusted her, so he brought her onto his charity's board of directors and then resigned, leaving everything to Ada.

"He's found his true love," Joker said, a lump in his throat.

Gio spent weeks putting together his new charity organization, and today was its official unveiling. He'd kept the details close to the vest, which Joker respected, even if he didn't understand it. Either way, he offered Gio whatever help he needed. Gio had worked hard for months, but he'd kept his word and didn't overdo it.

When the time came to launch the new charity organization, Gio asked him to work the event. Joker hadn't planned on missing it. He could have done without all the press, but he trusted Gio to know what he was doing. The place was packed, and Joker recognized a few faces. Some of them were politicians, others were from the police force, and half a dozen or so were from various branches of the military. Val, the fire chief, stood looking imposing in his dress uniform. He kept sneaking glances at Saint, who pretended—pretty poorly if you asked Joker—that he didn't notice. Something told Joker that Saint was in for a revelation or two.

King had hired extra security in case Joker decided he wanted to end his shift early. Why the hell he'd want to do that was anyone's guess, but whatever. It was King. Speaking of... Joker glanced at King, who looked a little too calm for his own good. Granted, King was always calm. Stoic wasn't just one of his traits, but a freaking mission statement. Still.

"There something you're not telling me?" Joker asked him.

King simply pointed to the front of the tent where Gio was taking the stage. Everyone clapped as he walked onto the stage with Cookie and stopped in front of the microphone. When everyone quieted down, he spoke.

"Thank you all so much for joining me on this new adventure. Those of you who know me, know I spent most of my adult life traveling the globe, helping people through my charity, an organization that is now in the beautiful hands of the amazing Ada." Gio motioned to Ada in the crowd, and she blew him a kiss as everyone clapped and cheered.

"It was during one of my trips that something happened, something that changed my life forever. It wasn't until recently that I discovered I was suffering from PTSD, and even then, it's taken me some time to come to terms with this new part of me. Thanks to my family and my loving partner, I know now that I'm not alone. That it's okay to ask for help, to lean on others. It was love that brought me this sweet boy right here. This is Cookie, my service dog." Gio smiled down at Cookie, who lifted his head and gazed at him in adoration.

"I'd been lost for a long time, and then one night, I sat on the couch watching TV, and I glanced over to find my boyfriend asleep on the couch with our two dogs sprawled on him, snoring softly. He looked so at peace, and it struck me then. I'd found my purpose. With that, I would love it if you'd join me in supporting my new charity, one that is extremely close to my heart of hearts."

Joker waited with bated breath as Gio pulled on the gold rope hanging from a huge white banner. The banner floated to the floor, and Joker gasped.

"Oh my God." Tears filled Joker's eyes, and his heart threatened to beat out of him. He took a step forward, his eyes glued to the sign.

Gio met Joker's gaze over the crowd and smiled. "In honor of one of our fallen heroes, I give you, the Echo K9 Foundation."

Joker put a fist to his mouth and shook his head. He turned to King, whose eyes looked suspiciously glassy.

"Yeah, definitely something," King said.

"Did you know about this?" Joker asked, his voice breaking.

King smiled warmly at him, patted his shoulder, and walked away.

The crowd was still clapping, cheering, and whistling. Gio held up a hand, and the crowd went quiet again. He wiped a tear from his eye and laughed softly. "As you can see, this charity means the world to me. The Echo K9 Foundation will provide service canines to military veterans at no cost to them, along with vet care, training, food, counseling, and a host of additional services to help them on this new path. Thank you. If you give me five minutes, I'll be over there to answer questions."

The crowd clapped and cheered, watching Gio as he made his way over to Joker, who'd wiped the tears from his eyes and cleared his throat. He pressed his PTT button, and King spoke before Joker could utter a word.

"Enjoy the rest of your day."

Joker shook his head. Fucking King. He pushed aside the flap in the tent and stepped outside with Chip, Gio and Cookie right behind them. Security was walking the grounds, and there were some people milling around chatting, but they'd have more privacy out here than inside the tent.

"I'm sorry I didn't tell you," Gio said. "I wanted it to be a surprise. I hope it's okay."

Joker stared up at him. "Is it okay that you named your charity after my dog?" He sighed as he brought Gio into his arms. "What am I going to do with you?"

"I can think of a few things," Gio teased quietly as he leaned in and kissed Joker's cheek. "There's also a bronze statue of her in the lobby of my organization's new building. Everyone who walks in will know what a hero she was."

Joker wrinkled his nose, the backs of his eyes stinging again. "Thank you."

"You're welcome." Gio laced their fingers together. "I love you, Sacha, and I hope that I get to spend the rest of my life showing you just how much."

"I love you too, Gio. And I plan on letting you show me how much you love me," Joker replied with a smile. "Especially since I've got something similar in mind."

Gio kissed him, and Joker leaned into it, his hand on Gio's waist. He squeezed him gently when he heard a camera click.

With a chuckle, Joker pulled back. "Go on. They're waiting for you."

"I'm going to grab some water and a quick snack before I start answering questions. Meet me after for dinner?"

"You got it."

Gio popped a quick kiss on Joker's cheek before heading back inside. For the first time in his life, Joker felt... settled. He was exactly where he belonged. A long time ago, he'd vowed never to lose his heart, when the truth was, over the years, he'd been giving away pieces of it to the people who'd claimed him as their own, to his found family. In return, they'd given him pieces of their own hearts, trusting him with something precious, and he hadn't realized that until Gio.

EPILOGUE

TWO MONTHS LATER.

"Are you trying to choke me?"

Joker glowered at Gio, but there was no real heat in his words, as evidenced by Gio's laugh. He finished fastening Joker's bow tie, then took a step back to run his gaze over him.

"There. You look gorgeous."

"This is stupid. Why is it always fucking tuxedos?" The damn penguin suits needed to die a fiery death. This was Florida. In August. Were they out of their minds?

"It's a wedding, love," Gio replied, turning to the dogs.

"It's a *beach* wedding. Outdoors. On the beach," Joker reminded him. "I can't believe you got the dogs matching tuxedo bandanas."

"It was the only way they could attend, and I'm not going anywhere without Cookie, and if Cookie goes, Chip goes."

Joker let out a heavy sigh. Gio was adorable. "Come

here." He pulled Gio into his arms and kissed him. As much as Joker hated tuxes, he couldn't deny Gio looked incredible in them. The tailored tux accentuated his broad shoulders and trim waist. He oozed elegance, while Joker just appeared uncomfortable. "What if instead of going to the wedding, we stay here and wreck each other in bed all day. I mean, we have our own beach. We don't need to use anyone else's."

Gio chuckled against Joker's lips. "As tempting as that is, we promised King we'd go."

Joker's groan was loud and petulant. Having friends was overrated. Stupid promises. "There better be good food is all I'm saying," Joker grumbled.

They had some time before they had to leave, so he would make the most of it. He kissed Gio, loving the feel of Gio's arms around him, his lips on Joker's, their tongues moving together. Gio's subtle cologne filled his nostrils, and Joker groaned. God, he loved the way his man smelled.

A little sigh escaped Gio that made Joker smile. Yeah, Gio was more than a little crazy about him. It was as if he couldn't keep his hands, or mouth, off Joker, whether it was a discreet hand against Joker's lower back while they were out, or their fingers laced together as they strolled down the beach in the evenings, or when their limbs tangled as they had sex. Not that Joker was complaining, especially since he was the same. How could he not want his hands on all that sleek muscle and soft skin?

"Are you trying to distract me?" Gio asked, sliding his hands down Joker's back to his ass.

"Is it working?"

"Always," Gio said, his smile wide. "Cookie, Chip, go with Saint."

The dogs trotted off, leaving the bedroom. Gio left Joker

and closed the door, then turned, the wicked gleam in his eyes sending a shiver through Joker. He motioned to the end of the room. "Hands on the glass."

Joker groaned and hurried to do as he was told. He placed his palms against the one-way glass windows in their bedroom and spread his legs. Anticipation had him thrumming with excitement and need. When it came to Gio, Joker was insatiable. The need to have Gio fill him, to feel Gio's come running down his legs... was enough to make him whimper.

"Please, baby."

Gio didn't waste any time. He unfastened Joker's dress slacks and shoved them down his legs along with his underwear. When he disappeared, Joker grunted a protest. The drawer to the nightstand opened, and a heartbeat later, Gio was back, his slick fingers stretching Joker.

He arched his back and pushed his ass against Gio, moaning at the ripples of pleasure as Gio prepped him. "Fuck, that feels so good." Gio crooked his finger, hitting that particular spot inside Joker, and he cried out, "Fuck! Yes, just like that. Fuck yeah."

"You're going to be thinking about me in your ass the entire time you're sitting there, remembering that burn is from my cock filling up your tight hole."

Joker groaned. He wasn't going to last long. He let his brow fall against the glass as Gio lined himself up and slowly pushed inside him, Gio's wide girth stretching him, the pain soon giving way to the most delicious pleasure. Gio stilled, completely buried inside Joker, their bodies pressed together, Joker's back to Gio's front.

"You feel so amazing," Gio murmured against Joker's temple. Slowly he pulled out, then snapped his hips.

Joker cried out, then demanded more. With every one

of Gio's thrusts, Joker met him with a thrust of his own until Gio was pounding his ass, their bodies smacking together as Gio claimed him. Gio shifted his angle, and Joker threw his head back with a loud groan. His body was a mass of thrumming energy, ready to take off like a Fourth of July firecracker. Every inch of him lit up from the inside out, and he grabbed his dick, stroking himself off in time to Gio's thrusts.

"That's it, sweetheart. Come for me."

Joker's orgasm exploded through him, and he came all over his hand and the glass just as Gio's hoarse cry filled the room, his come coating and warming Joker's insides. Their panting breath was the only sound in the room as they stood, bodies remaining joined together. Joker's knees wobbled a little, and Gio carefully slipped out of him. He kissed Joker's cheek.

"Don't move."

Joker did as he was told, his eyes on the blue waves sparkling beneath the sun's bright rays. His heart was whole, his soul soaring in a way he'd never experienced before, all because of the love he had. He'd spent so many years avoiding getting his heart involved, and in the end, this sweet, sinful man had somehow skillfully stolen Joker's heart right from under him. He smiled at the tender stroke of the washcloth between his legs. When Gio had finished cleaning him up, Joker pulled up his boxer briefs and pants. He sorted his clothes out and kissed Gio. It was a silly thought, but after what they just did, knowing that he had Gio to come home to every day made him feel like he could take on the world.

"Ready?" Gio asked, kissing the tip of Joker's nose.

"If I gotta," Joker grumbled. "You got the lint rollers?"

Gio held up the black designer duffel that contained

folding cooling mats—in sand color—pop-up water and food bowls for the boys, some water bottles, a couple of dog bones to keep them busy, treats, kibble, and several lint rollers because black tuxedos and golden retriever fur were mortal enemies.

They got the dogs secured in the back seat of the SUV, then climbed in after them. Joker had never been more grateful for air conditioning. The walk from the front door to the car alone had him sweating. Damn ceremony better be short. At least the reception afterward was inside the hotel.

The beach hosting the huge-ass wedding was behind a luxury hotel less than half an hour away. They walked through the lobby, guests gasping and cooing at Chip and Cookie trotting along in their matching tuxes. Gio had gotten Cookie a black service dog uniform so it would match the tux. Again, ridiculous. A huge ornate sign at the far end of the lobby near a pair of floor-to-ceiling glass doors announced the wedding, and they approached the two women standing behind the table beside it. Gio handed over their invite, and they were escorted outside onto the stone veranda and a set of wide steps that led down to an expansive patio and then the beach. They spotted their friends seated several rows down near the front and walked through *sand* to get to their seats. Well, "seats" was a strong word. Joker stared down at what Ace and Colton were sitting on.

"What the ever-loving-fuck is that?"

Ace grinned up at him. "Well, good morning, sunshine." He patted the space next to him.

"Don't call me that," Joker said through a grunt. Only Gio called him that. He pointed down to where someone expected him to park his ass. "I repeat, what the fuck is that?" Several of their coworkers were already seated around them, and they snickered at Joker.

"I believe it's driftwood," Ace replied, looking too damned happy for his own good.

Joker took a seat with a heavy sigh while Gio put down the cooling pads in the sand next to the end of the... dead tree or whatever the fuck it was they were sitting on. The dogs lay down and settled, though if it got too hot, he'd take them inside. He wasn't going to let his dogs get overheated because one of the grooms was an asshat.

The rest of their friends arrived, and Joker glanced around "their side" of the aisle. Pretty much the whole of Four Kings Security was here, along with a few people he didn't know—he assumed they were friends of groom number two.

"Why the fuck are we here again?" Joker asked, shifting uncomfortably in his seat, and had to catch himself before he toppled over. Whoever the fuck thought giant pieces of driftwood in the sand made for good seating needed to be smacked in the head. Not only was he sweating balls out here, but his shoes were full of sand. Who asked people to wear tuxes to a beach wedding? Again, in fucking *Florida*.

"We're here because King asked us to be here," Ace said, checking his watch for what seemed like the hundredth time.

Joker hated weddings. He especially hated themed weddings. The only exception he made where weddings were concerned was if it was someone close to him. Although he'd met Gage Kingston on occasion, Joker wasn't friends with the guy. King's cousin ran with a different crowd, and Joker had yet to meet someone who didn't immediately dislike the man's boyfriend after meeting him *once*. The guy was a total douche. He darted his gaze at the sea of people across the aisle. That's right. King had asked every available body at Four Kings Security to attend the wedding because Gage's asshole fiancé had thrown a tantrum when he realized he had ten times the number of guests as Gage, making the seating "uneven" and "sad."

Gage and King didn't strike Joker as being very close for some reason they knew nothing about. The guy was rarely around, but King was ready to call in the cavalry for Gage, so that had to mean something. Gage had been in the Navy —which had taken balls, considering the Kingston family was an Army family, but Joker never remembered what it was Gage had done in the Navy, only that he'd fulfilled his contract and then got out. The rest of their crew arrived, taking up two... trees. Leo took a seat next to Colton, and King sat beside him on the end.

Not long after, it looked like everyone had arrived, but the wedding had yet to start. Chip started panting, and Gio removed two of the pop-up dog bowls and filled them with water. As soon as Chip had some water, he was fine, but Joker didn't want him out here too much longer.

"Wasn't the wedding supposed to start, like, fifteen minutes ago?" Colton asked worriedly.

The priest stood at the end of the aisle beneath a massive archway also made of driftwood decorated in seashells, starfish, and... seaweed? It looked like seaweed. The wedding wasn't just on the beach and beach-themed; it was seashell-themed. There were seashells on *everything*.

"I think the groom is getting antsy," Jack said from behind Joker, leaning forward to speak quietly.

"Is that what we're calling it?" Joker murmured, studying the lanky blond man with wild hair. He was some kind of artist or something.

Lucky tapped Ace on the shoulder. "Bro, did he just pull out his phone? At the altar?"

"Yep, it would seem so. I'd also like to point out that his phone case has a giant seashell on it. How did that even fit in his pocket?"

"What's he doing?" Gio asked. "Is he on a video call?"

"I think he's filming himself," Jack replied.

"What's his name?" Leo asked, and Ace handed Leo the wedding program containing all the information about the grooms.

Leo tapped away at his phone. "He's talking to his social media followers. Yikes. That's not very nice."

"What'd he say?"

Joker cringed. That was King's not-happy voice.

"He's pissed off with Gage and saying how selfish he is, and how can he do this on *his* wedding day."

Joker frowned. *His* wedding day? Last time he checked, weddings involved two people. "Why is your cousin marrying this guy? He doesn't seem like Gage's type."

"I don't know, to be honest." King let out a weary sigh. "They've been on and off again for a long time, and every time I thought Gage was going to move on for good, his boyfriend would reel him back in."

A ginormous older man in a white linen suit approached the groom. He had to be the father, because the two had the same blond hair, blue eyes, and cat's-ass sour lips expression. Glancing around the space, people started to murmur and whisper among themselves; some of them glared in their direction. Joker narrowed his eyes at one guy who'd made the mistake of glaring at him, and the guy quickly darted his gaze somewhere else.

It was probably best if Joker didn't look over there. He leaned into Ace. "Thank you."

"For what?"

"For having a wedding with solid ground and no dead sea trees for seating."

Ace chuckled. "You're welcome."

"My ass is getting numb," Lucky muttered.

"Um, Ward?" Leo tugged on King's sleeve. "I think your cousin is trying to get your attention."

Joker turned, along with the rest of them, and sure enough, Gage was frantically waving at King from the small white tent on the patio. What the hell was going on?

Ace craned his neck. "Is Gage wearing a suit made of... seashells?"

"What the fuck?" Joker had to press his lips together to keep from laughing, because if he started laughing, he wasn't going to stop.

"I'm very concerned," Gio told Joker. "I hope the shells have been cleaned out properly."

Ace tapped Joker's shoulder. "Um... is it just me, or does that look like a claw?"

"Where?"

"By his crotch."

"Why are you staring at his crotch?" Joker teased.

"I wasn't staring at his crotch. Something dark moved, and it caught my eye. It happened to be in the vicinity of his crotch." Ace squinted. "I think it's a claw." He turned his attention to King. "Wait, doesn't your cousin have one of those weird aversions to crustaceans?"

"Really?" King grumbled. "You can't remember to order normal sticky notes at work instead of neon pink, but you remember my cousin's aversion to crustaceans?"

"It's not that I can't remember; I just choose not to."

Before King could reply, Colton smartly jumped in.

"King, maybe you should go check on your cousin. Make sure he's okay."

King stood and made his way toward the tent, then disappeared inside with his cousin. Something had to be going on. The wedding should have started by now. Maybe Gage was having wardrobe issues. Who the fuck knew? Maybe if Gage's fiancé went to talk to his soon-to-be-husband instead of ranting on social media, this whole thing would resolve quicker and they could get to the eating and drinking part of the day.

What seemed like a lifetime later, King returned, and judging by the look on his face, it would be an interesting day.

"What's going on?" Ace asked.

"There's a bit of a situation."

Shit. Were they going to need equipment? Was it a security issue? "What is it?" Joker asked, ready to spring into action.

King met his gaze, his expression somber.

"We've got a runaway groom."

WANT to know what happens with Gage? Preorder *Aisle Be There*, book one in the new Runaway Grooms series on Amazon.

WHAT HAPPENED during Joker and Gio's bachelor auction date? Check out the bonus scene here: https://readerlinks.com/l/1869833

A NOTE FROM THE AUTHOR

Thank you so much for reading *Sleight of Hand*, the thirds book in The Kings: Wild Cards series. I hope you enjoyed Joker and Gio's story, and if you did, please consider leaving a review on Amazon. Reviews can have a significant impact on a book's visibility on Amazon, so any support you show these fellas would be amazing. Preorder your copy of *Aisle Be There*, the first book in the upcoming Runaway Grooms series, part of the Four Kings Security Universe on Amazon.

Thinking of donating to a K9 military vet charity? Check out Paws and Stripes or K9s for Warriors.

Haven't read the Kings? Start with *Love in Spades*, available on Amazon and Kindle Unlimited.

Want to stay up-to-date on my releases and receive exclusive content? Sign up for my newsletter.

Follow me on Amazon to be notified of a new releases, and connect with me on social media, including my fun Facebook group, Donuts, Dog Tags, and Day Dreams, where we chat books, post pictures, have giveaways, and more!

Looking for inspirational photos of my books? Visit my book boards on Pinterest.

Thank you again for joining The Kings: Wild Cards on their adventures. We hope to see you soon!

ALSO BY CHARLIE COCHET

FOUR KINGS SECURITY UNIVERSE

STANDALONE TITLES

Beware of Geeks Bearing Gifts

FOUR KINGS SECURITY SERIES

Love in Spades

Be Still My Heart

Join the Club

Diamond in the Rough

LOCKE AND KEYES AGENCY SERIES

Kept in the Dark

THE KINGS: WILD CARDS SERIES

Stacking the Deck

Raising the Ante

Sleight of Hand

RUNAWAY GROOMS SERIES

Aisle Be There

THIRDS UNIVERSE

THIRDS SERIES

Hell & High Water

Blood & Thunder

Rack & Ruin

Rise & Fall

Against the Grain

Catch a Tiger by the Tail

Smoke & Mirror

Thick & Thin

Darkest Hour Before Dawn

Gummy Bears & Grenades

Tried & True

THIRDS BEYOND THE BOOKS SERIES

THIRDS Beyond the Books Volume 1

THIRDS Beyond the Books Volume 2

THIRDS: REBELS SERIES

Love and Payne

TIN SERIES

Gone But Not Forgotten

Go Down in Flames

PARANORMAL PRINCES SERIES

The Prince and His Bedeviled Bodyguard

The Prince and His Captivating Carpenter

The King and His Vigilant Valet

SOLDATI HEARTS SERIES

The Soldati Prince

The Foxling Soldati

The Soldati General

COMPROMISED SERIES

Center of Gravity

NORTH POLE CITY TALES SERIES

Mending Noel

The Heart of Frost

The Valor of Vixen

Loving Blitz

Disarming Donner

Courage and the King

North Pole City Tales Complete Series Boxset

STANDALONE TITLES

Forgive and Forget

Love in Retrograde

AUDIOBOOKS

Check out the audio versions on Audible.

ABOUT THE AUTHOR

Charlie Cochet is the international bestselling author of the THIRDS series. Born in Cuba and raised in the US, Charlie enjoys the best of both worlds, from her daily Cuban latte to her passion for classic rock.

Currently residing in Central Florida, Charlie is at the beck and call of a rascally Doxiepoo bent on world domination. When she isn't writing, she can usually be found devouring a book, releasing her creativity through art, or binge watching a new TV series. She runs on coffee, thrives on music, and loves to hear from readers.

www.charliecochet.com

Sign up for Charlie's newsletter:
https://newsletter.charliecochet.com

facebook.com/charliecochet

twitter.com/charliecochet

instagram.com/charliecochet

bookbub.com/authors/charliecochet

goodreads.com/CharlieCochet

pinterest.com/charliecochet

Made in the USA
Middletown, DE
16 July 2022

69514356R00172